OUT OF
TOUCH

Haleh Agar was born and raised in Montreal, Canada. She left to teach English Literature at international schools in Bahrain, Singapore and most recently London, where she now lives. Haleh has been published in literary magazines and journals, including *Mslexia*, *Viva Magazine*, *Fincham Press* and *LampLight*. Her short story 'Not Contagious' was Highly Commended by the judges of the 2019 Costa Short Story Award. She won the Brighton Prize for flash fiction and the *London Magazine*'s inaugural essay competition for her piece 'On Writing Ethnic Stories'. *Out of Touch* is her first novel.

OUT OF TOUCH

HALEH AGAR

WEIDENFELD & NICOLSON

First published in Great Britain in 2020 by Weidenfeld & Nicolson
an imprint of The Orion Publishing Group Ltd
Carmelite House, 50 Victoria Embankment
London EC4Y 0DZ

An Hachette UK Company

1 3 5 7 9 10 8 6 4 2

A CIP catalogue record for this book is
available from the British Library.

ISBN (Hardback) 978 1 4746 1224 1
ISBN (Export Trade Paperback) 978 1 4746 1225 8
ISBN (eBook) 978 1 4746 1227 2

Typeset by Input Data Services Ltd, Somerset

Printed in Great Britain by Clays Ltd, Elcograf S.p.A.

www.weidenfeldandnicolson.co.uk
www.orionbooks.co.uk

To Simon

SPRING

One

A man hit Ava with his car a few miles from her bungalow. He said he didn't mean to do it. Ava told him she believed him. *Of course I believe you*; she said it like that in the dark.

'It was an accident.'

'Of course . . .'

It wasn't possible to see what he looked like, lying on her side in that muddy ditch, and she didn't move her neck, afraid she'd cause it damage. The pain in her back and hips felt bright and urgent, and yet a calmness washed through Ava: she didn't need to decide what to do about her father's letter. Her mind could rest here.

The man phoned the emergency services and relayed questions to her. 'They're asking if you're bleeding anywhere.' He might have said that. Ava's attention wavered.

She felt him hovering over her but didn't mind because he smelt like a fresh bar of soap, clean and sharp.

'I can't be sure about the bleeding,' he said. 'It's hard to see in the dark.'

The urgency in his voice reminded Ava of her grand-mother Katerina and the rushed way she used to shout into the phone when she called her brother in Greece, trying to reach him across all that land and sea.

'The ambulance people want to know about your vision.' Two long and shaky fingers appeared in front of Ava's nose. 'How many is that?'

'Two.'

'Good.' The man's voice brightened. 'Yeah, she said the right number of fingers.'

But when the call ended, he spoke to her again with agitation.

'Why were you out here? It's dangerous walking on this road at night.'

'I needed to clear my head.'

Ava's eyes darted up, but all she could see were nettles. She thought of asking the man to look for her father's letter, but he was so full of anxiety, pacing back and forth above her, that she left it.

He introduced himself as Sam.

'Ava. I'd shake your hand, but . . .'

He didn't laugh. It was the same at work – jokes met with silence. If she survived this, she would learn to be funny.

'Do you mind if I smoke?' he said. 'It helps calm my nerves.'

'No, go ahead.'

Headlights cut through the darkness, but there were no sirens and soon the lights faded into the night. All they could do now was wait. Wait for the ambulance, wait to see if she would live or die or become a little disabled. Could she still feel her legs?

The brown thaw of spring lingered there in her nostrils, conjuring a memory of those awful white stockings she'd worn as a child, kicking a ball to her father on Hampstead Heath. When it rained, they'd become thick with mud – itchy stockings that rolled at her knees, at her ankles. Before her bath, Ava would paw at her legs, leaving red scratches all over her flesh. Her sexual experiences in adulthood often fell short of the satisfaction she'd felt as a girl, tearing off those thick white stockings and scratching. 'You're a mess,' her mother had told her, putting foam into the bath, and Ava had thought, *So are you*.

Sam asked where she lived.

'My bungalow's on the same side of the road. About five miles towards Welton.'

'It's too bad your house isn't facing the river.'

Ava laughed, and everything below her head tightened into thick knots of pain. 'Those houses on the river cost about a hundred grand more.'

'That much?'

'At least.'

She knew because she'd asked an estate agent when she'd been thinking of selling the place before Christmas. The agent had looked at Ava and pursed her showy red lips. 'Pity it's not facing the river,' she had said.

'I live near the high street with my parents,' Sam offered.

It surprised Ava that he should live with his parents. She had assumed from the deep tone of his voice that he was tall, broad-shouldered, approaching middle age. Had he taken over his parents' basement in the way some lost, lonely men did?

But Ava was in no position to judge, having lived with her mother until the day she'd died. In that time, she'd only ever brought one man back to the bungalow, and he'd liked staying late into the morning so he could have coffee with her mother. Watching them laugh and share stories, Ava had thought how they'd make a lovely pair. When she'd told her mother this – because there was nothing, nothing she'd wanted more than for her mother to be happy – the crease on her mother's forehead had deepened. Apart from this man, who eventually bored Ava like the others, no boyfriends ever came to the house. It was Ava who travelled out late at night to meet men who'd rather sleep alone. She preferred it that way, returning to her room and spreading out in her own bed.

'Hah!'

Sam asked what was funny.

'My mother died in a crash five months ago. It must mean something, surely. Both of us getting smashed up by cars.' She left out the part about the coroner's report and the alcohol in her mother's blood.

Sam apologised for her mother's death in the usual way, fumbling and awkward. His sympathy was marked by ellipses in his speech and it was hard to keep track of the number of times he said, 'Oh, God.'

'Thank you,' Ava said.

It was getting embarrassing, this new tendency of telling strangers about her mother – at gas stations, in supermarkets, in a ditch at the side of the road with her cheek planted in the cold mud. Her mother's death was always there on her tongue, ready to announce itself.

'Where were you headed?' Ava asked. She didn't want to think of her mother anymore.

'I was driving back from Brighton. My dad sent me there to collect terracotta curtains for his shop. I was on my way to drop off the order, but none of that matters now. God, I'm really sorry—'

'I like the beach in Brighton.' Ava smiled. 'I used to go there with my father when I was little.'

'Oh, yeah? The beach in Brighton is all right because it's all rocks. I'm not a huge fan of the sand, if I'm being honest. It gets into everything and when there's food involved, that's the worst feeling, having sand in your teeth. But who knows, maybe one day we could put all this behind us and smoke a joint out there together?'

Again, Ava pictured this man's bedroom in his parents' basement, a green glow from a lava lamp moving across his bedsheets, an expertly rolled joint drooping down from his lips.

'Sure. That sounds nice.'

Another car drove past, shaking the ground, sending a wave of pain through her. Ava's mind turned to Michael. Pain and Michael went hand in hand. If he'd received the same letter from their father, he would've thrown it in the bin. Her brother was above such things as family, too important for that.

It occurred to her that their father might be bluffing, that this whole thing was a big joke. *Ha, ha! I'm dying. Ha, ha!*

At last, Ava heard sirens in the distance.

Sam bent down and touched her shoulder. 'They're coming.'

Ava shut her eyes against the blue spinning lights, so bright and intense, drilling into her head. She heard doors open and slam, Sam saying something to the paramedics. She felt detached until he took her hand and it felt firm, his touch.

'There's a letter,' she said to Sam. 'It's only a page. Typed. I must've dropped it. Could you find it for me?'

He didn't respond. She wasn't sure he'd heard.

'It's important . . .'

A woman's voice asked her name.

She gave her mother's name instead of her own. 'Elena. Elena Agatha Andreadis.'

But she couldn't be sure she'd spoken at all. Snippets from her father's letter swirled in front of her eyes before disappearing into the tall grass: *Can we meet?*

A hazy picture of a family in early autumn, looking down at the rusting landscape below. Green turning orange, orange turning red, red turning to rot – and for a brief moment, the stockinged girl's mouth curved into a smile.

Two

More people were turning up to the bar in Gramercy. The *New Yorker* had published a glowing review, calling the story night the bar hosted every month a triumph and a miracle. A religious experience with all the heart and honesty of an AA meeting, except booze was allowed. That was what they'd written, and now Michael had to stand in a long line to get inside.

He didn't mind the wait too much – not with the early-evening sun falling over the sidewalk in blocks of amber. He could get sentimental about a thing like that, light shifting across the city he loved. And he didn't mind listening to the conversations of the people in front of him. Women in their early thirties passing their phones around, showing each other who they were dating, who they wanted to date. Michael felt glad in that moment that he'd met Layla before everything could be done through his mobile. He thought he would be very bad at it, dating through his phone, fussing over what photos made him look like the right man. He would choose the wrong ones and women would laugh at him, just as the group in front of him did now, staring into their screens. 'Another topless photo! Another rock-climbing shot!'

The line was finally moving. A few people joined behind Michael. They looked affluent, with their tailored suits and confident smiles, presumably having come straight from the office. He felt underdressed in his shabby blazer. He was starting to look like the rest of the Social Sciences faculty, fraying at the edges. He decided that after tonight he would throw the blazer out.

Even the doorman, in his powder-blue shirt, hair shorter at the sides than on top, looked smarter than him.

'What's that?' the doorman said.

Michael looked at the paper. He was holding out his father's letter. He flushed with embarrassment, feeling somehow that the doorman would be able to read and assess his whole life story in those few seconds of checking. He searched his other pocket, presented the ticket and the doorman let him through.

Inside, Michael felt an immediate shift as the day's troubles receded. He greeted strangers with a smile, feeling that he knew them, all these people here for the same reason.

The worn leather armchair near the front of the stage where Michael liked to sit was taken, so he bought a bottle of beer and settled at a table towards the back next to a young couple. He assumed they were on a first date, the way they groped each other with desire. It felt like that in restaurants and bars around the city, like everyone was out on a first date.

The lights dimmed. The first speaker – a short, stocky man in his fifties – stood on the stage with a microphone in front of him. There was a hunted look in his eyes. A light shone against the bald patch at the top of his head. When he swallowed, the sound of his dry mouth travelled through the speakers. The room was completely still, waiting for him to begin, to tell his story. He apologised and dry-swallowed again.

'It's hard to talk about these things, but . . . it is important,' he said in an accent Michael couldn't place.

When he'd collected himself, he spoke of returning to a country that was no longer home. War had changed the landscape of his childhood, the house he'd grown up in was no longer there, rubble left in its place. It wasn't just a physical change, though; his own cousins, loving and welcoming as they were, looked at him as an American now, a foreigner, and that's when he realised there was no place he truly belonged.

'Not here, not there . . .'

The young couple next to Michael kept talking, kissing each other's noses and eyes. Michael couldn't get into the talk. Like other new faces he'd seen come and go, the couple next to him were not there to listen, to reflect on what they heard and feel part of something bigger. To them, this was a thing to do. They might tell their friends the next day about where they'd been and their friends would say, 'Oh, we've heard about that place!'

When the man finished talking, there was a round of applause and Michael stood to change his seat, but the next speaker appeared too quickly, a woman in her late thirties, around Michael's own age. Projected onto the screen behind the stage was a photo of her in hospital, a tiny newborn asleep on her chest. Her eyes looked weary in the photo, the way Layla's had been after thirteen hours of labour, but she was smiling through her exhaustion.

'Her name is Clara,' the woman said, her voice steady and determined. 'She was born at thirty-two weeks and weighed five pounds, three ounces. Her blood type was O negative. She was a fussy feeder and she only lived for a day – that day.' She pointed to the photo, her hand shaking a little. 'It was the best and worst day of my life.' She paused, looking down briefly before focusing her eyes on some point in the distance.

'My family and friends told me not to worry. "You'll have another baby," they said. The doctors, my parents – nobody would call her by her name. To them, she was a tragedy, not a person. Not Clara.'

The young couple next to Michael kept talking. Michael tapped the guy's shoulder.

'Do you mind?' Michael said.

'What?'

'Would you pay attention, please?' Michael felt stupid for saying that. In his seminar classes, he'd never told a student to pay attention. Instead he'd paused and waited for silence.

'Relax.'

'Why did you even bother coming?'

A few people sitting at the table in front of Michael turned around and frowned at him.

'Chill,' the guy said, leaning forward, his big forehead looming as a threat.

Michael stood up and his chair scraped against the stone floor. More people turned to look at him. There were no free seats, so he leant against a brick wall by the side of the stage and listened.

'When we put Clara's things away almost a year later – her little sweaters and stuffed giraffe and all those bags

12

of Huggies diapers – when we boxed them up, it was hard.' The screen showed a picture of those baby things in a pale-yellow nursery. 'My mother, always practical, always scrimping and saving, said that none of it would go to waste – we would be able to use it again, and when we put our new baby into the crib, we'd feel happy instead of miserable. I looked at her, like, Ma, have you lost your mind? I told my mother again, "Her name is *Clara*. And these were Clara's things and we're going to celebrate her birthday in July, so expect an invitation in the mail . . ."'

Michael swallowed hard, and even after other speakers had taken the stage, it was this woman's story of her daughter and the denial of her humanity that he thought about on his commute home and how life was too flimsy; you couldn't count on it. He thought of his son, Jacob, the close call they'd had in September, and he checked his phone to see if there was any news from Layla. She'd sent a video.

Michael played the clip and watched Jacob count to fifteen, breezing through the single digits, stumbling a little over eleven, but he made it to fifteen without any mistakes. A few weeks ago, he would have stopped at ten. Jacob looked at his mother when he got to the end with large expectant eyes and she clapped for him and he smiled with all his small teeth. Michael found he was smiling too, happiness softening his face.

He wanted to show the video to the commuters sitting next to him. His son's latest achievement. But nobody returned his smile, and he remembered how complicated life was outside of the bar in Gramercy.

Above ground, the sun was gone. Michael looked

forward to summer, when the evenings would feel bright and fluid and endless.

In the apartment lift, he pressed the button to the fourth floor, but his keys didn't work in the door. He realised he was standing in front of his old place. They'd moved up to the sixth floor a few weeks ago when a bigger apartment had become available – one with a spare room for an office and more space to store things they didn't need. A graphic designer now lived in their old apartment. Michael had given him a hand last week, carrying his lemon trees up to their old balcony. Some of his other plants were private, the graphic designer had said.

'I'll bring over some lemonade once I'm settled in,' he'd promised, but Layla said they weren't having any.

'He's a total stoner. He'll put something in our drinks.' And then she'd paused and looked around the living room, all those boxes piled up. 'Come to think of it, yeah, let's get him over here. The sooner the better.'

Michael took the stairs up to the sixth floor, anticipating all the unpacking still ahead. Their lives were in boxes. They'd bought too many things, too many toys for Jacob. Building blocks and little trampolines and a pretend kitchen.

They'd said they were going to be minimalists and live like Scandinavians, everything pale and grey and bare. They'd never become one of those couples who gave up their living room to toys. This was the story they'd told themselves. But Michael was always stepping on something soft and noisy, and when a miniature soldier punctured his skin, Layla agreed to get rid of the whole platoon. A massacre, those tiny green soldiers falling into the trash.

The apartment was hazy. A burning smell wafted from

the kitchen. Michael usually cooked dinner, but Layla had insisted on doing it since she'd started her sabbatical. It makes sense, she'd said, though she hated cooking.

Jacob was still up. He was standing in front of the television in his rocket pyjamas, watching cartoons.

'Jacob,' Michael said. 'Jacob, sit here, would you? You're too close to the screen.' When he turned the volume down, his son looked up and frowned.

There was no resemblance between them – father and son. Jacob had his mother's big eyes and thick black hair. And there was something in his mouth that reminded him of Ava, the way it curved down a little. He felt a rush of guilt whenever he thought of his sister.

'Can you count to fifteen for me?'

Jacob shook his head and made a face. At times, he waltzed around the apartment like a comedian, pretending to fall over, shooting quick glances at his parents to check they were still watching him.

'Can't hear,' he said in a low whine, and pointed to his ear and then the television. When Michael turned the volume back up, his son grinned, happy again.

In the galley kitchen, Layla was throwing burnt vegetables into the trash.

'You're late.'

Michael scratched his chin and told his usual lie: he'd had a department meeting and papers to grade. It was easier that way.

'Jacob won't sleep,' Layla said, and threw up her hands. 'We'll have to order takeout.' Then she told Michael about her day. A woman at the park had let her child throw sand in Jacob's face. Fistfuls of the stuff. No apology. And then Jacob had started coughing in the afternoon. A dry

15

cough – but still, a cough. Was that why he was refusing to sleep now? Maybe she would take him to see Dr Fineman in the morning . . .

'We'll monitor it,' Michael said.

Since starting her sabbatical, Layla had given such accounts of her day to Michael, almost as soon as he walked through the door. A debrief on everything and nothing. He knew she missed work. She had achieved so much since qualifying: the Fraser-Williams merger she'd negotiated with little support, her promotion to senior associate. She reminded him often of such achievements at strange times and in strange places, like at the checkout line in a grocery store or at five in the morning, the bleary half-light of dawn there on her anxious face.

They kissed, leaning against the side of the fridge.

'You smell,' she said.

'Like what?' He thought for a moment she could taste the beer he'd had at the bar.

'The city.'

'I'll shower.'

'Wash the city off.' Layla smiled. 'That's something I *don't* miss – the grime of the subway.' She pointed to the dreaded task list on the fridge. 'I've made the coffee table, but the dining table still needs to be put together.'

'OK,' he said. 'I'll do that.'

In the shower, Michael thought of his father's letter.

Can we meet? I need to see you.

Michael imagined Lee at a big desk typing that. He could understand why his father would write to Ava. She had been his favourite. His eyes would glaze over when she came into the room. But when it was just Michael and his father together, without Ava and their mother there, Michael could sense his father's discomfort. He would shift in his armchair, or suddenly stand to leave. On several occasions, he'd said to Michael, 'Be more like your sister,' though he was older than her. Their mother would hang Michael's drawings on the fridge with magnets – pictures of landscapes and big blue skies. But his father didn't care for them. 'Try out for rugby,' he insisted, and when Michael didn't make the team, his father shook his head. 'You're pathetic,' he'd said to Michael more than once. But that had been a long time ago. They'd had no contact since he was fifteen, twenty years now.

Lee wanted to clear his conscience, that was why he'd sent the letter about his terminal illness and plan to end his life 'before things got bad', and Michael didn't see why he should help.

There were no towels on the drying rack. Layla must have washed the one he'd been using, and the others were probably still stuffed in a suitcase or in one of the garbage bags in the office. Michael walked through into the master bedroom, leaving puddles on the oak floor where he stepped, only remembering that they didn't have curtains when he looked out the window and saw a naked woman in the adjacent apartment. She saw him and laughed, and he laughed too as he covered himself with his hands. She waved goodbye and drew her blinds and, for a while, Michael couldn't stop thinking about it, the oddness of the encounter, seeing a stranger bare like that, being seen that way.

When he was dry and clothed, he took his son back to bed.

'Story,' Jacob said, pointing to a book on his shelf.

Michael's colleague Dr Susan Barker had given him the whole vegetable book series. Each story taught a moral lesson. That evening, Michael read about the racist carrots who excluded the asparagus because he was green, and the swede who shamed the carrots by saying how they were all vegetables and would rot into the same ground. God only knew where Susan found such books. The stories were admittedly weighty for a two-year-old, but Layla hoped they'd encourage Jacob to eat, because he rarely did.

In the apartment across the way, a light switched on. The naked woman was clothed in a T-shirt and shorts, her hair no longer wet, so he could see she had a blunt fringe cut just above her eyes. She sat on an IKEA futon that Michael recognised from his days at college, and ate her spaghetti in front of the television.

Jacob's eyes were finally heavy, and Michael stopped reading. He turned his attention back to the woman and felt a deep calmness watching her eat her spaghetti dinner. She must have a sense of humour, he thought. She must not worry too much, the way she'd laughed and waved. He imagined a life for her filled with travel and hobbies, movement and stillness; everything possible.

Layla reached around the back of his shoulders and he flinched, startled by her sudden presence, but he shut his eyes and leant into her.

'I ordered Chinese,' she said. 'We need to get curtains. I'll put it on the list.'

Three

There were two new cards on the table next to the hospital bed. One of them said, *Get Well Soon*, the other, *Sorry You're Unwell*. Ava wanted to make an aeroplane out of all those cards, with their meek-coloured sympathy, and fly out of the long-stay ward, go anywhere else.

She pressed a button by her bed and waited. She needed to wee. The nurses assisted with her toilet needs and, at first, she had felt a kind of shame and would apologise as they removed the filled bedpan from beneath her, but now she just went, because, what else was she going to do?

'How are you feeling today?' a nurse said, raising her bed. Ava couldn't tell the nurses apart. They were all the same to her – drifting in and out of focus as they took charge of her body, wrapping a blood-pressure cuff around her arm, or sticking a thermometer into her ear – poking and jabbing her flesh, and then leaving, their shoes light against the linoleum floors.

So long as they kept the morphine in her blood, Ava had no cause for complaint.

'I need to urinate,' Ava told the nurse, feeling heat rise to her cheeks.

A week before, a young doctor with a handsome face had told Ava that she'd fractured her pelvis and right tibia. When he'd stood close, listening with his stethoscope, she'd worried that she smelt of sweat and that without her bra, he would think her chest was flat.

He'd told her that the operations on her pelvis and leg had taken eight hours, had only been performed once they'd stabilised her blood pressure that'd fallen too low. And now there was metal in her flesh in the form of nails and plates.

He returned now to explain in detail. 'Think of your recovery as a journey,' he said and smiled at her. Ava noticed that his bottom teeth were crooked; it was something that pleased her a great deal, finding an imperfection like that on a person who seemed at first glance to be completely spotless.

The doctor gave her various time frames, all of them prefaced with, 'If there are no further complications, and there can always be complications . . .' He said she would be in a wheelchair for three months while the pelvis healed. The right leg would take four to six months, but she would be able to use crutches once the pelvis was strong. What struck Ava was the way he said '*the* pelvis', '*the* leg', like they were detached from her, and she was starting to feel that way, like her body was a foreign thing.

The cast on her leg went all the way up to her thigh. Only her toes were visible, a smear of dirty pink polish crowning each nail. She could hear her mother saying, 'Get a pedicure. Comb your hair.'

'You're like Jesus,' Jane said, sitting by the bed. 'All those nails drilled into you.' Her mother's friend was her first visitor. Ava wished it was somebody else in that chair. Someone who didn't mention Jesus so much.

Jane moved a strand of grey hair from her face and tucked it behind her ear. From this angle on the bed, a few hairs were visible on Jane's chin and Ava wondered if they'd always been there, those stray hairs, or whether she hadn't had a chance to get rid of them before this visit. It was something Ava thought about after Jane left, those hairs on her chin, how you could discover something new about a person when you looked at them from a different angle.

'You're looking better. There's more colour in your cheeks.'

'This isn't your first visit?'

Jane's eyes widened in shock. 'Who do you think was sleeping by your bed when they brought you in?' She straightened her back against the seat. 'I'm filling out papers from the lawyer I was telling you about. Henry Williams. He's a friend.'

'What for?'

'Compensation. You need to be compensated while you're off work.'

They talked about the department store. Ava told Jane she'd forgotten to order the Levi's trousers for Mrs Lambert. Mrs Lambert was one of those customers who thought the world was owed to her, that all the sales associates at Green's department store were there to satisfy her unreasonable demands. She expected the store to honour her returns without receipts. The items she tried to return had been used. An indiscreet stain here, a scuff there. She expected the staff to order in new stock when the warehouses were out. To bring brands in that they didn't sell. Ava was suddenly glad not to be at work.

21

'Don't worry about her. I'll put the order in tomorrow. I'll ask Pastor Lukas to include you in Friday prayers too.'

Ava opened her mouth to object about the prayers but didn't see the point – Jane did what she wanted.

A stout police officer with a red face came by to speak with her. Ten days had passed since the accident. One of the nurses told her he had been before, but she hadn't been able to answer his questions then. Her condition was only now deemed stable. Sometimes she could hear doctors and nurses discussing her on the other side of the curtain. *The tibia. The pelvis. The patient.* She had never felt more unstable in her life.

The police officer had a cold, indifferent way about him. He asked why she'd been walking along the road at night and whether she had any reflective gear on.

'I received a letter from my father,' Ava said, rubbing her temples. 'I needed to clear my head.'

'And the reflective gear?'

'Well, it wasn't dark when I left the house.' Ava wondered who wore reflective gear when they stepped out of their own front door. *I am here! Do not injure the tibia or the pelvis!*

He took notes and said he would send a copy of the report in a few days' time.

In the early afternoon, Ava began to feel desperately bored. She had asked one of the nurses about getting a television in the room, but the nurse shook her head. There were none available at present. She occupied the windowless quarter of the room, just a bare off-white wall to the left side of her bed. Three other women were recovering in this space. It was the room where broken women were sent to mend.

The elderly woman to her right had fallen out of her bathtub, thrown her hip out and broken her wrist. When her children had first come to visit her, she had pleaded with them to take her back to their flat. She was lonely in this room. No one listened to her. She could not watch her soap operas. If she had to stay, would they sit with her a little while longer?

Ava heard the children whisper to one of the nurses through the curtain. They asked about discharge arrangements. Would someone go to their mother's flat once she was back to change her ostomy bags? Could transport be organised by the hospital? They didn't think they could manage it themselves. They had jobs. Children. Other responsibilities. Ava got the impression that they felt a kind of shame, the way they lowered their voices, covering up their discomfort with polite language. They could not take care of their mother.

'Stay just a little while longer?' the woman said again to her children as they were leaving.

Ava wondered then about her father, his desperate plea to see her again. Hardly a word in twenty-two years, and then – *Can we meet?* He was dying, would be dead and gone before the year was out. No mention of what he was dying from, only that his fate was certain. There was a whole paragraph about pain and suffering and how he wouldn't let the pain take hold of him, how he was making arrangements to end his life.

He wanted a clean, civilised death. Perhaps it was the morphine in her system, but Ava thought what he'd written made sense. Why wait around for the big colourful mess of death?

He regretted their time apart. He'd written that too. His

lack of effort in keeping in contact when he'd moved to Sydney to be editor-in-chief at a national paper – it was something he would always regret. But he didn't apologise for Sandra Banks. He'd never acknowledged what had happened there. Ava remembered the story of his scandal printed in a popular women's magazine, thirteen years ago. Her mother had bought an issue, had slammed it onto the coffee table for Ava to read.

'See,' she'd said, her eyes large. 'I knew it all along.'

Ava remembered her father's terse response to the allegations. *Yes, it's true she fell pregnant, but I never threatened her to have the abortion . . .*

What surprised Ava most was that her father was dying. She had not thought him capable of this vulnerability. She had no memories of him ill in bed. Unable to move. A pain that he could not overcome. Even with a hangover, he'd stayed relatively pleasant. She had assumed that he would always be some place in the distance, on the very edge of her life, there when she needed to conjure him up.

She was desperate for a distraction from the hospital and her father. She wanted to dream of a crush, the prospect of a happy future awaiting her when she recovered.

There weren't any particularly interesting memories of previous lovers to look fondly upon now, like an old, romantic film reel. At most, there was Marcus O'Neil's long and girthy penis to think about, the half-blur of it that last night they'd been together in his car. 'Does it hurt, having a penis like that?' she'd asked, and he'd looked at her like she was a clown. They'd met up a few times, always in the back seat of his Fiat, but now he was dating a girl who liked to sail and they'd done a sailing trip together in France, so apparently it was serious. Ava would have to look elsewhere for that sort of comfort.

The last date she had been on was with Kyle from the shoe department. He had no conversation or charm and had spoken mostly about work and people they both knew. He had spent a great deal of time talking about a female customer whose feet were a size eleven and how she'd been appalled that he had nothing to show her in that size. Ava had smiled and looked at her watch. When, at the end of the night, despite her best efforts to discourage him, he'd pressed his lips to hers, Ava had felt pale and depressed. It was one of those dates that made her question everything about her life – how she ended up there, where she was headed next.

She had never felt as lifeless and unattractive as she did now, overly warm in her hospital bed, clammy with sweat, bristles of hair growing under her armpits and in the space between her eyebrows. Michael was made in their father's image, fair and tall, while she had inherited her mother's features, that slight bump on her nose and dark, prominent eyebrows – a look that required constant care and maintenance. A boy at school had called her exotic once, like she was something colourful and feathered, and she had felt her eyes widen in shock. She had seen how her mother waged war against her own hair, plucking, straightening, colouring.

The diary Ava kept in her handbag was full of appointments for waxing and threading, the goal always to remove the hair by the root. For a few weeks following a wax, Ava would have the confidence to giggle at bars, sometimes looking to get close to someone just so they could feel her skin, raw and inflamed, but more importantly, hairless. At work, she found she could look customers in the eye, raise her freshly shaped eyebrows at them when they wanted to refund swimming costumes with stains in the white crotch flap. There was a sense of being completely unstoppable when everything was tidy like that, and she invited people to inspect, to judge her worthy. But, inevitably, the hairs returned, and Ava was again her mother's daughter.

A young man she'd never seen before pulled the curtain back and stood at the foot of her bed. He was tall and thin, and his brown eyes were sullen. He carried a pink orchid between his hands. Ava hoped he was delivering the flower to her because she loved orchids, the subtle, romantic bend of the stem. But there was no one who would send her this gift. Jane didn't believe in frivolities.

'How are you feeling?' the young man asked, and Ava knew at once he was the man who'd hit her with his car.

He looked to be in his early twenties, much younger than she'd thought – the deep gravel of his voice was deceptive – and she hadn't imagined him ethnic either.

'I'm alive,' she said.

It wasn't something that she'd expected to feel, but there was an expansion of warmth inside, meeting him again. She remembered his touch, how he'd held her hand.

Ava didn't recall his name when he said it was Sam Ghadimi. Almost two weeks had passed since the accident. The details were hazy. He'd apologised, and that she remembered well.

'Do you mind that I'm here?' he said. 'I don't want to make you uncomfortable or anything.'

Ava smiled. 'I don't mind.'

He turned and nodded to a man and a woman who were hovering by the door. The woman edged closer and asked Ava if they could come in. She nodded and they joined Sam at the foot of her bed, smiling like they were all good friends. Sam introduced the couple as his parents, which was easy to tell; he had his father's protruding chin and his mother's brown eyes, except hers had dark crescents beneath them, like she'd known life's hardship. Now it felt crowded, and Ava began to worry about the way her hair looked and her elevated leg on display, her toenails rough and discoloured.

Sam's father cleared his throat. 'Sam will take care of you for as long as necessary. He explained to us your situation.'

'What situation?'

'That you are alone,' said Mrs Ghadimi. 'We are sorry about your mother.'

Sam glared at his mother, before they all started speaking quickly to each other in a language she couldn't understand. Ava thought perhaps this was all a hallucination, something that happened when there was too much morphine in the system.

'He is telling us to leave the room because we are disturbing you,' Mrs Ghadimi said, and Sam rolled his eyes like an embarrassed teenager. His parents said they would wait outside.

Once they were alone, Sam apologised for his parents. 'We can't stay, actually. There's a big shipment coming into the shop from Manchester. But do you mind if I come by every now and then to visit? Without my parents.'

'You really don't have to do that.'

'I want to,' he said, and then his eyes shifted to her leg. 'Are you in pain?'

She shook her head.

He looked relieved and moved in closer. 'I went back to

that ditch on Bath Road,' he said, pulling out her father's letter from his pocket. 'You said it was important.'

Ava took the letter, feeling her chest tighten with a sense of panic. 'Thank you,' she said, her voice thin and low. Her first thought was that Sam had read the letter and the prospect of someone else knowing brought an incredible sense of relief, the closest thing to happiness. She heard herself ask: 'Did you read it?'

Sam placed the orchid on the table next to the cards. He nodded reluctantly. And then he looked to the doorway where his parents were waiting.

Ava said, 'Come back soon.'

Four

Michael's first landlord on the Lower East Side had told him to lower his expectations. He'd shown Michael around a studio apartment, barely 300 square feet, the eaves grazing the top of his head. People were always telling him to lower his expectations at that time in his life, but these were tired people with little imagination.

Layla had laughed when Michael told her this, blowing smoke from the corner of her mouth. They were on a first date. 'Not everyone has the *luxury* of an imagination. An imagination costs time. It costs money.' Michael thought she looked beautiful, the way the candlelight flickered over her face.

She took him back to her apartment that same night and poured coffee into little glass cups and told him about Lebanon, how the moon was different there. Large and yellow. Closer. He drank the coffee, which was bitter on his tongue, and then she kissed him and told him to take off his pants.

Michael knew it was love when she said they ought to break up before things got serious. She'd been accepted to do a master's in Melbourne, the other side of the world.

They would disappoint each other, the way couples did in long-distance relationships. What was the point in that? She'd explained it that way, and Michael had agreed.

At the encouragement of friends, Michael had started seeing a political science major, Nancy Brockman, a few months later. Nancy Brockman, with her swimmer's shoulders and easy smile, fell in love with Michael, but he did not love her back. Still, they laughed when they went to see films together, and Nancy spent a lot of time with her pale calves on either side of Michael's head, rocking gently with pleasure. When she bought him an iPod shuffle for his birthday, with dozens of songs already uploaded, he told her that his heart was elsewhere, specifically in Melbourne. Nancy asked if she could keep the iPod shuffle and he said that it was only right that she did.

Michael took a red-eye flight to Melbourne on New Year's Day. He'd drunk too much the night before and turned up at Layla's place smelling of beer and sweat, his eyes sagging with tiredness, but she had looked at him with confused happiness. They had bacon on sourdough bread and made love in her living room because her roommate was away. When her course ended a few months later, she moved back to New York.

'I don't want kids,' she'd said when they moved into their first apartment together. All their furniture was second-hand, found in different garage sales in the suburbs surrounding the city, everything used except for the bed. She'd wanted that to be new so they could break it in together.

The idea of children had felt distant then, a different life. 'I just want you,' Michael had told her in the darkness of their bedroom, and they had both slept soundly.

When Michael had asked Layla to marry him a few years later in a quiet corner of Central Park, the season's flu stuffed up their noses, she had said yes and then they had both cried and coughed. They passed around celebratory three-ply tissues and held each other in the snow, their teeth chattering from the excitement and fever. On the way home, the diamond ring shone on her finger, even under the dull fluorescent lights of the bus. Before they got off at their stop, Layla said again that she didn't want to have children.

'You're all I need,' Michael had replied, but that night he found that he couldn't sleep, even after two doses of cough syrup, his mouth full of that bitter peppermint taste.

When Michael turned thirty-three, he told Layla that he wanted to be a father. For months, he'd been suffering quietly, walking past families and feeling a deep sadness. He could name the thing that was missing in his life: he wanted to be a father. 'It's important to me,' he had said to her, and then she cried a little and left the apartment for some space to think. When she returned a few hours later, her eyes swollen from crying, he told her that if she didn't want to have children, then that would be the end of it. They could be one of those couples who spent winter holidays trekking in the Andes.

'I don't want to become somebody else,' Layla had said later that night, holding her head in her palms. 'I'm afraid I'll turn into someone else if we have a kid.'

They talked about how she could still work and go out with her friends and they would still have sex in different positions, not just quiet missionary like other couples probably did once they had children. They could be different from their friends, he said, the ones with the screeching babies. Modern parents – clever and stylish, taking their children on holidays to places like Borneo. They could stay in a treetop hotel. She had laughed, and said, 'All right, let's do this.'

That first time they tried for a baby, Layla was shy and nervous. Michael's throat was completely dry. It was like they had never been together. The gentleness of the act, their faces looking into each other: Love. After the first couple of months without luck, they fucked hard and fast in all positions, and like that, they conceived Jacob.

Their friend Bonnie had told them to forget their expectations when it came to raising children. She'd been the first of the group to have a baby.

'Things never turn out the way you plan them,' she'd said, making room for Layla on her couch, which was barely visible under all the toys. 'You learn to appreciate the small things when you've got kids, things you used to take for granted. Like headaches! I can't wait for a headache to strike me down so that I can make the room dark and get under the covers, let Steve deal with the little hellion.'

Laughter, laughter, but Layla paled as she ran an anxious hand over her swollen stomach. One child – they'd agreed later that night.

When Jacob was born, Layla had turned to Michael after hours of sweating and pushing and vomiting into a bucket. 'We're parents,' she'd said, ashen, strong as marble.

He had kissed her damp forehead, and when he held his son, looked at his perfectly formed mouth, all that dark hair matted on his head, Michael had thought how none of it mattered anymore. The past, his family – it was all distant and muffled now when he held his son. He would behave differently from his parents.

Another envelope came through the mail from his father. Michael took out a picture of him and Ava, standing side by side on Primrose Hill, their heads craning up. *Thought you'd want to have this*, his father had scribbled on the back. *I hope you'll get in touch.*

'What's come in the mail?' Layla called from the sitting room.

'It's just coupons.'

Michael shoved the picture into the back pocket of his jeans. The shame encasing his childhood was a cold, solid thing; it was difficult to look at, and even more difficult to explain.

Layla was unpacking picture frames from the last of their cardboard boxes. She placed them on different surfaces and then stood back, decided the photograph was not in the right place and started over again.

Jacob was colouring at his crafting table. Michael patted him on the head and told him to stay on the page. He tried to settle down to some work, but the morning sun was shining brightly through the balcony windows onto his laptop, causing him to squint as he pulled passages from recent political speeches.

> *This country was built by those who believed in more, those who rose above their circumstances . . .*
> *And all it takes is to roll up our sleeves . . .*
> *Everything is possible . . .*

Michael felt a headache edging forward. It was Saturday and he needed a break from work. He told Layla that he was popping out to the coffee shop down the street.

'Do you want anything?'

Layla was standing at a distance from a photograph of them on a beach in Sri Lanka, before Jacob was born. Michael's nose was sunburnt badly in the picture, while her brown complexion glowed.

'Yes,' she said, not moving her gaze from the picture, like she was searching for something there. 'Black coffee with lots of sugar.'

The communal garden where they took Jacob to play was full of colour – as it should have been with the extortionate fees they paid for building maintenance. Bees hummed from flower to flower. There had been a big push last spring from the residents of the apartments to save the dwindling bee population; all sorts of pamphlets and petitions had been slipped under their door, and he knew certain flowers had been planted for the bees so that they could thrive. A letter came from a woman on the third floor, objecting to these plans, saying how her son had allergies to pollen and bee stings. That was when the door-to-door visits started from the bee supporters. Michael refused to let them in, did not want any part in the building politics. The next morning, when he'd stepped out for work, he'd knocked over a jar of honey that had been left on the doormat.

Layla said the woman and her child had moved out last winter. They were living beyond their means. It was the way of the city: adapt or move out. The area where they lived belonged to the bee lovers. Hot-yoga enthusiasts. Michael felt like a fraud, the socialist things he wrote in his middle-class apartment, spending twelve dollars on Americanos. He swatted a bee away.

The coffee shop had opened last month, and it was

impossible to get a table. Inside, it was packed with people in their late twenties hunched over laptops, nesting for hours, and Michael had to wait in line for ten minutes and then squeeze himself into a space by the window to spoon brown sugar into Layla's coffee from a Mason jar – everything in Mason jars.

He was ready to leave when a sudden knocking of glass startled him. On the other side was a woman with thick-rimmed glasses, a half-smile across her thin red lips. Michael had no idea who she was at first – perhaps a student, he thought, but she was older, and he knew all of his mature students because they always sat at the front and asked too many questions and called him Michael instead of Professor Bridges. It was her bluntly cut fringe that brought to mind the naked woman from the apartment across.

Michael felt warmth rush to his face, remembering that she had seen him completely bare, wet testicles and all. He mouthed 'Hello' through the glass, and she gestured at the empty seat at her table, inviting him to join her.

Outside, they shook hands formally like they were meeting at a conference. She said her name was Sarah Addams.

'We're getting curtains today,' Michael said, 'so the free show's over, I'm afraid.'

'Ah, that's a shame.' She spoke in an English accent, and Michael asked if she was from London.

'Camden Town. Do you know it?'

'I grew up in Hampstead, so not far.'

'Not far at all.' She gestured again for him to sit, and he accepted her invitation, resting the two hot coffees on the metal table. 'Where's your English accent?'

Michael shrugged. 'I must've just lost it over time.' But it was something deliberate, losing his accent, erasing any traces of the past that way. 'When did you move from London?'

'Just a few weeks ago. I'm only here till September. I'm teaching a summer course at NYU.'

'What do you teach?'

'Art.'

He leant forward a little. 'I'm actually a lecturer.'

His pride in his role was matched by a kind of embarrassment at the university and he dreaded the follow-up question, which was always, 'Where do you work?' He felt a slight shame whenever he named the university, which ranked somewhere in the bottom of all the league tables, except in Bakery Science, a new degree programme that was getting a lot of buzz and attention, and much of the university's funding had been diverted there.

A few years ago, Michael had applied for a professorship position in the Social Studies department at NYU. He had prepped for days and bought a new tie with blue diagonals running across it. Layla had made him a big breakfast that morning, and they had both been excited, but the position went to somebody else. For days, he'd reviewed the interview in his mind, reliving the mistakes he'd made, until Layla told him to stop torturing himself.

Sarah didn't ask where he worked and he felt relieved when she wanted to know instead about his research. He said his work focused on policy discourse analysis.

'It's a lot more interesting than it sounds,' he said, always keen to show how his work was exciting and relevant. He told her a little of what he was researching, the stories politicians told. They were familiar stories – rags to riches, against all odds, David and Goliath, that sort of thing.

'People hear these stories and are supposed to feel safe and empowered. But while politicians are telling us these stories, they're also making cuts to things like affordable-housing programmes, and people who need support suddenly can't afford rent. And failure rests on the individual's shoulders because, according to the stories – the ones we love and watch and believe in – if you work hard, then you'll rise above your circumstances.'

Sarah smiled politely. Michael thought he had bored her, or perhaps she thought he was being condescending, the way he'd explained his research like she was an under-grad student instead of an accomplished academic.

She said, 'I think I'd turn cynical if my research focused on that.'

'Yes, well . . .' He cleared his throat. 'Are you a prac-tising artist?'

She nodded her head and took out a box of cigarettes from her large tote bag, stuck one in the corner of her mouth and lit it. Those thick-rimmed glasses made it diffi-cult to guess her age, but perhaps early forties, he thought.

'I'd offer you a cigarette, but most men don't like these thin ones. They find them effeminate.'

'I don't smoke. Not for a few years. But thanks.'

She leant back into her chair. 'I make sculptures. One of my pieces is being exhibited at the Grey Art Gallery. They've put me in one of the tiny rooms next to the toilets on the second floor.' Her green eyes settled on Michael. 'I've noticed you have a son.'

'I do.'

She smiled. 'He's a sweet little thing. How old is he? One?'

'He turned two in September. He's just learnt to count to fifteen.'

'Oh?' she said, and it was clear by the way she answered that she knew little about children. 'I've actually been meaning to do a collection on fathers and sons for some time.' She hesitated then, pulling on her cigarette before continuing. 'This might sound strange, but would you consider modelling for my collection? With your son.'

'Modelling?' Michael laughed in that false, high-pitched way he hated, a laugh he had used in his failed NYU interview when the dean had said something about the weather. 'I don't really think—'

'It's actually not as strange as it sounds. Let me explain.' She blew smoke from the corner of her thin mouth. 'I just need to observe. The trouble is that it's rare seeing a father and son together on their own. It really is! You know the playground behind our apartments? I've never seen a father there without a mother or another father around. It changes the whole dynamic when there's another parent.'

'So, you'd be watching us in the playground?'

'Something like that,' she said. 'From a bench, out of the way. You'd just send me a quick message beforehand and I'd pop down with my sketchpad. I promise it's not as strange as it sounds.'

She kept repeating that, and Michael thought how her request was the strangest he'd ever received.

She took out her business card. 'This is my New York cell,' she said, writing her number on the back.

She eyed him then, some knowledge behind her gaze. 'I can immortalise you. Father and son.'

They both laughed, but he felt again like he was standing in front of her, naked.

She put her cigarette out in an empty orange juice bottle and smiled. Her teeth were white and straight, the work of expensive dentistry. 'See you around,' she said.

*

It had taken them three hours to look through curtains in specialist shops on the Lower East Side. Every time they'd gotten close to choosing, Layla had found a new way to discredit the fabric or shape. Too dark, too bright, too avant-garde, too lacy. In the end, she'd decided on grey blinds, and Michael didn't mind either way by that point.

'They go with the couch,' Layla said, playing around with several picture frames on the side table. 'Makes sense.'

Michael nodded from behind his laptop. There was an email from his editor, Lima Bardour, saying she wanted to bring forward the publication date of the book he was contributing to, so they could capitalise on the recent buzz in the news on cuts to affordable housing. She needed his chapter by the end of next week.

'Story,' Jacob said, climbing onto the chair next to his father at the table.

'It's not time for a story.'

'Story!' Jacob whined.

'Layla? Do you mind? I've really got to get this email out. It's about the book.'

'Jacob, come help Mommy,' she said, taking a photo from its frame and replacing it with another one. 'You know what? I was just thinking about how I used to *love* writing. In high school, I won a prize for a short story. Did I ever tell you that? It was about cyber-dating. A girl goes out to meet some guy she's been chatting with

39

online. Thinks she's in love. But it turns out to be her father.'

'You should start writing again,' he said, and then he wrote that in the email: *You should start writing again.*

'Story!' Jacob slammed his tiny fists onto the table. Michael shot his son a look of warning.

'It's been years since I've written anything. I'm probably very rusty.'

Jacob slammed his fists down again and knocked over his drink. A flood of orange juice rushed to the laptop. Michael picked it up and threw it down on the couch. Anger rolled through him. He spun around and shouted into his son's face.

'Why have you got to be such a little *shit*?'

Jacob's mouth fell open with a choking cry, so that there was no sound before the apartment rang with his shrill complaints.

Layla looked at Michael, stunned. 'What's got into you?' She lifted their son into her arms and took him to his bedroom.

Michael touched his face, wanting to pull out every strand of hair there. But it was true – his son was being a little shit. He wanted one of those thin cigarettes Sarah Addams had been smoking. How could he have shouted that?

The lights came on automatically when he stepped out onto the balcony. From there, he watched steam rise from the ground in front of the bakery at the end of the street.

From the back pocket of his jeans, Michael removed the picture of himself and Ava. There was little resemblance between them, brother and sister, and yet they both held the same blank expression, looking up at their father. The sun would have been behind him, the way they were struggling to keep their eyes open.

He longed then to speak to his sister. Apologise to her. Would she hang up if he called?

The steam obscured the people moving in the street below. It brought him calm, watching strangers go about their business. Michael stayed out on the balcony, staring into the billowy grey confusion, until it was close to Jacob's bedtime.

He knocked on his son's bedroom door.

'Can Daddy come in?' Layla asked, on the other side.

Michael put his ear to the door; it was all stillness.

'He says you can come in,' she called out.

Jacob was already in his rocket pyjamas, building a tower out of his blocks. Layla got up from where she was sitting next to him, stood in the doorway and watched from there.

Michael moved in closer to his son, though Jacob ignored him at first and carried on building his tower. In one swift motion, he knocked the tower down and then he looked up at his father, his gaze testing.

'I'm sorry.' Michael looked into his son's very dark eyes. 'I'm sorry I shouted before.'

Jacob didn't say anything, just handed his father a red block, and like that they built the tower back up. It was only a short while before Jacob was smiling again, like he'd forgotten about before, and it broke Michael's heart that he should so easily forget.

Jacob passed a green block to his father and told him to build a sky.

★

Michael remembered this: his father sitting across from him at the family table, the vein above his left eye getting larger.

'How are you going to turn this around?' His father's tone was sharp against his reasonable question.

Tears slid down Michael's face at the very moment he wished to appear strong. Lee shook his head. He grabbed Michael's wrist. The words written in permanent marker on his arm were still faintly visible, though he had scrubbed until his skin had turned red.

'Do you want them to keep writing *fag* and *pussy* on your arms? Is that what you want?'

'No.'

Lee dropped his son's arm and it flopped down on the dining table. Michael hoped that his father would leave it there, that he'd carry on eating and talk about work or an upcoming party and just ignore him as he did most of the time, but he leant into the back of his chair and looked at Michael from across the table with disgust.

'From over here, it looks like you want that. You *want* them to continue treating you like rubbish. You like it when they write *cocksucker* on your arm.'

'I don't . . .'

Lee frowned. 'If that's true, if that's what you *really* feel, then toughen up. Stop drawing eyes on your bloody binders like a girl. And if they come after you, you don't fucking cry. You put a bag of shit in each of their lockers.'

'I hate—'

'What? What is it that you hate? Speak up if you've got something to say!' Lee shouted, his face red with hatred. 'It's how you make people listen.'

He shook Michael's shoulder hard, but the force of this

sudden violence just caused Michael to sob more loudly, and Michael despised himself in that moment, more than he did his father.

'Christ!' Lee threw up his hands. 'I haven't even *touched* you. My father would punch me right in the face. Blood everywhere. I lost a front tooth when I was nine.' He moved his top lip, baring his teeth. 'Look,' he said, pointing to an incisor. 'It's a false tooth. My father knocked the real one right out of my mouth and I didn't cry like this. Not even close.'

Michael heard his mother say, 'Leave him,' but beyond that, no protest. He used her interjection to leave the table. She didn't follow as he'd hoped.

He waited for her in his room, lying on his bed, fists squeezed tight, but when he heard her footsteps at last, she went into her own bedroom and switched on the transistor radio. Michael listened to her soft humming.

She was getting ready for a party, and soon the house would be quiet.

Five

The old woman who'd fallen out of her bathtub was discharged from hospital. Her hip and wrists had mended. She asked about her children, whether the hospital had phoned them to say she was free to go. They would want to take her home, she was sure of this. But when the nurses said that they'd arranged an ambulance to take her home, that her children couldn't make it, the old woman muttered her disappointment.

'All they do is take. I give them birthday money. I helped with their flat deposits. And when I need something from them, where the hell are they?'

Ava thought of her mother then, how so many times she'd said to Ava, bleary from drink, 'All you do is take.' But Ava couldn't think of what she'd meant. She was the one who gave her time, her attentions, her money – her life – to her mother.

When the old woman was gone, Ava asked an Irish nurse if she could move to that part of the room. She desperately wanted to see out of the window.

They moved her bed and things. Sam's orchid rested

there on the window ledge, sunlight dappling it through the glass.

Sam came to visit a few days after he'd brought the orchid and letter. He took her out to the courtyard in a wheelchair. Two nurses who had been tending to her were sitting at a nearby table having their sandwiches, and it was nice to see them that way, smiling and breezy. Outside the hospital ward, they were not caregivers, fussing over her body, but regular people, enjoying the sun.

Sam had brought games with him. Snakes and ladders, backgammon and draughts. Two-person games that felt completely outdated. Games her grandparents might have played when they were children. He looked stylish in his T-shirt and fitted jeans, his hair all in his face like the guitarist in a band.

He said he was turning twenty-one at the end of July. 'I feel so old.'

Ava arched her eyebrows in exaggerated offence. He said how she looked young for thirty-one, but sitting in that wheelchair, playing draughts, it was difficult to feel anything but geriatric.

'Really, you've got a good face,' Sam said, moving one of his pieces on the board. 'It's a happy face, you know? Some people look sad all the time, but your face isn't like that. You could be a presenter on a children's show.'

Ava laughed. 'And that's a good thing?'

'Yeah. Definitely.'

Sam relaxed as he began to win; there was an ease and confidence about him, as if those moments of focus made him forget that he'd hit her with his car, and he could be himself, instead of repentant and timid. He jumped over one of her pieces, kinged himself and then apologised, but there was a look of quiet satisfaction on his face. Any move Ava made now would result in another piece being taken.

'Your father pronounced your name differently.'

'Yes.'

'Where are you from originally?' she asked.

'Welton.'

'I meant—'

'I know what you meant.' Sam took two of her pieces in one go, another king. 'I'm Iranian. But I was born in Welton.'

Sam went on to explain about his parents leaving Iran when they were students in their early twenties, before the Iranian Revolution. He'd seen black-and-white photographs of them in wide bell-bottomed jeans in Tehran, his mother without the headscarves the government now imposed.

'The worst was finding pictures of my dad and uncles in Speedos at a beach. They loved wearing those things,' he said.

'Have you ever been to Iran?'

'No,' he said. 'But all of my cousins are there. Twelve boys between four families. One of them reached out to me in an email last year.'

'What did he say?'

'He asked if I was a virgin.' Sam laughed, and Ava wondered briefly what answer he'd given his cousin. She thought he was probably not a virgin, and she suspected that he'd had a few lovers. His easy smile – when he relaxed – and the lovely glow of his skin were enough to convince someone, if not several people.

'What about you?' he said.

Ava thought for a moment that he was asking about her virginity, but she remembered that they were talking about their heritage.

'My mother was Greek.'

'Can you speak the language?'

'No,' Ava said.

Her mother never spoke it at home. When Ava had asked her mother why she always spoke English, Elena had said that her father wanted her to integrate into British life when they'd moved from Cyprus when she was seven. And Ava's grandmother, Katerina, used to laugh at Elena's broken Cypriot accent. When they went to gatherings in London with other Greeks, Elena's speech had been slow and halting. No confidence behind her words and they always seemed to be the wrong ones. She'd felt stupid after those gatherings and her mother hadn't helped. 'That is not how *my* side of the family speaks in Athens,' Katerina had told her daughter.

Ava was finally able to move a piece forward without an immediate threat of danger.

Sam's phone was always vibrating in his jeans and he often waited a couple of minutes before discreetly checking it as he did now. Ava's own phone's battery had died a few days after the accident and no one had a charger for it because it was an old model – no internet, just a basic flip phone. Sam had laughed when he'd seen it on her side table, like it was an artefact, some relic from the past. When he asked why she hadn't upgraded, Ava told him she had the internet at home and didn't need to take it with her, though she realised it would have been useful in hospital. She was growing more and more desperate for entertainment.

His phone buzzed again, and Ava asked if he had a girl-friend who was trying to get in touch.

'Yes,' he said, his eyes focused on the board. 'She texts a lot because she's back in Nottingham now that uni's out. Long distance is tough.'

Ava didn't say that Nottingham was only a few hours' drive from Welton, so hardly long distance.

A few years ago, she'd dated an accountant from Singapore. They'd met on a chatroom and arranged to have simultaneous meals together a couple of times a week, though the time difference meant she was having lunch while he had his dinner. He told her she was beautiful and how much he looked forward to seeing her in the flesh, and then he went on to list all the things he would do to her once they met, moving his hands vigorously beneath the keyboard. His enthusiasm filled her up, the way he lusted after her. A few times, when Ava had sat topless and cold in front of the webcam, he'd shown her just how excited he was, but the image was pixelated and none of it appealed. The noises he made, his desperate need for her, was enough. When he said he thought it might be love and spoke of expensing a trip to London to his firm, Ava's heart sank a little. The distance had been reassuring; she didn't want anything serious, too real. She began to avoid his Skype calls and, like that, it – whatever it was – fizzled out.

Ava liked being outside, away from the white walls of her room, but the sun in the courtyard was strong and her chest grew damp. Her leg beneath the long cast was itchy, and a faint animal smell rose from it. She felt trapped in the wheelchair and lonely suddenly, knowing that Sam would leave soon and she would have to return to the silent room.

She looked at Sam. His eyes rarely met hers. It was her move, but she couldn't see what to do: everywhere there was danger.

'What did you think of my father's letter?'

'What do you mean?'

'Do you think he really is sick?'

'I assume so. I mean, that's what he said. I don't know, though. Why would he lie?'

Ava told Sam that her father had often lied. She told him that she hadn't seen him in twenty years. She and Michael were supposed to have visited Sydney the first summer after her father had moved away. Michael hadn't wanted to go, but she'd been looking forward to it all year, seeing her father again, going to all the places he'd mentioned on the phone. *Let's go to the Opera House! Let's go see the dolphins! Let's go! Let's go!* But when it was time to buy their plane tickets, their father said to hold tight. It was a bad time for him. Very busy. Christmas would be better, but then Christmas was no good either. He'd met someone and she was taking him to New Zealand to meet her parents. The pattern repeated and then he stopped sending cards, making calls.

Her father had tried to get in touch ten years ago, when he'd moved back to London and was divorced again, but by then it was too late. She could not forgive him.

She left out the part about Sandra Banks and the scandal of her father's affair because she thought it might taint the picture too much.

Sam didn't say anything. She wasn't sure what she expected from him, what she'd hoped to achieve by telling this story. Some reassurance, perhaps, that it was not unreasonable for her to want to see her father again and that, by the same token, she would be completely justified in forsaking him.

Ava moved her piece on the board, and he jumped over her few remaining pieces. She was glad for the game to be over. The nurses on the table across stood, their metal chairs scraping against the pavement. They threw their sandwich wrappers into the bin before passing through the glass doors that led back to the ward.

'Do you think I should see him?'

'I can't really tell you what to do.' Sam shifted in his seat again, and it irritated Ava how he couldn't sit still or give a straight answer.

'Would you take me back inside, then?'

Ava helped him put all the playing pieces into the worn box and then he wheeled her back to her room, parking the wheelchair against the side of the bed so she could push herself up with her arms.

'Thanks for visiting,' Ava said, and Sam looked like he was about to say something, but he just smiled and left.

★

Being in hospital meant too many hours in a day. It meant staring at a wall for an afternoon and getting angry at people you hadn't thought about in years and missing others. It meant over-plucking eyebrows in front of a small, dirty hand mirror, a mirror that magnified everything to monstrous proportions.

Ava asked for the papers every morning. Her mother had banned the news from the bungalow, because it reminded her too much of Lee.

'Who needs to know about what's happening in London or China? Those things will never touch us.'

And she was right, they never seemed to, and for years

they lived that way, in their own blind vacuum, outside of space and time. Except there were a few cases when the wider world infiltrated the bubble.

'Another terror attack,' someone would say in the department-store staffroom. 'These immigrants . . .'

Ava read the *Welton Standard* first. Boy Fined for Selling Gin Lemonade on Riverside. Council Tax Hikes. Danger of Death on Days Road. She read the article about the road, and waited to feel something, the mild thrill that came with exploring danger from a safe distance, but she felt only disappointment. The article wasn't news so much as speculation. No accidents had been reported recently. A few locals gave interviews, saying how they'd like to see a zebra crossing, how there would be a catastrophic accident there one day and someone would pay the price with their life. It was a symptom of living in a town like Welton, people having the time to think of 'one day', giving interviews about 'one day'.

The *Messenger* had been her father's paper after he'd moved back to London. There was a new editor-in-chief, Kathy Roberts. Ava wondered what her father thought about a woman sitting in 'his' chair. It'd taken her completely by surprise when two years ago, on a rainy afternoon in November, Ava's mother had mentioned that Lee was retiring from the paper.

Elena had been sitting in her corner of the sofa by the window, her feet up on the coffee table. Her ankles looked so thin, the bones sticking out at the sides. When she spoke about Lee, her small made-up eyes were focused on the fashion magazine between her hands. She flipped through the pages decidedly.

She had been, it seemed, keeping tabs on him. She'd

said how, in front of colleagues, Lee would have given praise to Kathy Roberts, telling everyone that she would make a much better editor than him. His words and facial expressions would have been carefully chosen, her mother had said, all the time her eyes focused on the magazine. In private, he would probably claim she was unsuitable for the job. He would say that she'd try to undo all the good he'd implemented just to prove she was in charge. 'Because nobody could ever be better than your father. Especially not a woman.'

Ava's mother had often talked about Lee. Drunk or sober, and after years of separation, she had spoken of him in a spiteful tone. Even the happy memories were framed by suspicion.

Ava pieced together the story of her parents' meeting, filling in the gaps where her mother had stayed silent.

Elena had been sharing a flat with two Greek-Cypriot girls in Camden. A year before that, her father had died of a stroke. The summer they buried him in the Greek Orthodox part of Hendon Cemetery, the IRA had planted bombs in three train stations – Euston, King's Cross and Victoria. Katerina had announced she was done with this country. What reason did she have to stay? She had no intention of being blown up by the Irish. She'd take her chances with the junta in Greece.

'I'm staying,' Elena had said, surprising her mother. For years, she had dreamt of owning a clothing boutique like her father's friend Costas in Camden. She'd worked for him for a few years, at first in his factory alongside her mother as a machinist, and then in his showroom. She loved watching customers admire the sturdy, discreet hemline of a skirt. When her mother returned to Greece, she found a job in Women's Apparel at Selfridges. It was a start, and it meant she could support herself and stay in London.

She had met Lee one cold evening in December. He was looking to buy a silk scarf for his mother for Christmas. His parents lived in the Midlands. His father was a miner who thought his son had lost his mind, moving to London to be a journalist. Lee told her all of this while she showed him delicate scarves. He didn't pay attention to the scarves, just said, 'The soft pink one will do.' He said his mother was Irish, so she would scold him and say, 'Now what did you go and buy this for?'

He also told Elena that she had beautiful eyes. He had a smile that told a thousand lies. Elena had said this to Ava with a smirk, and Ava couldn't tell if her mother fully disapproved of his charm.

Lee asked Elena to dinner that same night and they met outside the store when her shift was over. They ate at a French restaurant. He made recommendations on the menu and she said, 'I'll have the same,' when they ordered.

Lee's eyes lit up when Elena said she was from Cyprus. He asked questions like he was interviewing her for a feature. When did her family move to London? How old was she? What did she think of enosis? What of the junta? What did she think of their fall? Was she affected by the Turkish invasion in the north?

Elena couldn't tell if his questions and interest had anything to do with her. But she liked how he took chances, the way he spoke with ease and confidence. She could tell even then, by the way the waitress spoke to him, by the way the other diners kept glancing over, that he could command attention.

After dinner, Lee suggested a walk through the city to the river. As they were strolling along Seymour Mews – an explosion. Glass fell from the sky like rain. People screamed and shouted and then a mob of frightened people rushed towards them. Lee looked at Elena. He led her out of the chaos, to Manchester Square where there were trees, away from all that broken glass.

Ava imagined her father brave and strong, ensuring her mother's safety before leaving her to investigate. But Elena said that she'd felt abandoned, the way he took off, and she should've known it then – that his work would always come first.

He weaved through the running people, towards danger to get his story. Elena waited for twenty minutes in the cold green park before she made her way back to her flat, shaken.

They hadn't exchanged numbers so she didn't think she would see him again. Later, on the radio, she heard a bomb had gone off outside Selfridges, and the following morning she saw a picture in the paper of a mannequin's severed head lying in all that glass. They opened the store even with the missing windows. She called in sick for her evening shift. Her flatmates asked if she was OK because she kept to her room. And then another explosion, this time in the furniture department at Harrods.

Elena phoned her mother. 'Come to Athens,' Katerina said. 'Things are better here.'

Jennifer Spitfields, Elena's boss, called to tell Elena that if she was serious about keeping her job, she would have to come into work. She had called in sick a few times at this point. Elena went in the following morning and there was Lee, loitering by the leather gloves display. He told her he'd returned every day since the explosion to see if she was working. He apologised for leaving her that night.

'It's just the nature of my job,' he said. Elena told Ava how he loved saying that, and how, over the years, she grew sick to death of hearing it.

They got married a few months later. Elena told Ava she married Lee because he was attentive, when he wanted to be. She was lonely and the Greek-Cypriot flatmates were getting married too.

She was careful not to say it was love – that she had loved Lee, and that was why she'd married him. She couldn't admit to a thing like that. When she gave her reasons for not leaving the marriage sooner, she hadn't mentioned love then either. She said she'd stayed because of Ava and Michael. The church demanded it. They were both Catholic. Her mother disapproved of divorce. It was for financial security that she'd stayed so long. She never, ever said that it was for love, though Ava knew she'd loved him desperately, the way she'd laughed at his jokes, her eyes smiling when he brought home gossip from the office, speculations he couldn't publish about film stars and politicians. And she giggled when he grabbed her to dance in the kitchen and she closed her eyes, happiness there on her face. She couldn't tell Ava that all she'd ever wanted was to hold her husband's attention.

They spent their wedding night at the Hilton. A few weeks later, a bomb went off in that same hotel lobby, killing two people and injuring dozens.

'Our relationship from the start was born out of conflict,' Elena said. 'In London. Abroad. There was always violence around us. Your father is a sadist. He's drawn to conflict.'

Ava had thought, *So are you.*

★

'Knock, knock,' the solicitor, Henry Williams, announced himself on the other side of the curtain. Ava told him he was all right to draw it back.

'How are you doing now?' he asked, his gaze somewhere just above her head.

'Surviving.'

He sucked on a blackcurrant cough drop, the smell sickly. Ava's answer seemed to please him a great deal because he started speaking quickly and with animation about the car insurance, how it would likely cover the physiotherapy she required once discharged from hospital and her salary from the department store too, until she could work again.

'This is all good news,' Ava said.

'Yes, but there's something else I wanted to talk to you about. Another route we could explore.' He looked at Ava for the first time, his long face settling into a more serious shape. 'Sam Ghadimi's parents own a profitable curtain shop in Sheffield. The car he was driving the night he hit you is also used for company purposes. We could potentially file a suit against their business.'

It was then that Ava thought how Mr Williams reminded her of those advertisements on television – a middle-aged, balding lawyer with a concerned, serious look fixed on him, a phone number flashing across the screen in a cheap red font.

'If my salary and medical bills are covered, that's all I really need.'

'Oh, I'd give it more thought,' he said, biting into the cough drop. 'You could live with debilitating pain for the rest of your life. Not to mention the psychological trauma. We're talking about the possibility of a six-figure settlement here.'

Six

Michael's in-laws were driving down from Chicago to stay for the long weekend. He looked forward to their visits. It was Layla who would go to bed and leave him on the sofa with her parents having another sherry. She usually shot them a look: 'Shouldn't you all be getting some sleep?' Mrs Zaytoon liked to call her daughter a party pooper, an expression she'd picked up from daytime television.

On some level, Michael knew his enthusiasm irritated Layla. She was on edge for days before her parents arrived. They cleaned the apartment together, but Layla continued, scrubbed aggressively in places no one could see, like behind the couch and in wardrobe cupboards. When Michael pointed out how her efforts were unnecessary, Layla paused from her cleaning, looked at him, her dark eyes grave and wide, and said, 'My mother will see. She sees everything.'

When Michael arrived home from work, the Zaytoons were there drinking tea – Mrs Zaytoon on the sofa with Layla and Mr Zaytoon on the floor playing with Jacob. They stood to greet Michael, kissing him on both cheeks. Layla asked her parents if they wanted more tea.

'Sit down,' Mrs Zaytoon commanded. 'We have had *too much* tea. Yacoob,' she said, '*yallah*, come here.' Jacob was in a shy, weary phase, staying close to Layla.

'How are you, Michael? How is work?' Mr Zaytoon said.

'Good. Work is good.'

The Zaytoons never asked about Michael's family. Layla had told them it was a delicate subject. 'They won't understand,' Layla had said when Michael told her that he didn't want to invite his mother to their wedding. 'They're Lebanese. These things matter to them. You need to invite your family.'

Michael had told Layla that his mother was an alcoholic. He avoided details. He didn't tell her about the time his mother had harassed a cashier at their local bank, calling him ugly and a selfish lover (she suspected) because he'd refused to let her withdraw money she didn't have. It was sunny and she'd made her way through too many gin and tonics and went to the bank, demanding to withdraw four-hundred thousand pounds from her account, although her credit was twenty-two pounds and thirty-five pence. She'd wanted to buy a house on the other side of the road with a view of the river in her bedroom. Michael didn't tell Layla that his mother had been arrested for drunk-driving, swerving home one night, the River Derwent to her right, dark like the paved road ahead. She'd lost her licence and Ava had had to drive her into work for a year. He didn't tell her that his sister sent him urgent emails about their mother, and he never knew what to say.

Michael didn't trust his mother not to ruin his wedding. He couldn't risk the embarrassment. And he couldn't invite Ava to the wedding without including his mother.

In the end, he sent the wedding invitation home three weeks before the day. As the days passed and no answer came, he felt more relaxed, but then, on the day, a sense of guilt like a dark fog hovered close, when he posed for photographs, cut the cake, danced his first dance as husband. All the things that should've brought joy on his wedding day had been spoilt by this sick feeling of guilt. He sent home a picture of himself and Layla and received a letter back from his mother a few weeks later. Her handwriting was sloppy, the letters drooping the way they did when she'd had too much to drink. She congratulated him on his marriage and said she hoped their children would not inherit his wife's enormous nostrils. She signed with all her love and told him to come home soon. Ava sent a card separately, saying only, *Congratulations.*

Layla had made reservations for an early dinner at a Lebanese restaurant a few blocks from the apartment. The Zaytoons liked eating there, and it was their habit to visit at least once when they came to stay.

The evening was pleasant and warm, and Michael felt relaxed walking along the street with his mother-in-law, through the shadows of oak trees, leaves wavering softly in the breeze. Her strides were short, her pace impossibly slow, and Layla and her father were much further ahead with Jacob. He knew their slow amble was a nuisance for the men and women in suits hurrying past them, eager to get home after a long day in the office, but he didn't want to rush her.

'Do you mind if I take your arm?' Mrs Zaytoon asked.

'No,' Michael said, 'of course not.' He extended his arm out to her and smiled as she took it. It pleased him to be able to support her, to have her close.

'My doctor keeps telling me, "Lose weight, you are too fat."'

'Your doctor calls you fat?'

'He's from Lebanon so it is OK.'

Michael's smile widened.

'How is Layla doing at home?'

Michael thought for a moment before responding. He didn't want to reveal everything to Mrs Zaytoon, the anxiety and various checking behaviours Layla seemed to have developed recently. He couldn't imagine anything worse than Mrs Zaytoon asking Layla about it.

'I think she's having a hard time adjusting. She loved her job. I think she misses going to the office.'

'Jacob is most important,' Mrs Zaytoon said simply, and Michael was relieved she didn't say anything more about the thing that had happened to Jacob in September.

A man stepped out from behind them into the road. 'Fucking ridiculous,' he said as he passed.

'Have you got a problem?' Michael shot out, suddenly hot with anger.

The man turned to face him and Mrs Zaytoon. He looked affronted and adjusted his glasses as if he was the one who'd been sworn at. 'Well, yes. You're walking at a snail's pace and taking up the whole sidewalk.' He tucked his briefcase under his arm, and it was obvious by the way his gaze shifted around that he was anxious. 'I haven't got time for this.'

Mrs Zaytoon didn't speak until the man was out of earshot. 'Michael, you should be careful. You do not know if a stranger is a crazy man with a gun. You cannot be sure in this country.'

She picked up her pace then, and her breathing became

laboured, quick and shallow. Michael was sorry and said he didn't mean to upset her, that there was no need to walk so quickly. She gave him a light, playful shove with her elbow, and he knew he was forgiven.

At dinner, Layla and her parents spoke mostly in Arabic, even to the waitress, and it was easy to tell how proud they felt being able to speak their own language. Michael was used to it. He didn't mind not understanding what they were saying. It was a relief not to have to pay attention to their words, not to have to participate. Their open bodies and hand gestures and laughter confirmed that all was well in the family.

Turning to Michael at the end of the meal, Mrs Zaytoon said in English, 'Did you like your food?'

'Yes,' Michael said. 'Not as good as your cooking, though.'

And here, Layla whispered, 'Suck-up,' her eyes gleaming, and Mrs Zaytoon asked her daughter to translate.

After the plates were cleared and Mrs Zaytoon had fretted over how little Jacob had eaten, there was the usual battle over who would pay the bill. Mr Zaytoon reached out first and kept the bill close to his chest while he reviewed it, his round glasses low on the bridge of his nose. Michael wanted to pay, insisting that they were his guests, but Mr Zaytoon's voice rose in protest, while the waitress looked tired and bored, standing over their table with the card machine between her hands. It became necessary for Michael to back down. Layla and Michael thanked Mr Zaytoon for the meal.

'My pleasure,' he said proudly, slipping his wallet back into his grey suit jacket.

That night, the Zaytoons slept on the sofa bed in the

living room. They always refused to take Layla and Michael's bed, though it was offered. Their snoring filled every corner of the apartment.

In the darkness of their bedroom, behind the protection of the shut door, Layla complained about her mother. 'She thinks Jacob is losing touch with his roots. What am I supposed to do? I can't exactly speak to him in a language you don't understand.'

Michael listened. Sometimes when Layla complained like this, he defended her mother and she would say, 'You *always* take her side.'

When he didn't offer a view, Layla brought up his roots, his mother. 'Why won't you talk about her?'

Michael's eyes opened in the dark. He could not bring himself to say: my mother died six months ago. My sister phoned and asked me to the funeral. I sent flowers and went to work. He couldn't tell her that. It was shameful. Ugly. She would tell him to go back and visit his mother's grave, see his sister and do the decent thing. But he was not ready to face the past, these people. And even after her death, he still resented his mother.

'I told you, she's an unstable person. What more is there to know?'

In the morning, Layla kissed Michael on the bridge of his nose. She looked at Michael with love, said she cared for him, that was why she asked about his family. Then she reached down and grabbed hold of him – this was something she liked doing, Michael had learnt over the years: having sex while her parents were in the same house. Michael would have preferred to wait until they'd gone, but she climbed on top of him and they both covered their mouths and tried not to make any noise. When they were done, Layla said she'd found a beginner's writing course that met every Thursday.

'You should do it,' Michael said.

She kissed his eyes and reached down again, but Michael said they ought to get out of bed.

In the living room, the Zaytoons had already tidied the sofa area, folding the duvet and pillowcases and putting everything to one side of the room, out of the way. Layla wanted to take her parents to Greenwich Village. Michael had final exams to grade and Mrs Zaytoon had a sore stomach, so they both stayed behind while Layla took her father sightseeing with Jacob.

It was midday when he took a break to check on Mrs Zaytoon. He found her sitting out on the balcony.

'Would you like anything?' he asked her. 'A cup of tea?'

She shook her head and smiled. 'Do you mind, Michael, if I smoke?'

'No. Of course not. I didn't know you smoked.'

'I don't tell Layla. You know what she is like.' She winked at him. 'Sometimes it is better to have secrets.'

She took a packet out of her cardigan pocket and stuck a cigarette into her mouth. Michael had never imagined her like that, a closet smoker.

'Are you sure it doesn't bother you, the smoke?'

'No, no. It doesn't bother me.'

In the final year of his doctorate, Michael had gone through a smoking phase. Long nights without rest working on his thesis, ashtrays filled with stubs. Watching Mrs Zaytoon with her cigarette reminded him of how comforting it had been, the warm glow, blowing out smoke that disappeared in the wind. She must have caught his look of longing because she extended the box out to him.

'No, thank you,' he said, with much difficulty.

She had brought her own glass ashtray, flecked her cigarette there.

It was a muggy day and the streets were quiet. People had packed up and left the city for the long weekend, probably off to the Hamptons or Lake Placid, in search of green and blue.

'Yacoob. He is becoming bigger now, *mashallah*.'

'Yes,' Michael said. 'It feels like every day he's changing in some way. His hair getting shaggy, his legs stretching out, or his moods swinging.'

As they slipped into a comfortable silence, Michael felt that he could have stayed out on the balcony with Mrs Zaytoon all day. Her softness made him feel at ease in a way that he didn't around others – not even Layla, and certainly never around his own mother. He found that he wanted to confide in her.

'I'm worried about screwing things up with Jacob. Being a bad father. Just the other day I yelled at him for spilling juice.'

She blew smoke out from the corner of her mouth. 'You are a good father. You work, you teach him manners. I have learnt something from raising Layla and I see it with my nieces too.' She fixed her moistened gaze on Michael. 'It is always the mother they blame. I know Layla does this. She blames me for things in her life.' Mrs Zaytoon raised a palm – stopping Michael as he tried to interrupt. 'No, I know it's true. She blames me. So you don't have to worry. The father never has to worry.'

Michael thought of his own parents, and how he had blamed his mother for the hardship he'd endured – it was true – but he blamed his father more. He wanted to tell

Mrs Zaytoon then that his mother had been killed in a crash. Her blood alcohol level three times above the limit. He could've tried to save his mother instead of hiding from her in New York. Mostly, he wanted to talk about Ava. All the strain of their mother's illness on her shoulders.

Mrs Zaytoon stubbed out her cigarette and the moment seemed lost.

When it was time for Layla's parents to return to Chicago, Jacob latched onto Mr Zaytoon. It was the same every time – his initial scepticism melting into love. Mrs Zaytoon winked at her son-in-law behind Layla's shoulder.

'That wasn't terrible,' Layla said, when the door shut behind them.

*

Years ago, Michael didn't know that his mother was Greek and, by extension, that he was part Greek. His father called her Elle or Ellie.

Every couple of weeks, Elena sat on the white porcelain lid of the toilet seat in a silk robe, flipping through a fashion magazine while the dye under her shower cap silenced the dark roots that were coming in. She coloured her eyebrows to match and Michael asked his mother if it stung, having that toffee goo so close to her eyes, and she said no, because she was careful. He would lie in the empty bathtub reading fantasy books until it was time to wash the dye out. After she'd showered and dried her hair, it was a blaze of blonde, her scalp a little red where she parted her hair down the middle. She used to leave the bathroom full of steam, and Michael wondered that she wasn't cooking herself under those hot showers. He liked going into the bathroom right after his mother and spelling out his name on the mirror – a reminder that he was there. Between the dinner parties she hosted, the time and energy she spent accusing Lee of various transgressions, it often felt like she'd forgotten him altogether.

Elena's mother, Katerina, flew in from Athens after Ava was born and stayed for a couple of days in their Hampstead house. Michael was only five and it was a long day for him at school, thinking about Ava. He liked the smell of her head, though his mother said not to touch there, and it felt like that sometimes, when he was stroking or kissing her, his love for his sister was so urgent and large that he might hurt her with it.

When Michael met his grandmother Katerina, he thought how much she looked like his mother, despite her dark tresses and the lines around her mouth. He found it strange that she rarely spoke during the day but was incredibly talkative at night, words seeming to fall out of her mouth then. She kept to the armchair by the window, where she looked out onto the small patch of grass that was their garden in the day.

With Katerina in the house, Michael realised there was much he did not know about his mother. Up until that point, he hadn't realised she was Greek and that she spoke the language. Watching those vowels and consonants push out of his mother's mouth, he thought she was a magician. Abracadabra! Like that, she transformed into someone else. Elena and Lee spoke to each other warmly across the dinner table with Katerina there. Lee even asked Michael about school.

At night, in the silence of his bedroom, Katerina told him things.

'Never marry for love. Your grandfather had a good heart, yes. But he was a bad match. My father was a prosperous accountant in Athens. Your grandfather didn't have any money or influence. And he thought the Turks were like us. Like us!'

His grandmother looked dead, lying on that mattress across his bedroom floor, her dark hair around her like a bunch of dead snakes. 'Your mother must accept her choice. She knew what your father was from the start.'

Michael was glad when his grandmother returned to Athens. The room smelt like her, even after she was gone. A warm, cabbagey smell, with something sweet and floral mixed in, like rose water.

Their routines resumed, no need to pretend once company had left. All the window dressings of their family life were pulled down. Lee stayed out late, either at work or at his club, and when he was at home, he kept to his office. One night, when Lee was still not back, Elena said to Michael, 'For every hour he's not home, I'm going to cut up a new tie.'

Her scissors had bright red handles, and there was a cold, focused expression on her face when she cut his work ties into tiny pieces.

In Year Eight, Michael's English teacher did a unit on Greek myths and Michael was reminded of his Greekness. He had no idea what it meant to be Greek because no one had explained it to him. It became an obsession, reading those myths, and he read beyond the assigned school texts, checked out books from the Hampstead Heath library. He read under the warm glow of his bedside lamp, late into the night.

It comforted him, how dysfunctional the families were in most of the myths: fathers eating their children, children slaying their parents and mothers throwing their sons down mountaintops. Gods, petty and jealous and vengeful like his own parents, who at times seemed hell-bent on gnashing through each other, tearing skin and tissue to get to the marrow, that place where words like failure and cheat and crazy could settle, make a permanent home.

The story of Medea, an anguished woman in an unhappy marriage, resonated with him most, because he recognised his mother in the portrait, and he began to worry that, like Medea, she would someday kill him and Ava to get back at their father, hurt him that way. He thought his father stayed because of Ava, that his only reason for returning to the house was her.

A couple of years later, when Ava was ten and Michael fifteen, Elena said to Lee over breakfast, 'Robert Embringham wants to have an affair. He told me last night at the party.'

Dishes were piled up by the sink from the night before. Lee didn't lift his eyes from the paper in front of him. Michael and Ava spread butter on their toast cautiously.

They'd both gone down to say hello at the start of the party, a dozen people in fine dresses and crisp shirts saying, 'Look how you've grown!'

Lee, with his hair slicked back and his golden-boy smile, said, 'It's funny, that. We give them food and they grow.'

An explosion of laughter, women flashing their teeth.

Elena had been standing by the open window overlooking the back garden, speaking to the TV actor Robert Embringham. She had a champagne flute in her hand, raised it to her lips and then spilt a little down her dress when she laughed at something he said.

'Ava's made the football team,' Lee told the men and women huddled around him.

Michael could see pride there, spreading across his father's red face. And then, as an afterthought, he said Michael was doing well in English.

'Maybe he'll be a journalist like his father.'

'No. I don't think so,' Michael said, and his father frowned at him.

Michael and Ava went back to their rooms but struggled to sleep with the noise from below: laughter, people speaking over each other, voices rising higher, and then sometime after midnight, a woman shouting, 'Get your pants back on!'

Elena looked at her husband in the kitchen, waiting for some reaction to what she'd said about Robert Embringham making a pass at her. She slapped a wet dish towel on the table across his newspaper.

'Perhaps you misunderstood him, Ellie.'

'No. He wants to have an affair with me,' she said. 'And can you blame him for asking? You were flirting with Penny all night. He probably thinks our marriage is a sham.'

'Another misunderstanding on your mother's part,' he said to Ava and Michael. He moved the towel so he could continue reading his article.

Elena's eyes grew large, a swell of dark clouds gathering. Her mouth curved up, a snarl of a smile. 'I suppose that kind of lewd behaviour is to be expected. The flirting. The disregard. How can I expect more from someone like *you*?'

And here, Lee folded his newspaper, set it down on the table next to his plate of bacon. She had his attention now.

'What's that supposed to mean?'

'It means you're a miner's son. Ask the children and they'll tell you what that means.'

Lee turned his accusing gaze to Ava and Michael, who said nothing. Often, Lee and Elena asked their children to act as referee, decide who was right, who was wrong. They never knew what to say. Any position they took resulted in one of their parents getting angry.

'Your parents worked in a clothing factory. How is that any better?'

'That's *different*. They were immigrants with few choices. They're completely different from *your* family.'

'If I hadn't married you, you'd still be working shifts at the department store.' The whole house shook with his voice. Elena's faced was flushed. She looked alive when Lee shouted back, his eyes on her.

'Your mother's the stingiest woman I know. So stingy! All she ever talks about is money and finding bargains. It's tacky and embarrassing. She's an *embarrassment*.'

'At least my mother isn't a cold, heartless *bitch* like yours. Your mother thinks she's better than everyone – the Queen included – and she's from Greece! Who does she think she is? No wonder you're such a spoilt piece of work.'

Elena took a dirty plate from the pile of dishes by the sink and smashed it against the wall above their father's head.

'You're *crazy*.'

'I know you're having an affair.'

Michael took Ava to the heath. They walked quickly, away from the house, and slowed their pace only once they got to the park entrance. The sun was out, the full

71

bloom of spring around them. A Dalmatian chased after a green ball, ran back to his owner with it.

'Don't worry,' Michael said to his sister.

'I'm not worried. You're worried.'

Michael realised that he was the one with tears in his eyes. Ava patted her brother's back.

They stayed in the heath for a few hours. Walking, sitting on the grass. Talking about school. They made their way back when they thought their parents would have retreated to their corners of the house. Lee in his office, Elena in the kitchen or upstairs, curled up in bed.

A young woman was standing by their front door. She was the most beautiful woman Michael had ever seen, with a perfect symmetrical face. She looked pale when she turned to Ava and Michael.

'Is Lee home?' she said, her voice thin and shaky.

Michael thought perhaps she'd left something at the house. But he hadn't seen her at the party. He had never seen her before. He would've remembered someone like her.

'He's not home,' Michael said, thinking it would be a mistake to send her in after the morning row.

The girl backed away from them. 'Can you tell him Sandra's trying to reach him? Sandra Banks.'

Seven

The physiotherapist, Marie, helped Ava stretch, move her left leg around. Six weeks had passed since the accident, and her pelvis was healing. When the doctor had shown Ava a recent X-ray, she was amazed. Amid the grey haze of skin and muscle, her pelvic bone gleamed white, and there, draped decoratively like a chain necklace, were the plates and nails that held her together. On the surface, she was untidy, with hairs growing long and wild, but beneath, at the level of bone, she was beaming and fancy. She longed to thrust her pelvis into someone. To feel pleasure there instead of pain. She wanted to ask Marie when it would be safe to have sex again but shied away from the question.

Marie said the strength in her hips was improving. 'It could be a lot worse, for sure.'

She took care of her appearance, Marie; her hair highlighted blonde, heavy make-up on her skin. Ava wondered what she looked like without all that eyeliner. She had been bringing Ava fashion and home magazines, but this time she'd given her a book called *The Happiness Hexagon*.

'You need to keep your spirits up,' she said. 'Especially when you're back home. It might come as a shock, going back in a wheelchair.'

When their session was over, Marie took Ava to the courtyard. The weather was fine, wispy clouds moving across the sun. They had iced tea and talked about being thirty and single.

'Read that book,' Marie said. '*The Happiness Hexagon*. It'll give you something positive to focus on.'

When she was back in the hospital bed, Ava read the blurb on the back of the book, the promises it made. A picture of the author was there, Dr Edgar Wandsworth. He was handsome, with a strong, confident jawline. Ava remembered watching him on a chat show, dressed in a navy suit, speaking about his book and how it was changing lives. There were people there who'd been through terrible tragedies, explaining how they'd fallen into despair but found a way out after reading his book and learning to wield the power of the hexagon. They learnt to overcome their pain. Ava couldn't think of what the hexagon meant, only that Dr Wandsworth spoke about how people accessed happiness through the senses.

The book made her think of a documentary she'd seen about a man who had no arms or legs and he said how content he was with life, happier than he'd ever been when his limbs were intact. Ava didn't believe him at first, because how could anyone be happy when they couldn't butter their own bread? He spoke about faking his happiness in the beginning, though he'd felt miserable inside. He hadn't let his pain show in front of his family or friends. He'd met interesting people who'd survived terrible tragedies like himself and he'd felt inspired by their courage. Eventually, he'd forgotten about being unhappy and had transformed into the bright, hopeful person he'd been pretending to be all along.

Ava thought she would try to be like this limbless man – one of those people who rose above their circumstances – and even the idea that she could change her story like that sent a rush of energy through her.

That day, when the nurses did their rounds to check her blood pressure and heart rate, Ava smiled at them, asked how their day was going, instead of lying there like a lost cause, pale and depressed. They looked at her, as if for the first time, their tired eyes softening with kindness. Before, they'd rushed in and out of the room, jotting down their illegible notes, moving on to the next invalid, with their white shoes light against the floors so that when they left the room, it was as if they'd vanished into thin air. But now, when Ava smiled and took an interest, they lingered and talked about their tiresome children and low wages, their lack of rest and other responsibilities. Ava nodded her head that was splitting with pain and said how she hoped their circumstances improved.

But she didn't feel any happier than before. In fact, she preferred the earlier silence of their visits to their newfound chattiness, particularly when the size and shape of her pain was large. Still, it was something she was determined to do: overcome her tragedy.

Kyle from the shoe department came to visit. He brought with him a lovely bunch of yellow and purple tulips.

'I remember how you said you liked tulips.' He kissed

her cheek. At least his teeth were straight – a shade of sepia, but straight.

'That's very thoughtful of you.'

He placed them in front of the orchid and Ava thought how, once he was gone, she would ask one of the nurses to move the tulips so that they weren't blocking the orchid.

'It's horrible seeing you like this,' he said.

'Oh, well. I'm sure it looks much worse than it is.'

He looked about the room, as if searching for something to say, then finding himself at a loss, he brought up work.

'Everyone's asking about you,' he said. 'People from all departments. Upstairs and downstairs. Even the snobs at the perfume counters. They'll want me to give them a full report.'

'You can tell them I'm doing a lot better.'

He nodded and put his hand on Ava's shoulder. She struggled not to flinch.

'If you need anything at all,' he said, and here his gaze settled on her with fierce devotion, 'you call me. You've still got my number, haven't you?'

'Thank you. I think I do.'

'Well, in case you don't.' He handed her a business card she'd seen before. Ava had spent an afternoon laughing at this card with her colleagues in Menswear. He had ordered them from a website – there was a picture of him in the right-hand corner, serious and unsmiling, his name in bold and a title he'd fixed for himself, Shoe Specialist.

'Isn't he the most ridiculous man?' she'd said to Jane, but Jane had been quick to shame her.

'He's an honest, hard-working man and you'd be lucky to have him.' Her chin was high, superiority etched into her brow.

When Kyle left, Ava thought perhaps Jane had been right and she'd been harsh, dismissing him after their first date. There was no attraction and Ava couldn't pretend there was, but all this time in hospital was making her question things she'd taken as givens. Like whether the sun actually rose if you didn't see it that day, or whether attraction was necessary for happiness in a relationship. She'd never been comfortable with any man, usually ending things after a few short months, pulling out before she ever felt or heard 'I love you'. She imagined herself running away or else laughing nervously between her teeth if a man ever said those words to her.

Ava's friend Claire from Women's Accessories stopped by the next morning. She brought Ava a cheap powder-blue scarf that was reduced in the clearance. Her three-year-old son Tyler looked at Ava like she was a monster in that bed.

'Lizzy *really* wanted to come, but her daughter's got norovirus. Projectile vomiting everywhere.'

Claire spoke about Tyler for most of the visit. His performance in nursery, the things he said that made her laugh. Occasionally, she'd ask Ava a question, but when Ava answered, Claire's eyes moved down to Tyler. And she followed him around the hospital room as he ducked under curtains where other women were resting.

Ava was glad when they left. Her friends, the ones who were still in Welton, had all amalgamated into the same person: women who spoke about their children. And before that, women who phoned her up to have drinks when their husbands were busy. She had no time for these people, except she had all the time in the world, in this hospital bed, in this sleepy town. What else was she going to do?

A new patient was wheeled into the room by a porter. She was younger than Ava, her neck and head supported by a brace and collar – that whole area immobilised – but her eyes, small and dark, moved around the room. Her sullen gaze settled on Ava. A middle-aged woman with the same dark eyes stood next to the girl and then pulled the curtain across. 'I still don't understand how you could do this to yourself. *How?*' And then, a few minutes later, 'And for what? For who? A stupid boy you won't remember in five years.'

Hours later, a doctor came by and Ava got the full picture. The girl had broken her neck. She'd thrown herself down some stairs. And when the doctor had left, her mother kept saying, '*What for? What for?*'

Ava thought of that issue of *Glamour* magazine with Sandra Banks on the cover. The interview in which she'd detailed her affair with Lee: the promises he'd made to help advance her career and then his threats when she'd told him about the pregnancy. She said she'd felt so lonely she'd thought of ending her life. Drowning herself in a bath.

Ava remembered Sandra's pale face, that day, standing at the door of their Hampstead home.

Across the hospital room, she heard, 'What for? What for?'

★

Marie had been out to the bungalow to make assessments. Her team put in ramps so that Ava could wheel her way up the front porch. They put a white plastic seat in the bathtub so that she wouldn't slip and crack open her skull.

The rest of the house didn't need adjusting as everything was on the same floor.

Ava was supposed to go back home last week, but a fever had come over her on Tuesday afternoon and her ankles had swelled. In bed, she'd smiled like the courageous limbless man, and all the while she'd felt she was vanishing beneath the bleached hospital sheets.

They'd put antibiotics through an IV drip because her temperature had climbed too high. Ava had been hallucinating, thinking her mother was sitting at her bedside with her head in her hands when it'd been Marie sitting in that chair.

'Don't worry,' Ava told her mother. She was thinking of the night she'd returned to the bungalow after staying out late at a bar in Sheffield. Her mother had been drinking too, and when she'd stood to go to bed, she'd lost her balance and fallen forwards onto the glass coffee table, smashing through it.

'I'm not worried one bit,' her mother had said, as Ava cleaned up her blood.

More tests had been ordered and different parts of Ava scanned and checked for clots. But all the results came back normal and her fever had subsided by Saturday.

The day Ava was due to leave hospital, Marie arrived in the ward, holding out a bunch of daisies.

'You didn't need to trouble yourself, Marie,' Ava said, accepting the flowers. She smiled, thinking how she would put them on the windowsill in her sitting room.

Ava wore her favourite blue dress on the morning she was leaving. She had asked Sam to collect it a few days ago. He was always offering to help with something. The fabric felt familiar, but the shape of the dress had changed, or rather, Ava had changed beneath it, her arms narrower and stomach practically concave. But, of course, the dress was an improvement to the hospital gowns, those pale, shapeless things, always gaping at the front or back depending on the test, leaving her with little dignity.

Once, waiting for an X-ray, Ava had seen an old man's underpants peeking out the back of his gown. They had pictures of superhero characters on them, like they belonged to a child. She heard him talking to the technician about the war. Ava wasn't sure which war, but he said how there was a war going on now in Britain. Us versus them. Them versus Us. 'The grocer near my house has turned into a bloody kebab shop,' he said. 'It's happening more and more.' It filled Ava with great satisfaction, knowing that the technician would see the cartoon figures printed on his saggy bottom.

As Ava packed her things, she felt a passing sadness. Although she'd been desperate to leave the hospital, there was a familiarity now, a sense of home after these seven weeks. The stain at the bottom of the separating curtain, the ebb and flow of the heart-rate monitor, these were the details that had populated the landscape of her days. She had found the numbers of the monitor moving up and down a relief – she was alive! And the orchid was her pride, with the nurses all saying how lovely it was when they came to check her vitals.

There was also something deeply comforting about having curtains in the place of doors. The soft movement of them, the swishing sound they made when someone pulled them back, the way they brushed the floors gently, light making its way through. Ava thought how, once she returned to the bungalow, she'd get all the doors knocked down, put in curtains instead, live like a hippy.

Marie's van, when it pulled up, was spacious and smelt of pineapples. Ava sat in the front next to Marie, with the seat all the way back to allow room for her plaster cast. She rolled down her window as they set off so she could feel the air on her arm. Along Days Road, the river was metal blue. A red sailboat lulled on the water, and it was easy to smile then.

'I love this song,' Marie said. She turned the dial up to 'Imagine', John Lennon's light baritone unfolding in her van, and sang along.

Ava looked at her with amazement. 'You've got a really nice voice. You should try out for one of those singing competitions.'

She smacked Ava playfully on the shoulder. 'I'm too old to be doing singing competitions on telly.'

Advertisements played on the radio. People buying furniture, others selling it. A food festival announced on the high street in Welton. A woman proudly declaring that a charity run for breast cancer had been a success. All this life happening around her felt dizzying after weeks of nothing.

Ava had swallowed one of her morphine tablets before leaving hospital and so felt no pain, no shadow over this moment. She should have waited another hour for her dose, until she was home. Marie had warned about taking more than the prescribed dosage, but she wasn't the one in agony. The bottle in her bag was full and it was a relief to be in charge of her own body again.

They passed the locks, busy with activity on this Friday afternoon. Old men without shirts on, waxing their boats in the late-May sun, the rolling hills smiling down on them.

Ava remembered when they'd first moved to Welton. The long drive from London, her mother at the wheel, Michael in the passenger seat. A strip of sun there on the dashboard.

Elena had been in touch with her old boss at Selfridges, Mrs Spitfields. Her niece, Jane, was a manager at a department store in Welton. They were hiring in Menswear. She would put in a good word for Elena.

The look on her mother's face when she said she'd got the job – it was like nothing could ever touch her. She bought a new pair of trousers and a navy silk blouse. She dyed her hair brown, closer to her natural colour. She spoke to Lee calmly about selling the house, how they would divide their finances, and he reassured her about the maintenance he'd pay, though a few years later, the payments stopped coming through. For all the noise and chaos of their marriage, Lee and Elena's divorce had been quiet and gentle, like a parting gift.

Ava had wanted to stay with her father, the parent who looked at her with love. He'd stayed up with her all night when she'd had that painful earache. He'd slept there on her bedroom floor and she'd watched him and felt his love.

Marie pulled up now behind Ava's silver Peugeot, the soft sound of tyres against the gravelled driveway. It was like meeting an old friend, seeing the house again, but had it always been so small? Her whole life between those walls.

Marie busied herself getting the wheelchair out of the boot. The front lawn was unruly, violent shocks of dandelion sprouting up here and there. It needed tending – work Ava couldn't do now. She wondered then if the neighbours had noticed her absence. Mrs Miller would have noticed the lawn, probably had a few things to say about the state of it.

Marie assisted Ava into the chair and pushed her along the path to the house. Ava unlocked the front door and at once was hit by the heavy smell of mothballs. Had the bungalow always smelt this way? It was something Ava worried about – an unpleasant smell lingering, her nose immune to it. Marie said she was going back to the car for her bag and the groceries.

Rolling through the entrance into the darkened sitting room, Ava thought how the house looked tired. She'd leafed through home magazines to pass the time in hospital. Marie had brought in all her previous issues of *Beautiful Homes* and she'd earmarked dozens of pages, putting together her ideal home, piece by piece. And now, looking at the beige carpet and the floral wallpaper with water stains at the edges, Ava felt like she was in somebody else's home. The floor-to-ceiling wall mirror, once a proud feature of the room, was an abomination from the nineties. Her reflection looked distorted somehow, skeletal. Even the brown leather couch made her recoil in the wheelchair. It was worn out, but not in a tasteful, distressed sort of way. It looked beaten down, suicidal. Her mother had once taken pride in furnishing their home. And now Ava felt that this place would never be her own.

'I'll come by Tuesdays and Thursdays for physio,' Marie said. She settled her gaze on Ava, her kohl-lined eyes too large for her face. 'You all right?'

'Oh, yes.' Ava fixed a more pleasant expression on her face. 'It's just strange being back.'

Marie unpacked the shopping in the kitchen and returned with the daisies in a vase. Ava pointed to the windowsill where she'd already placed Sam's orchid.

'The groceries are in the fridge, on the lower shelves where you can reach,' she said, arranging the flowers. 'Remember your exercises between our appointments. But don't push yourself too hard either.'

Ava nodded like a good student. In a corner of the sitting room, Marie had cleared a space for the equipment they used in their hospital sessions, all sorts of straps and blocks.

'Thank you. I don't know what I'd have done without you,' Ava said, wanting to ask Marie to stay – to beg her not to go. She was afraid of the silence between these walls. Her mother's ghost. But Marie smiled and let herself out.

Ava thought again about selling the bungalow, moving somewhere that had no marks or reminders of the past. She wouldn't take a single piece of furniture. She wanted everything new.

In bed with the laptop propped up on her lap, she looked at properties. Smart-looking flats in Sheffield city centre. She assessed floor plans and it gave her a mild thrill, imagining herself moving through those spaces. When she tired of property, Ava searched for information on the psychology conversion course at Sheffield. She still had the brochures on her desk. Her history degree hadn't amounted to much – a part-time job at the mining museum in Matlock Spa. She was more of a tour guide, performing for an audience, giving the same information several times a day, every day. Once or twice, she'd been asked questions that made her speak with excitement— about the lives of women and the coal mines, but mostly she'd spent her days exhausted with boredom. When she finally succumbed to her mother's cajoling and accepted a full-time job at the department store, she earnt double the salary. Her mother was pleased. They drove into work together, played the radio.

Ava had insisted it was only temporary, until she worked out what she wanted to do, but Elena had been adamant. 'You can't leave like Michael,' she'd said, and Ava knew it was true. Her mother wouldn't survive another separation. She really believed that.

But here was Ava's chance. There was still time to apply; the course's start date was not until the end of September. The idea of studying psychology made her weary with excitement.

At that moment, wind blew through the open window, causing the kitchen door to slam shut, and for the rest of the evening, Ava felt unnerved, sensing her mother's disapproval at the idea of selling her house and starting a new life. Leaving her behind. 'Just like your brother,' Ava heard her say.

Sometime in the night, Ava ordered a blue rug online. Her mother would have winced at the colour and its patterned geometry. She would've called it busy. Attention-seeking. But Ava smiled in bed, thinking of her new blue rug with all those shapes printed on it, and she imagined it in a different sitting room, bright and airy.

★

Ava's mobile rang early the following morning. It was Sam on the other end.

'Did I wake you up?'

'No.'

'Good, good.'

'Is everything OK?'

'Well, yes, everything's fine. I'm actually in your driveway.'

'Really?' Ava felt something between joy and confusion. 'Do you want to come in?' She dropped her body gracelessly into the wheelchair, the height of this mattress different from the one she'd grown accustomed to in hospital.

In the kitchen, Sam drank a whole pint of water. Ava worried the glasses smelt musty after so many weeks in the old wooden cupboards. She was on edge in the sitting room, looking at the vast mirror that needed dusting. He'd surprised her and she didn't feel ready. She lit a vanilla bean candle and hoped she could change the air that way.

He sat on the sofa but kept his leather jacket on, his long arm resting gently against a flat cushion. He had a carrier bag between his knees.

'What's in the bag?'

He smiled broadly, and she realised he'd been waiting for her to ask the question. 'I was in a charity shop and found the most incredible thing.'

He removed an ancient-looking box from the bag. It had an illustration of a man and woman on the front, and in block letters: THE GAME OF MARRIAGE. The woman had one arm looped through her husband's, and with the other she held onto a sturdy vacuum cleaner, one of the old ones where you could see the bag. The man in his slick suit had a thick cigar in his mouth.

'I bought it for six pounds,' Sam said, excitement in his voice. 'It's from the sixties.'

They had exhausted two-player games at this point: draughts, Battleship, noughts and crosses, and more obscure ones like Exploding Puppies.

'Do you fancy playing?'

'Yes,' Ava said, and then she wondered about Sam. Why he wasn't still in his bed or lying next to a woman he'd met at a bar. He looked fresh, no signs of a hangover. In her twenties, Ava would not have been awake at this hour on a Saturday, except if she had to work.

He cleared some space on her coffee table and laid out the board, which was still in good condition. There were two starting points at opposite sides of the board, one labelled as 'Man', the other 'Wife', and there was a heart in the middle, the words 'Happily Ever After' printed there.

Sam read out the yellowed rule sheet. 'The objective is for Man and Wife to meet in the middle so that they live happily ever after.'

Ava rolled her eyes, but Sam still had that look of excitement across his face.

'Isn't this fascinating? From a sociological point of view, I mean. It's the kind of thing I studied at uni last year – family dynamics in the fifties and sixties and gender roles.'

His enthusiasm made Ava smile, pulling her out of her cynicism. There were two silver moving pieces in the box – the woman with her vacuum cleaner and the man with his big cigar.

'So how do we meet in the middle?'

'There are blue and pink marriage cards,' he said.

'Of course there are.'

He cleared his throat. 'For best results, we recommend playing the Game of Marriage *before* an official proposal of marriage is made to gauge compatibility.' They both laughed and looked at each other, and Ava nodded for him to proceed.

'The marriage cards comprise scenarios you will

undoubtedly encounter in your married life. For instance, Wife may want to splash out by spending seven pounds on a new dress, but Husband might think it imprudent. You can only take a step forward towards Happily Ever After if you both come to an agreement. For example, Wife agrees with Husband that it is better to spend that money on a big Sunday roast dinner for the whole family instead of a new dress.' Sam smiled. 'This is *amazing.*'

'I'm telling you now, I'm buying that dress.'

Ava adjusted the throw over her leg, conscious that her good leg hadn't been shaved since the accident. The thin dressing gown she had on felt flimsy. She tightened the belt around her waist.

'Right, let's start,' she said. 'Would you like to be Man or Wife?'

Sam took the Man moving piece and read the first card. 'Your in-laws want to stay for a month while they renovate their house. Will you let them stay? Discuss and only take a step forward once you've come to an agreement.'

'That's an easy one for you since my parents aren't around,' Ava said. 'I don't see why they can't stay in a hotel, honestly. A month is a long time and I've only got the one toilet.'

'You'd make my parents stay in a hotel?'

Their moving pieces remained on Start.

Ava felt more relaxed as she read the next card. 'Husband gets a promotion at work. How do you celebrate? Discuss and only take a step forward once you've come to an agreement.'

They both agreed on sex, their first step forward, and yet their happy ending was nowhere in sight. Ava didn't want to move on from the question. She wanted to ask what position. There was a growing desire in her now to shock Sam, to see how he would handle her.

But Sam picked up another marriage card and brought up children. 'Discuss the number of children you want to have and only take a step forward once you've come to an agreement.' He looked at Ava, then sat up a little more on the sofa. 'Two,' he said.

'One. Or none.'

'You don't want children?'

'Not really.'

'Why not?'

'They're annoying. And it's a selfish thing to do.'

'What, having children?'

'Well, yes,' Ava said, straightening in the wheelchair. She felt her dressing gown pull apart a little and saw how Sam's eyes moved to her chest briefly. Ava adjusted her robe and explained. 'Isn't having children really just to fulfil your own personal desire of legacy or to keep you from boredom or divorce?'

Sam scratched his head.

'I just don't want to be a mother.' She shrugged. 'I think it's safe to say that under no circumstances should we consider getting married.'

'Agreed.'

They started putting the game away.

'Have you sent that email to your father?'

'I've given up on that,' Ava said flatly. In hospital, Ava had written out a few email drafts she'd been thinking of sending her father. She'd read a version out to Sam while they were playing Jenga, their hands shaky, the tower unstable. He'd told her it was a bit confusing. It was Sam's move that had brought the Jenga tower crashing down, their mouths open as they watched it fall to pieces.

Ava had redrafted the email, writing out each question on a separate line.

Why did you cut us out when you moved to Australia?
What are you dying from exactly?
Have you heard from Michael?

Ava deleted the message. She felt like a little girl in a film, searching for answers.

Sam stood now from the tired leather sofa. He rested his hand on her shoulder. 'If you want to go to London and see him, just say the word. I'll take you, if that's what you want to do.'

Ava returned to bed after Sam left. She thought of his offer to drive her to London. Would Michael go? She opened the drawer in her bedside table, pulled out her hardback copy of Machiavelli's *The Prince*. She'd read it in her first year of university and liked thinking about the psychology of this man, his sense of duplicity, how he manipulated others. On page sixty-eight, she found dried-up rose petals, now blood-brown. The bouquet of red carnations and roses had arrived with a note:

Sorry I can't make it. Michael

It was pathetic, an insult, her brother sending those flowers. He had been quiet over the phone when she'd told him about their mother. She'd thought he must be shocked, upset, struggling to find the words, as she was. He said he would be at the funeral, that he'd buy his plane ticket as soon as he hung up. And three days before the funeral, that bouquet had been delivered. She'd thrown it away, a few petals coming loose as she struggled to fit the stems in the bin. Then, in the middle of the night, she'd retrieved a single rose from the rubbish and hung it upside down until it had dried. She'd plucked the petals off one by one and kept a couple in this book. They were a reminder not to rely on other people, especially not her brother.

Eight

Dr Susan Barker told Michael to drop by her office. They worked on the same floor, but her office was much bigger and airier, with two large windows overlooking the manicured lawn. His office faced the parking lot. Michael often dropped in to see her when he was stuck on an idea. She was very good at unpicking the knots in his mind. It was Susan who had introduced him to Bar Five in Gramercy. She had said her best research questions had been inspired by the stories people told there. And it was not only what they said, but how they said it, what their bodies were communicating. Michael had gone along with her after work and been moved by the exposure and honesty of the stories he'd heard. The guilt and vulnerability left there on the stage. He felt less alone in the bar and so he kept returning every month.

When he knocked on the side of her office door, Dr Susan Barker was taking notes on a video she was watching on her computer. He told her he would come back later when she wasn't busy.

'No,' she said, and gestured with her long, thin hand for him to come inside. The thick rings on her creased fingers made her look like a fortune teller, and it was true that Michael thought this about Dr Barker, that she could see into the future, her sharp perceptive mind ahead of time. On the RateMyProfessors website, students had said she was strict but SO knowledgeable. Passionate and hot for an old person. Michael had checked his own ratings and saw that his score was 3.1 out of 5, lower than he'd expected. He read all twenty-three comments. Some just said, 'Fun class!' or 'Learnt a lot!' but others were much longer and told about how there was little room for opposition in his classes, how he pushed his own political agenda, and worse still was the anonymous comment that called him 'a condescending anarchist with bad taste in shoes'.

'Take a doughnut,' she said, extending a small box of Dunkin' Donuts to him, and he bit into a powdered one filled with jelly, felt a sudden squirt on his chin.

'I emailed you because I want you to watch this. You'll appreciate the narrative.'

Susan passed some tissues to Michael so that he could wipe the jelly mess from his chin while she explained the context of the video. She'd been conducting interviews with people who'd been recently diagnosed with breast cancer. She'd asked them open-ended questions to see how they identified with their diagnosis.

'I'll replay this one,' she said, the glare of her computer screen reflected by her round glasses.

Susan pressed play and they watched a woman in her early forties in a whitewashed conference room talk about her cancer diagnosis.

'It was hard at first. Of course, it was hard.' She looked down at her hands resting on the white table. 'But life will throw things at you . . . The strangest thing for me was

93

how the disease was spreading in my body, and I had no idea. Like, how could this body be me? Do you get what I mean?'

She wiped discreet tears from her eyes, a tight smile forming on her mouth. 'But like I said, life will throw things at you. And I'm doing meditation and I'm keeping positive. I'm taking vitamins and renting a lot of rom-coms. They're stupid, but I read somewhere that laughter's supposed to help.' Then she laughed. 'I know that I'll beat this. There's a lot of support out there for me. My sister's doing this run in April.' She scratched her nose. 'I'll come out of this a stronger person.'

Dr Susan Barker paused the video. Michael felt strange, having watched this intimate monologue. Of course, the woman would have consented to the filming and Dr Barker would have informed her about other colleagues watching for analysis. Still, something murky moved through him, a grey sludge in his veins. This was different from those Thursday talks at the bar in Gramercy where speakers at the front could at least see their audience.

'Almost all of them tell the same story,' Dr Barker said, sweeping doughnut sprinkles from her desk. 'They'll defeat the monster. But their bodies are contradicting them.'

She rewound the clip again and pointed out where the woman averted her gaze or sighed, when the heart-rate monitor under her sweater registered a sharp rise.

'See?' she said, pointing out when her pupils dilated. 'She's terrified. Of course, she is. And this is the problem, isn't it? How there's no space for us to say, "Hey – I am terrified of this thing!" No, she has to say that she'll slay the monster and everyone around her can relax.'

Michael nodded. He thought of his father, saying in his

letter that he would not let his illness progress to the point where he was suffering. He wondered if he was just as terrified as the woman in the video who smiled and spoke of overcoming her illness.

Lee had contacted Michael again. He had sent an email this time. It wasn't a long message. He'd asked if Michael had received his last letter. Then he'd said he'd been walking through Hampstead Heath and thought of their walks together. There was always that Dalmatian running around. Rupert? Was that the dog's name? Did Michael remember? He saw a Dalmatian today in the park and had thought of Michael.

Susan asked Michael about his plans for the weekend. He said he was doing nothing. Something with the family.

'What will you do?'

She shrugged. 'Make polenta.'

Michael walked to the NYU campus to pick up a book on healthcare reform he'd reserved from the library. Students were laid out on the grass like dead, unmoving things, sun-bathing, or else eating sandwiches under shaded trees. A girl in a grey vest top tousled through the tight ringlets of the boy sitting next to her. He grabbed her chin, kissed it. When Michael had been a student, he had often sat under trees, in all kinds of weather, writing out his life goals in a tatty journal that he took everywhere with him. He drew timelines and graphs, and it was through this kind of forward planning that Michael realised he could never be happy in Welton, that he would always feel guilty until he broke with his life there. A card sent home at Christmas, a life update given that way, sure, maybe birthday flowers – but nothing more than that.

Across Washington Square Park, the Grey Art Gallery came into view with its perfect white columns. The building reminded Michael of a drama his mother used to watch, wherein a young woman, dissatisfied with living in a tired pocket of London, reimagined her neighbourhood. The scenery around her changed as she moved her gaze up and down the high street. The chip shop on the corner transformed into a tea room; the interiors painted duck egg, scones and sandwiches sitting on tiered plates. The abandoned shoe factory in the distance turned into something white and polished and columned like the art building in front of him. But the thing that stayed with Michael was when the woman settled her gaze on a homeless man curled up in a doorway, reimagining him instead as an attractive lamp post, upright and glowing. He remembered his mother telling him to keep walking, to keep his eyes straight ahead when they walked past someone like that.

He thought of Sarah Addams, how she had her work in the Grey Art Gallery. She had mentioned it when they'd had that coffee. It was easy enough to find her installation there, in a tiny room next to the toilets on the second floor.

The moths were in flight, suspended from the ceiling by thin wires. They were made entirely of soda cans, some pieces cut very fine to achieve delicate details on the wings, like veins on a dying leaf. The left wings of all the moths were partially torn, but they kept flight. *The Human Experience*, it was called.

Michael stood there for a while, admiring the installation. He thought of the speakers who told their stories at Bar Five. Their exposure. The installation made him think of them.

He left the gallery after a couple of minutes and sent a response to his father:

We never had a relationship. I don't see the point in building one now. Sorry you're unwell. Please don't write again.

A light rain fell on Michael's head as he made his way home. He saw Sarah Addams smoking her thin cigarettes in the courtyard between their buildings. She nodded at him.

'It's either too cold or too hot in this country,' she said, and smiled. She was wearing a big yellow raincoat with flip-flops on her feet.

He walked over to where she was standing. 'I saw your installation today. The moths with the damaged wings. I liked it very much.'

Her round face lit up. She wasn't wearing her thick-rimmed glasses and without them her eyes looked far apart. 'That's nice to hear.' She drew in smoke and slowly released it from the side of her mouth.

'The way you use soda cans is really clever.'

'Thank you,' she said, her gaze moving to the sidewalk. 'I can show you how I do it, if you want to come up and see.'

'Right now?'

She shrugged. 'Right now works.'

The metal doors of her building lift closed in front of them. 'What inspired your piece?' Michael asked, standing in his corner of the lift.

'My experience with breaking into the art scene. People tried to knock me down, but I kept flight.'

The elevator pinged when it reached the right floor. Sarah's apartment was compact and messy. Clothes piled up in different corners of the living room. Paintbrushes, scissors, precision knives and glue guns flung out in disarray on a long table where she did her work. A bicycle was suspended on a back wall; at least that was out of the way. When Sarah took off her yellow coat, she was wearing a flimsy navy tank top and shorts underneath. She offered ginger ale or 7-Up.

'No, thanks.'

'Please, have one,' she said, handing him the 7-Up. 'You'll be doing me a favour. I need the cans empty.'

She gestured for him to sit in a chair at the end of the long table where her cutting tools were laid out beside a few cans of Coca-Cola.

Looking out of the window, Michael saw Jacob's empty room across the way. His son was probably watching TV with Layla in the sitting room. He should not be here, he realised. He should be on the other side. But he was already cutting a can open with scissors.

Sarah put on her glasses and her eyes no longer looked so far apart. 'What made you move to New York?' she asked.

'I got a scholarship to study at NYU.'

'There are plenty of good universities in England.' Her eyes were focused on cutting the Coke can, and she did it with ease, while Michael struggled with the small scissors, creating sharp, uneven edges. She leant in close and said to lead with the end of the blades. He thought of his mother and the scissors with the red handles she'd used to cut up his father's ties. *Snip, snip.*

'I left to get away from my family,' he said.

She moved her chair closer, inspecting the edges of the can he was working on. 'Now cut off the top and bottom. Then you're going to use this rolling pin to flatten the middle.'

For a while, they worked quietly, cutting and flattening the large rectangular middle of their cans. Michael asked what drew her to New York.

She didn't look up from her cutting. 'Fresh perspective,' she said. 'And, like you, I've got family things. My mother keeps asking when I'll settle down with a nice man.'

'What do you tell her?'

She laughed. 'I tell her I don't want a nice man. I want someone naughty.' Sarah looked at Michael, her green eyes wide and steady. 'Stop rolling for a moment.' She ran her pale hand over the aluminium. 'Good. Now turn it over to the other side.' She started drawing a pattern in permanent marker on her flattened piece of aluminium. 'Copy that.'

He looked at the oval shapes, small at the centre, getting larger as they fanned out, and Michael realised he was making a rose.

He cut along the pattern and spoke of his father. 'He's been in touch after twenty-two years.' It surprised him that he should tell her this personal thing.

'Is that good?'

'Not really. He says he's dying and he'll kill himself before things get bad.' He laughed.

She looked up from her cutting, and Michael continued following the shape of the template.

'He wants to meet.'

'Will you go?'

'No.'

Once the pattern was cut out, they curled the petals and the aluminium started taking the shape of a flower.

'Now, the final thing is to turn the petals out,' she said.

And there it was, a Coca-Cola rose.

'You should take that home to your wife.'

He held the flower for a moment. 'I really did love your moths. I'll let you know next time I'm at the park with Jacob. For your sketches.'

She smiled. 'Thank you.' And then she leant in and kissed his cheek.

It was still raining outside in the courtyard between their apartments. Cold, heavy drops that felt like ice, but his cheek, the place where she'd kissed him, was still warm.

That night, Michael went to Jacob when he woke up in the night. His son was afraid. He couldn't name the thing that frightened him. He just said, 'I'm scared.'

Michael read him a story and sat with him until he fell asleep again, his chest rising and falling in a steady rhythm.

Sometime later, when the room was beginning to glow with the early-morning light, Layla tapped Michael lightly on the shoulder. 'You did it again,' she whispered. 'You fell asleep on his floor.'

Gently, she guided him back to their room, pulled the duvet over them. 'Your feet are so cold,' she said, and he crossed them over her warm legs.

Nine

Ava wrote to her father. She said she would be in London visiting a friend next week. She was thinking of stopping by to see him. Within a couple of minutes of sending the email, there was a response waiting in her inbox. He asked about dinner. Would she have dinner with him? He would cook whatever she liked. Did she have allergies? Sometimes allergies developed later in life. He couldn't have dairy anymore, not really, without paying for it. Was gluten an issue? How long would she be in London? Overnight? Did she need a place to stay? He had three spare beds. How was she doing, anyway?

Ava didn't respond.

She shut the lid of her old bulky laptop. A sense of panic rushed through her. It had been impulsive, sending that message when she still had doubts.

Jane was in her driveway. She was taking Ava to the department store to visit the sales team and Ava welcomed this distraction from her father's questions. The team had been wondering when she'd return, and she'd looked forward to this visit, getting out of the house again.

In the car, Jane talked about her solicitor friend, Henry Williams.

'I'm glad you're thinking about it at least,' she said, brushing a loose strand of hair from her face. 'It could be a lot of money.'

Mr Williams kept pestering her about filing a suit against the Ghadimis. He'd stopped by in the morning with a thick stack of papers and left them on Ava's coffee table for light reading.

'The police report says that Mr Ghadimi was returning from a pick-up for his parents' curtain shop when he hit you. An errand for the business.' Mr Williams smiled with his large teeth. 'It means we have a case. But we've got to move on this soon.'

He'd only asked how she was feeling on his way out, his gaze moving past her to the front door. From the bay window, she'd watched him drive off in his shiny blue car.

'Oh, they'll be nice to you, these Ga-dee-mees,' Jane said. 'They're not daft. They know that you can come after them and raise hell. Don't you forget that.'

Ava didn't tell Jane how Sam was a regular visitor to the house, how they watched Netflix together and he helped her change the sheets on her bed. He said to hold out her arms in a victory pose and draped the duvet cover over her head. He laughed and said she looked like a ghost out to seek revenge on those who'd wronged her.

'Well, you're top of that list,' Ava had said. 'Running over someone is definite cause for a haunting.'

Ava had laughed, but Sam was quiet, and she couldn't see his face because the cover was still on her head, her arms sprung out like a starfish. When she found her way out, there was pain in his eyes. They were not yet in a place to joke about the accident, it seemed.

Ava knew what Jane would have to say about her and Sam spending time together. In Jane, there was a constant battle between her born-again Christian self and another part that doubted everyone, expecting the worst.

Jane wheeled her through the perfume counters. A new smell lingered, floral and sweet, the samples at the counters lighter for the summer season. In winter, it smelt of luxury and parties in this corner of the department store.

Ava stopped to speak to some of the women who came out from behind their counters and greeted her warmly, even when they'd rarely spoken before.

'It's just awful,' Laura from Clinique said, shaking her big head. She had dyed her hair red when it had been brown, and the colour didn't suit her flushed complexion. 'At least you're alive.'

'Yes. Lucky that.'

Jane said they had other people to see. They passed the shoe department and everything that had been full price before her accident was now marked down. Yellow sale stickers everywhere. Kyle wasn't working. There was a young man with a small piercing in his ear behind the till. In Menswear, the team fussed over her and she was happy to see them. Sharmaine was in charge in Ava's absence.

'Don't worry about a thing,' Sharmaine said, and Ava really didn't.

The clothes on the mannequins were different, the pastels for spring replaced by white shorts and brightly coloured T-shirts. Taking in all the changes, she felt a creeping sense of her own irrelevance.

The staffroom smelt of fish. Someone had heated up

leftover salmon in the microwave and it sent a wave of complaints through the room; every person who walked in making that sour face.

People approached Ava with interest, people from the furniture department and Childrenswear, and others who worked on the ground floor.

'It's great to see you,' they said, and she smiled shyly, not used to being the centre of attention at work.

They even laughed at a joke she made about the wheelchair, a joke she instantly regretted because it wasn't funny – but they laughed, and it made her feel terribly depressed how their pity for her extended so far.

When the novelty of seeing her in the wheelchair wore off, people went back to eating their lunches, scrolling through their phones, flipping through newspapers and magazines that were scattered across the tables.

It felt suddenly too cold, the air conditioning on too high. Had it always been this cold here?

They didn't stay long. Jane was hungry, and Ava didn't mind the idea of lunch. At the food court, they both ordered meatball sandwiches and large strawberry and banana smoothies, and then complained of sore heads when they drank too quickly.

'Everything seems to be running smoothly in Menswear,' Ava said.

'What did you expect?'

Ava shrugged. 'I've been thinking about doing a psychology conversion course.'

'What in the world is a conversion course?'

'It means that even though I studied history, I could continue on with psychology, once I've completed the course.'

'Since when do you want to be a therapist?' A big dollop of meatball fell from Jane's mouth. She quickly cleaned it up with a napkin.

'I've always been interested in the mind. How we remember things. It's fascinating.'

'Does this mean you're not returning to Green's?'

'I'm not sure.'

Jane looked deeply offended. But Ava had never planned to stay. She didn't take pleasure in the work as Jane did – Jane, who enjoyed circling exchange and refund policies on customer receipts. Nothing pleased her more than inspecting an item a customer had returned, her glasses low on her pointed nose. She relished discovering stains on items and telling customers like Mrs Lambert that the clothes had obviously been worn, that they could not be returned in that condition. The job had always been temporary for Ava, until she could find a way to heal her mother. She couldn't have left with her mother like that. During her degree, she'd lived at home and commuted to Sheffield, too afraid to leave her mother alone.

Jane discreetly belched into her hand. 'You're going to have to do something for money. Call your solicitor. Tell him you want to proceed with the Ga-dee-mee suit.'

Ava suddenly tired of this visit. She wanted to go back to the bungalow. Jane insisted on pushing her in the wheelchair.

'I appreciate your help, but really, I can do it myself.'

Jane sighed. 'But I still have to walk alongside you, and you're too slow for my pace. And how will that look if I'm just walking next to you while you're doing all that work? A fine friend I'd be . . .'

Ava thought how earnestly Jane had explained her need

to help and the way others arranged their faces with sympathy when they saw them – the notion that if these rituals weren't performed there was something defective about her, that she would appear unfeeling to herself and others. The vulnerable must be protected and pitied. Ava had to play her part as the good patient, and she was sick of it.

She squinted at the bright lights in the stores, music beating out of them. A group of adolescent girls searched through sale bins of scanty underwear in a nearby shop and Ava thought of her own underwear – plain cotton, sagging at the back. If Jane hadn't been with her, she would have gone into that shop and picked up a couple of pairs from those bins. Something with lace or satin, so she might feel a bit different.

A flash of teal in another shop window caught her eye. 'Jane, do you mind stopping for a moment over there?'

Jane wheeled her towards the window display. It was a beautiful dress: teal silk with capped sleeves, A-line, cut just past the knees. A first-date dress. An afternoon-tea dress. Money dress. If she went to London, she would wear it.

Jane was hovering behind her, impatient. Her fingers tapped against the wheelchair handles.

'You wanna go in?'

Ava shook her head, and then they left.

★

At home, Ava thought of the teal dress, imagined the hem moving in a light breeze. She wanted to greet her father in it.

She sent a response to his email, short and to the point. She said she had no allergies and would see him in a few days. Her heart felt like it was doing sprints.

Elena had got rid of all the photos of Ava's father when they moved from London. She went years without seeing his face, never having the courage to search for his name online. Then, when he'd retired from the *Messenger*, they'd put up a picture of him in the paper. It was the same black-and-white photo they'd been using for the past twenty years: a wry smile on his mouth, his blond hair slicked back with gel. You could feel the largeness of this man, the look in his eyes, like he was watching everything at once. Editor of the *Messenger. News Today. Tomorrow. Always.* She had kept the page hidden in an old dictionary, though the ink had bled into a haze of grey now. She wondered how his face had changed, the hard shape it might've taken. How would she feel now seeing her father again?

Marie came by for physio. Her eyes were painted a deep purple and they looked even larger than usual. Ava wondered what kind of friends she kept, what she did on her weekends to pass the time, whether she went to the clubs on Church Road. Ava used to go often to those places when she'd still been in secondary school, spending the night at her friends' houses, telling her mother they were watching films when they were out dancing, meeting boys who were too old for them.

Marie smiled at Ava. 'Right, let's start.'

Ava had been diligent with the exercises, bringing her legs up in bed, rotating from side to side. Marie said she was doing well. It reminded Ava of being in school and getting a gold star – that's how she felt around Marie.

'Your pelvis is getting stronger,' Marie said.

At the end of every session, Ava asked the same questions about when she could walk.

'Crutches,' Marie said. 'Keep this up and we'll ease you out of the chair and onto crutches in about a week or two.'

'And . . . sex?' Ava said, her voice trailing off. 'When can I do that?'

Marie smiled. 'Not yet.'

Ava felt impatient. 'The cast is very itchy.'

'Just keep it dry.' Marie started packing her things. She asked Ava if she had any weekend plans.

'I'm going to London,' Ava said. Until this point, London had seemed like some intangible place, an abstraction, too big to touch. But telling Marie made it real.

Marie looked up from the bag she was packing. 'How long will you be gone for?'

'Probably back the same day,' Ava said, not having discussed such details with Sam. When she'd asked him in a text if he could take her, he'd said, 'Of course. Yes.'

Marie said it was just over a three-hour drive, and to make sure she was stretching, keeping the blood circulating.

Ava asked Marie what she was doing at the weekend, and she said she was seeing friends, going to the cinema. Ava wanted to ask if she'd like to go out sometime, not as her physiotherapist, but as a friend, but she thought Marie probably had better things to do.

'I forgot to give these to you,' Marie said, handing her a CD labelled *Music for Movement*, as well as a small poster – of ninety hexagons. 'They go with the book I gave you. *The Happiness Hexagon*. I'll hang the poster on your fridge.'

Ava had no idea what she was supposed to do with the poster or the disc, but she trusted Marie.

'Have you read the book?'

'Not yet.'

'Read the book,' Marie said. 'It'll change your life.'

When Marie left, Ava phoned Sam.

'Everything OK?' he said, his voice always stricken with panic when she called.

'I wondered if you could do me a favour.'

She told him about the teal dress on the mannequin, asked if he could pick up a size ten.

'Yup. I'll stop by yours around seven.'

When he knocked on the door that evening, Ava had been nodding in and out of sleep, dreaming she was swimming in a lake, all the sound muffled underwater, and everywhere she turned, there were shadows. She'd been having dreams like that since her mother died and she thought it was just something that happened to people who suffered a loss; the mind playing out its dark miseries in the world of dreams, where it was distant and safe.

'You all right?' he said, moving into the sitting room.

'Fine.' Ava yawned, still groggy from her nap.

He made himself comfortable on the sofa. 'My mum sent you dinner.' He held up a Tupperware container, left it on the coffee table.

Ava wondered if her own mother would've been so kind had the situation been reversed. She imagined her sitting in the passenger seat after they'd hit a man, telling her in that agitated way she sometimes spoke to step on the gas; no one had seen.

'That's very nice of her,' Ava said. 'You'll have to thank her for me.'

'And,' Sam said, reaching for another bag on the side of the sofa, 'the dress. What's the occasion?'

'London.' Ava felt heat rush to her face. 'I want to look nice.' She gestured to the console table. 'My handbag is just there.'

He shook his head. 'You don't have to pay me back.'

'Of course I *have to* pay you. You're already doing me a huge favour by driving me all the way to London.'

And here, Ava looked at Sam, this young man with his perfectly formed mouth and bright eyes hiding beneath a thick mound of hair and shame.

'I haven't been to London in months,' he said.

Ava told him she didn't remember much about the city beyond home and school and the high street close to where they'd lived. 'The heath wasn't far. I used to get lost in there with Michael.' She thought of them as children, waving long sticks in a pond at the edge of the heath, fat-headed tadpoles dispersing, doing their quick zigzag swim. The memories from that time in her life came in flashes, never more than a few images strung together like that.

'I've broken things off with Kendall,' Sam said.

Immediately, Ava was pleased, and this feeling confused her. She wasn't sure what tone to take. 'Are you all right?' she said neutrally.

'Yeah, I'm OK. She's not.' He scratched his head. 'It wasn't fair to string her along if I wasn't serious. She keeps phoning me. It's exhausting.'

'I'm sorry,' she said.

'It is what it is.' He paused, as if he were expecting her to say more. 'I've got an early shift at the shop.'

Ava fixed a serious look on her face. 'Please take what I owe you for the dress.'

He shook his head. 'You're all right.'

That night, Ava read Dr Wandsworth's book on happiness. She read it all in one sitting, finding herself unable to pull away from it. A bright feeling of excitement moved through her, like she'd found something that fit after a long and tiresome search.

Dr Wandsworth's theory wasn't groundbreaking. She might have read similar ideas in other books. The hexagon of happiness, as he called it, was all about the senses, how you could access happiness that way. He said movement was the sixth sense that was often neglected. But it was the most important of the senses, allowing access to 'the feeling body'. Ava didn't know what he meant exactly, only that since the accident her confidence in her body had been shattered and here was a chance to restore it, even find happiness through it. There were instructions outlined for ninety days and Ava liked the practicality of the exercises. The thought of a project to occupy her time brought a sense of purpose and relief.

It wasn't just the book that helped to lift her spirits. Ava became deeply interested in Dr Wandsworth and spent the following day collecting information about him on the internet: where he was from, where he lived now, whether he was attached to anyone glamorous. She felt connected to him, as if he were there on her sitting-room sofa, or else lying next to her in bed. She imagined he would be a cheerful husband, always offering advice and support.

Jane phoned while she was engaged in the first exercise – eating a cookie. She sniffed it, contemplated its shape.

'Have you decided about filing the suit against the Ghadimis?' Jane asked.

'I won't be doing that.'

Jane breathed heavily into the receiver. 'Well, Ava, it's your choice. Of course, it's *your* choice, but still. I only want what's best for you. You know that, don't you?'

Ten

Bar Five sometimes held its story evenings in strange places, like in the middle of a marshland or at the edge of a cliff. At-your-own-risk waivers were signed before those more adventurous meet-ups. But it added something to the stories people told, being someplace like that, stranded, or else on the verge of total collapse, and nowhere had Michael felt more acutely a sense of his own doom than the night they'd met in an old crumbling Victorian house in Brooklyn. It wasn't clear whether they were legally allowed to be there, but the organisers had sent an email to a chosen few, those who regularly attended the talks, and asked them to RSVP so they could ensure they had enough hard hats.

The building had once been a lingerie boutique. It'd been transformed into a family home sometime in the forties. The twin girls who'd lived there had gone missing and some said that they'd been killed by their uncle, though this was just speculation.

The roof had collapsed some time ago, and the moon could be seen intermittently through fast-moving clouds on the night they gathered to hear people tell their stories.

Michael imagined a bright crystal chandelier hanging above them in the place of those stars when it had been a family home. There were plans to knock the house down and build new apartments that would sell to the highest bidder. It surprised Michael that it had taken so long for developers to grab hold of this place when space was at a premium.

Jamila, the event organiser, projected an image of a tarot card on one of the remaining walls – a burning tower, mortar coming loose and people throwing themselves out of windows. A watchful eye sat above all that collapse, its pupil big and red.

That evening, people told their stories of self-destruction and devastation. Drug addictions and crimes. How they ruined the lives of those they claimed to love. Others told of devastations that came from outside, circumstances out of their control, and how they watched helplessly as their lives collapsed around them. Spouses and children inflicted with illness. A house burning down on a quiet street, someone still left inside. They called those stories the Burning Tower stories.

Michael's Burning Tower story had unfolded in September last year. Jacob's nursery had tried to reach them, leaving messages on Michael's and Layla's phones while she was in a meeting and he was teaching a seminar. By the time they'd received the voicemails, their son was already in hospital. Jacob had collapsed in the middle of playtime. Michael imagined his little body on the nursery carpet, bright pictures of zoo animals beneath him. It was bacterial meningitis, turning septic. There was a chance they'd have to put him in a coma to keep his organs from failing.

This was their son. They couldn't have it right, Michael

and Layla said to each other. But it was his small body on the bed they'd wheeled away to the intensive care unit. Michael held his wife while they both cried in the orange plastic seats of the waiting room. When the tears stopped, they asked questions. How had they not noticed he'd been unwell?

All those hours in hospital waiting for news, they kept pacing back and forth, going over details, something they'd overlooked that morning. He'd had no appetite at breakfast, but he was always a fussy eater. His cheeks – had they been warm? Layla sat with her head in her hands, a run through her stockings. She'd come straight from work, hadn't used the toilet in hours.

In the middle of the night, Layla said that this was happening because neither of them believed in God. Between the two of them, they couldn't produce a single deity to keep watch over their family.

She blamed herself, she blamed Michael, she blamed her parents who were not practising Muslims. They ate pork and celebrated Christmas – not the Jesus part of it, but the bright tree part, and the presents part and the same songs being repeated part.

Michael said it was the same in his house, though his father had turned himself into a kind of god, which was probably worse. He thought of those trips to Box Hill, his father parking the car at the foot of the hill and making the whole family climb up while he called out to them, always ahead, 'Come on, keep up!'

When they got to the viewing point, his father would look down on the rolling landscape, like he'd willed it into existence. Once, when he'd been standing there, he'd told Michael, 'I made myself,' and Michael had pictured his father putting himself together, limb by limb, rolling his head out of snow.

Things turned around for Jacob a few days later. The antibiotics were working, the fluid treatments stabilising his blood pressure. And when his eyes flittered open, it was like the day he was born – the happiness across Layla's and Michael's faces, the promises they made. *You are safe here. We will keep you safe.*

For days, he was pale and irritable, drowsy from the fever. But he smiled behind his pacifier when Michael retrieved a coin from behind his ear, his little hands searching at the back of his head, and then groans of frustration when he couldn't find anything there. The needle sticking into his hand, that little bit of blood in the IV tube – Michael thought, if there was a God, then he was a sick bastard.

How were they to go back to living as they had before? They couldn't trust that life would be kind to their son. Layla wouldn't leave things to chance. Every niggling change in him aroused her suspicion. What was his body trying to tell them? Why did he eat so little? She took a sabbatical from work to keep watch. She would be the Eye, the God their family needed. But it was getting out of hand: the googling, the hand sanitising, the safety items she ordered from Amazon.

'I forgot the hammer,' Layla had said when they'd been driving to see her parents in Chicago. 'I can't believe I forgot to bring the hammer with me.' She'd read an article about a family whose car had swerved into a lake, and they'd all drowned, stuck inside the car. The little girl was only two.

'Can you imagine?' she'd said, a wild fear in her eyes. 'Watching your child drown next to you?'

Layla had ordered one of those small emergency hammers and every time they rented a car, she brought it with her, ready to smash open some windows.

'Layla, this is too much,' he'd said when she first placed it in the glove compartment. 'We don't need a hammer.'

'Just a precaution. It's because I love you.'

Michael rested a hand on her knee, and she told him to drive with both hands.

A few weeks later, when an apartment block went up in flames in Queens and fifty tenants perished, she ordered fire masks and a ladder you could throw out of the window.

Layla was reinforcing their tower, padding it with cushions, building a moat around it out of antibacterial gel, but it would all come down some day, like the derelict building in Brooklyn, the blinking moon there in the place of a roof.

★

'I'm really struggling with this,' Layla said, biting on the end of a pencil. She was writing a story for her beginners' writing class.

Jacob was growing restless inside the apartment, dumping his toys on every surface. Michael said that he would take Jacob to the park; that way, she could focus.

'That would be great,' she said, her eyes still on the notebook. It made Michael happy, seeing Layla like that, preoccupied with something else.

Michael pulled the curtains back in Jacob's bedroom and saw Sarah Addams sitting on her IKEA sofa with a paper between her hands. Her work on the moth was still something he thought about, and he'd gone back to see it – *The Human Experience*. He sent her a message to say that he was heading to the park with Jacob, if she wanted to do her sketches for her exhibition on fathers and sons. He watched her look at her phone and read his text and she looked across and waved, and Michael and Jacob waved back.

It was a real job, getting Jacob ready to go out. Michael lathered sunscreen on his arms and legs and Jacob laughed, told him to stop. He picked out a yellow hat for himself that was too big, and when his father suggested the red one, which fit better, he said, 'No.'

It was already too hot, hotter than any June Michael could remember. When they reached the park just beyond the apartment, Sarah Addams was already there, sitting casually on a bench with a sketchpad between her hands, pencil ready. She smiled a little and then looked down at her notebook. Was she sketching their approach? Michael tried to pretend she wasn't there. But she was watching him, and it was all he could think about. Her eyes on him.

'Swings,' Jacob said, pointing up, but all the swings were taken.

'Why don't we start with the slide?' Michael suggested, and reluctantly Jacob nodded his yellow-capped head.

He stayed close as his son climbed the stairs to the slide, so he would be able to catch him if he fell backwards, but he made it to the top and Michael moved to the foot of the slide. Jacob stayed up there for some time, frozen. Another kid behind him peered out, anxious to get down.

'Come on, Jake,' Michael said, walking up to him. 'Come down.'

Jacob shook his head, so Michael gave him a gentle shove. He slid a little, then stopped halfway down the slide and walked the rest of the way.

'Swings,' he said, but they were still occupied. A few mothers smiled at Michael and he smiled back at them in parent solidarity. He noticed that his son's shoelaces were untied and got down, tied them up, three knots so they were secure.

Eventually, one of the mothers removed her son from the swing. When he shrieked, she threatened to take away his iPad and then he was quiet.

Jacob smiled on the swing, his little teeth flashing happiness. He liked it when Michael pushed higher, throwing his head back a little, that pale bit under his chin, looking up, up.

Michael dreaded the moment he'd have to remove Jacob from the swing. He wouldn't leave quietly. And sure enough, when he said it was time to go, Jacob cried, his face red and blotchy while his father carried him home. He hoped this scene would not be the focus of Sarah's sketches, but when he looked over, she wasn't there; the bench where she'd been sitting was now empty. Michael felt short-changed somehow. Hadn't they been convincing subjects?

'All right,' Michael said to his screeching son. 'All right.'

When he was back in the apartment, Michael saw that Sarah had sent him a message:

Thank you.

★

Layla wanted Michael to read her story. 'I mean, only if you want to. You can say no if you feel weird about it.'

'Of course. I'd love to read it.'

She handed him four printed pages with the corners folded over because they were out of staples. She said she couldn't watch him read. While Jacob was napping, she left the apartment to get some things from the Saturday market.

'Studio Apartment' was the title of her story, and Michael suddenly felt like an intruder, the same way he'd felt watching that intimate interview of the woman speaking about her cancer diagnosis.

He didn't know why he should feel that way, with his own wife. He pushed through his discomfort, but when he reached the end of the story, he was confused about what to do, how to interpret it.

The story was about a woman in her late thirties who lived in Melbourne, where Layla had once lived. She had her own studio apartment, no children or husband. Nothing much happened in the story, apart from Mali going about her life, working in the city, seeing friends and being happy. It seemed like the alternate life Layla could have had, free of Jacob, free of Michael. Did she want him to read it so he'd know of her regrets, her fantasies? Was she aware that she was writing about herself?

'What did you think?' Layla said, putting away the olives and fruit she'd got from the market.

'It was inspiring,' Michael said. 'Mali's a strong character.'

She removed her head from the fridge. 'You think so? You don't think it's a bit flat, the story itself? I'm wondering if more should have happened.'

'I think the story does the job of telling us about Mali's life.'

She beamed, lines appearing at the corners of her eyes. 'Thank you for reading. I really appreciate it.'

That evening, when she went to her writing class, Jacob asked to go to the aquarium shop. It was nearly his bedtime, but the weather was fine and Michael wanted some air, so he agreed to take him. The walk was pleasant. It was still warm from the day's sun baking into the asphalt.

At the aquarium, Jacob pointed to brightly coloured fish moving in the tanks. Like the last time they'd been, he smiled and pointed at things and said, 'Look, look, look!'

'See these ones?' Michael said, lifting his son up to the tank so he could see the zebra-striped fish.

Jacob giggled, then gestured for his father to put him down so that he could explore on his own.

'Stay close.'

There were only a handful of people around, the hour of closing near.

'Star,' Jacob said, pointing to a starfish, the fleshy beige of it startling.

A girl who looked to be a few years older than Jacob asked her mother about buying a turtle, and the mother asked a sales clerk about what a turtle needed in terms of environment and food.

A few tanks above, at eye level, was a jellyfish. It was a small, translucent thing. The big disc of its head and the slow, soft, alien movement of it drew you in. Michael turned to show Jacob, but he wasn't there. A wild panic rushed through him, his heart beating in his ears as he looked down different aisles in the shop.

'Jacob?'

'Have you seen a boy?' Michael said to the woman and her daughter who were now at the till buying a bunch of turtle things.

'No, sorry,' the woman said, and while she spoke, Michael's eyes caught a glimpse of the door, wide open, and the cars moving beyond the pavement.

He ran out of the shop, up and down the street, but no luck. His chest felt tight, the world constricting around him.

A man from the aquarium with a lanyard around his neck called out to Michael, waved to him. Michael ran back to the shop, and there was Jacob, standing next to the man.

'He was hiding in a corner, behind the coral tanks,' the man said, in a bored way, like he'd seen this kind of thing happen many times before, children hiding and their weary parents in a panic. 'We're closing now.'

Michael grabbed his son, relief and anger moving through him. 'Thank you,' he said to the man, who started locking up.

Michael got down so he was level with Jacob. 'You never, *ever* hide from me again.'

Jacob's gaze moved to his shoes.

'You never, *ever* hide when we're outside.'

Perhaps Layla had been right about the leash. Jacob finally nodded his head and, slowly, they made their way home.

Jacob slept almost as soon as he was in bed and Michael sat on the carpet. For a brief moment, he entertained an alternative to the evening, one in which Jacob could not be found and he'd had to call the police and fill out forms. Layla would collapse on the pavement, her whole world gone, and she would leave Michael. He could imagine it too well.

It felt necessary in that moment to tell someone what had happened, to say, 'Hey, this bad thing happened because of me,' so he sent a message to Sarah Addams and told her how he'd lost his son at the aquarium.

She responded a few minutes later, asking if he'd found him and Michael told her that he had. He was a terrible father, he said.

She wrote back sometime later, saying that if he'd found Jacob, that was all that mattered.

But it wasn't. There was the other story, the one of his missing son, his life in ruins.

Layla returned from class, a look of exhaustion across her face. Michael put his arms around her, and she stayed there.

'The class thinks I should write about being Lebanese,' she said, speaking into his shoulder. 'Apparently there's no story to my story.'

For a while, they both stood there, holding each other.

Eleven

The summer before Michael had left for New York, Elena had started a casual affair with the TV actor Robert Embringham. He'd made a handful of visits to Welton and brought Marks & Spencer's biscuits in tins shaped like London buses and postboxes.

'Oh, hello,' he said, when Michael answered the door.

He played the role of Stephan Turner, an anaesthesiologist who committed murders on a mediocre soap opera. Ava had never liked her father's friend, the way he threw his head back when he laughed and said, 'You're killing me!' pretending to wipe away a tear. 'No, really, you are!' and then he'd slap his knee like a cartoon character, two-dimensional and loud.

He sat on the sofa, pretending to watch television while he waited for their mother.

'So,' he said. 'So, how's school?'

Ava said fine, though she was doing poorly in maths. Michael said he was going to study in New York in the autumn. And then he asked, 'How's Tracey?'

Tracey was Robert's wife.

Robert's mouth fell open – a moment's delay before he

threw his head back and laughed. 'You're killing me!'

Robert stood immediately from the sofa when Elena walked into the sitting room. She wore her old dinner party dresses when Robert came to visit, colourful silky things that were too flashy for Welton.

She looked happy.

Previously, when Robert had been to visit, Elena had stayed out all night and returned the next morning in the same dress. She had made an omelette breakfast for Ava and Michael and suggested a walk along the river.

But that night she returned early with a frown on her made-up face. She stomped into her room and shut the door, the affair having ended suddenly, though Elena never mentioned the reason.

The next weekend, she said, 'Welton's so dull. Is there a duller place in the world than Welton?'

And then, 'People are idiots! A customer asked why she couldn't return underwear. Everyone's stupid. Why am I working in that dump?'

And then, 'I'm going to Spinolli's.'

Spinolli's was a restaurant bar. A pianist played there on Fridays – an elegant, brittle woman in her early fifties. Elena liked watching her play. She said her father used to play the piano. It made her think of him.

Around midnight, she phoned home from Spinolli's.

'They've taken my keys,' she said to Ava, her voice a slippery drawl. 'Tell your brother to come get me.'

Years later, when Elena had lost her licence swerving home from Spinolli's.

Ava said, 'You have a problem,' and her mother had laughed, a flirtatious sort of laugh, breezy and dismissive.

'You need to do something about the nest of acne

between your eyebrows. Now that's a problem,' Elena said, narrowing her eyes at her daughter.

Elena was good at hiding her addiction at work, around others. Her public outbursts were rare. She carried a toothbrush and mouthwash in her large handbag. Only once, Jane had said, 'Put a mint in your mouth.' But for Ava, it was the last straw when she'd lost her licence and had nearly got herself killed.

Ava brought pamphlets home, books on addiction, gave Elena phone numbers for support groups.

'I'll give them a call if you come to Spinolli's with me.'

Ava told her mother, 'All right. Let's go.'

At the bar, Elena ordered two gin and tonics. Ava said she was driving, and Elena batted her hand.

'It's one drink.'

They sat at a table near the pianoforte. The room was dimly lit with tea lights and rain fell heavy against the large Georgian windows behind the piano. Ava worried the road to the bungalow would flood as it sometimes did when it rained like this.

The pianist, Maria Gonzales, wore an elegant white dress that fell just above her ankles. She didn't look at the people around her having their meals, chewing their food softly. She just started playing, and Elena smiled, her attention focused on the music, her eyes on Maria, who played with her whole body.

It was easy to get swept into the song, the large crescendo swell of it. Ava had planned to confront her mother about the drinking.

But when Maria took a break, Elena talked.

She talked about growing up in Kyrenia, the harbour town where her father had lived most of his life. She was there until the age of seven, before they'd moved to London.

In Kyrenia, they had a piano in the front room. Her father played the 'Moonlight Sonata' with great proficiency and feeling. She remembered his hands, the burning frenzy of them, playing the third movement. The ferocious life in that movement! Elena's eyes widened all the time, telling Ava.

She often thought of the harbour in Kyrenia, the shimmering water. Her father had a little boat and they took it out to sea when the weather was fine. Sometimes she pretended the River Derwent on the other side of the road was the sea and she was back in Cyprus.

'The Turkish military invaded when I was in London,' she said, drinking the last of her gin and tonic. 'So many families displaced. My father had died a year before the invasion.' She looked at Ava's glass. 'Are you going to drink that?'

Ava shook her head and her mother helped herself.

She continued. 'I was never political. But I took part in a demonstration to protest the invasion. This was in London. I hadn't planned to go until the last minute.'

She said she'd marched with hundreds of others from the Greek Embassy to the Grosvenor Hotel. The deposed Archbishop Makarios was there and he had come out and waved to the crowd. The excitement when he came out! Elena couldn't see him. But there was a renewed energy among the demonstrators as they moved on to the Turkish Embassy in Belgrave Square.

'That's when the violence broke out. Hundreds of police officers were standing in front of the embassy, waiting for us,' she said. 'Some demonstrators were pulled by the hair, even by the nose, and dragged into vans. One of the demonstrators dropped a large stone and I picked it up.'

Her eyes sparkled as she told Ava what happened next. 'I threw the stone at the embassy window.'

It was clear to Ava, the way Elena told the story, that her mother had felt a thrill, hurling the stone at the embassy, satisfied that the window had shattered.

'I'd never done a thing like that before,' Elena said. 'I just kept thinking of my father's piano in Kyrenia and how he would never play it again.'

Ava felt pity for her mother, listening to her story. Elena had never mentioned her father's piano before. She wanted to know more about her mother's Cypriot side of the family. But Ava watched Elena drain the rest of the gin and tonic and gesture to the waitress to bring another, and she remembered then why she'd agreed to come to Spinolli's.

'That sounds tough,' she said, and straightened her back against the chair. 'There are a lot of ways to deal with pain. Support groups and books . . .'

Her mother was rummaging through her handbag. Ava sighed. It felt hopeless. There was nothing she could say or do. Michael was no help, hiding in New York. She was alone in this, a small feather floating above a big grey sea.

Elena retrieved a receipt and pen from her handbag and wrote MOONLIGHT SONATA. She folded the receipt and placed her request on the piano stool.

The waitress came over with another gin and tonic. 'Thanks, Shirley,' Elena said before introducing Ava, who smiled awkwardly.

When the pianist returned, she unfolded the receipt and

turned to face the room for the first time. She saw Elena and gave her a knowing nod and played.

The music, slow and delicate, unfolded into the room like a beautiful death. Ava watched, not the pianist but her mother, the shape of her eyes. The ghosts moving across them. Ava felt a tingling in her skin, her heart. She wanted so desperately to save her mother.

When the song ended, Elena leant into Ava. 'My father used to say that all of life was contained in this sonata.' She ran her thin fingers along the rim of the empty glass. 'Your father, with all of his faults, understood this too.'

Elena gestured to Shirley for another drink. She looked far away, in a different place.

'I wish I could be better. For you and Michael. Things would've turned out differently with your father if I wasn't so angry.'

Ava felt a stinging in her eyes. She thought of the article in *Glamour* magazine. Her father's affair printed there. The humiliation her mother had endured. And Ava remembered all of her father's excuses when he'd moved to Sydney. *It's a bad time to visit, but maybe next year . . .*

'He lied to you. He cheated and he neglected us.' It was the first time she had spoken against her father, and it was clear then that a line had been drawn. Ava was on her mother's side, and would stay there.

The drink arrived. Elena wasted no time, took a large sip. The pianist played a more cheerful song, less complicated.

Ava wiped the tears that had slipped away. 'You'll call that support group in the morning.'

★

Ava started getting ready at five in the morning, though they weren't leaving for London until two o'clock in the afternoon. She hadn't slept well, anticipating the day ahead, and the pain in her leg had kept her up. Ava had lost track of her tablets, how many she'd taken. The bottle didn't rattle as much.

The teal dress Sam had brought over was a bit loose in the chest. Since the accident, Ava had lost weight and her breasts were always the first to disappear. A cruel punishment. She wore a white cardigan to hide the narrowness of her shoulders. She thought she looked sickly, not slim and attractive.

For the first time in months, she wore make-up – a deep red lipstick – and she moisturised her skin, put on perfume that smelt of roses. It was the same perfume her mother used to wear. For years, Elena had worn that scent, the room smelling of roses when she walked in. Today, it felt important to have her close.

Elena had taught her there was such a thing as wearing too much make-up and it made all the difference to what people thought of you.

'Subtlety,' she'd said, standing in front of the mirror above her dresser that needed cleaning. 'Just a daub of red here, a brush of rouge there.' She'd demonstrated and Ava had copied. 'The main thing is that you don't want to look like a prostitute.'

Elena had licked her finger and wiped it ever so gently over Ava's eyelids, smudging the kohl so it didn't look so harsh. She'd been getting ready for her first school disco.

'You've got very pretty eyes. The same brown as your grandfather.' There was sadness behind Elena's gaze. When Ava felt frustrated or upset with her mother, mad enough even to leave, she reminded herself how her mother had once said she had pretty eyes.

Ava waited on the front porch for Sam. She listened to chirping birds, the sound of cars muffling their delicate songs. She wanted to skip stones on the river. It was what she did with her mother on Saturday mornings. They would drive out to a clearing along the River Derwent, pick out all the smooth, flat stones and release them into the water. A wonderful feeling of lightness followed; something cold and heavy lifted from their hearts, and afterwards they went for ice cream or coffee, depending on the season.

'Michael's punishing me,' Elena had once said, hurling stones into the choppy water. 'Maybe I deserve it.'

When she used to talk like that, Ava didn't say anything; didn't think her mother cared for an opinion, especially one that would confirm all her fears, that, yes, he was punishing her and perhaps she did deserve it. With her mother, it was more a matter of getting the thing out than receiving an opinion.

'If I had any kind of sense, I'd have left your father years ago. Did you know he started his career in the tabloids? The sort of trash his mother used to read. He'd never admit to a thing like that. No. He's a *serious* editor-in-chief at a *serious* national paper.'

Her long, thin arms extended out in front of her and Ava thought how thin she'd become since Michael had left.

'Forget Michael. If he wants us out of his life, there's no sense in holding on.'

They'd received his wedding invitation only weeks before the set date. Ava had told her mother, 'Michael doesn't want us there,' because Elena was going to buy two tickets, expensive last-minute seats she couldn't afford.

She was ready to do that, to see her son on his special day. She had loved him the most.

'I'm still here,' Ava had said, and Elena had smiled then, a soft, resigned smile that seemed to say, *You'll never take his place.*

Ava stayed with her mother. All those years, she stayed. But now, Ava was going to London and it felt like a betrayal.

She caught a glimpse of the water, deep and cold like steel, through the leaves of the willow tree across the road. It was a grey day – overcast with rain threatening – and the willow's branches bristled in quick agitation. Ava curled her hands around her cooling cup of coffee. She didn't normally have coffee but was on her third cup, hoping it would help her to wake up, sharpening her reactions after such a long, sleepless night. By the time Sam arrived, she was drinking her fourth.

She wondered if the black Ford he was driving was the same car that had hit her that night on the road. It was a strange thought, that she would be sitting in it for the next three to four hours, this car that had caused her damage.

Sam looked different, his hair out of his face, slicked back with gel, and it was clear he'd chosen his clothes carefully: a navy collared shirt and khaki trousers instead of his usual T-shirt and jeans. Ava preferred him in his T-shirts but felt a quiet pleasure in thinking he might have made this effort for her.

Sam said the teal colour of the dress suited her, and Ava smiled. 'Thank you.'

'Have you got any bags for me to put in the boot?'

'No, just my handbag.'

Sam had the passenger seat pushed back so that she had plenty of legroom. His car smelt of soap and pine, a freshness that made her hungry, and her stomach started making embarrassing gurgling noises as soon as they pulled out of the drive. She was grateful when Sam turned on the radio, muffling the sounds of her digestive tract. A few drops of rain splattered on the windshield.

'Kendall kept phoning last night,' he said as they merged onto the A6. 'She thinks I've broken it off with her because of you.' An odd laughter escaped from him, like the sound of a hiccup.

Ava wasn't sure what to say, though a part of her was pleased his girlfriend believed this. It wasn't that Ava had anything against her or that she wanted to cause her grief – she knew nothing about this Kendall beyond her Barbie-doll name and the few details Sam had shared. But she was intrigued by the idea that Sam could be attracted to her despite the eleven-year age gap between them. Ava imagined his type: young, blonde. Kendall. But then, he'd broken up with her.

He turned on the windscreen wipers.

'Have you given Kendall a reason to be jealous?'

'I guess. A while ago,' he said. 'I kissed one of her friends during freshers' week.'

Ava was surprised, and even encouraged. 'Well, that'll do it.'

He scratched the back of his head. 'We weren't official or anything at the time. I hadn't thought so. Not sure what makes a relationship "official". We'd been on something like six dates? That doesn't seem so long to me. Anyway, I was smashed, and this girl was really, really fit.' He turned to Ava. 'What about you? How's your love life?'

Ava laughed, pointed down to her leg. 'No love life.'

'Before . . . the accident. Why are you still single?'

It was a question she was often asked by people at work, even regular customers who came in. 'But you've got those lovely brown eyes! And you're skinny. Exotic! Are you Italian? Egyptian? What hope is there for the rest of us?'

There was always the offer of a set-up. A nephew or a second cousin, or someone else working in sales – as if it was enough to have that in common: folding clothes, circling non-refundable policies on receipts.

When Ava was a teenager in bed at night, she used to dream about her future husband, imagining what he might look like, what he might be up to at that very moment, brushing his teeth or kissing some other girl. And then she thought how someday they would meet and not be strangers anymore, and he would be brushing his teeth in their house, kissing her instead of a silly girlfriend. But with her own parents, Ava had seen what relationships could do, how people punished each other with threats and silence. A sudden withdrawal of affection. Why would she want that?

'I don't see the point in settling down with someone out of boredom or loneliness,' Ava said.

Sam smiled. 'Exactly.' And he relaxed into his seat, his hands looser on the steering wheel, when before they'd been stiff and focused. 'For me, a relationship is just another thing tying me down to Welton.'

'You want to leave?'

He shrugged. 'Yeah. I want to try something new. But there's the family business.'

'Is that what you're going to do after uni, run the curtain shop?'

'It's what my parents want.'

Ava nodded. 'I understand about pressure. I stayed close for uni so that I could live at home with my mother.' A pause. 'She had a problem with alcohol.'

Ava could sense she'd extinguished the lightness of their talk, bringing up her mother and her struggle. She quickly changed the subject.

'I've sent in my application. For that psychology conversion course.'

'So, you're doing it, then?'

'I am.'

They settled into a semi-comfortable silence. Ava thought of her days as a student. The seminars where they chewed over dense passages of text. Sometimes Ava read a sentence three, maybe four times before the meaning became clear to her. Others in the class had sharp, intelligent comments to make. Some had attended private schools. They could make accusations – 'Churchill was wrong' – confidence in their voice and in the way they held themselves in expensive but casual-seeming clothes, like nothing could touch them. They questioned big thinkers and leaders without apology, and were praised for their boldness. They took risks and were rewarded.

Ava had taken to writing out her comments before those seminars and was the first to raise her hand so that her courage wouldn't falter later when others made points she'd never considered. Once, in her second year, she had drunk half a bottle of Johnnie Walker to celebrate her friend Phoebe's birthday. She'd been kissing a boy who didn't matter on a worn-out student sofa when she remembered too late about her evening seminar. But she went and her hand shot up about a dozen times in that class, asking questions, making comments. The instructor had looked at her like a proud mother.

'Nice to see you come out of your shell,' she'd told Ava, who spent the rest of the night with her head in the toilet.

Ava hoped her psychology course would be different. That she would take chances because she had the confidence to speak up, not because she was hammered.

Sam shut off the wipers. He asked why she wanted to study psychology.

'It gives us answers.'

'To what?'

'Who we are. Everything. Have you heard of Dr Wandsworth?'

'Doesn't he have some crack theory about happiness? A triangle, or a square, some random shape that's supposed to mean something?'

'It's not a crack theory,' Ava said, surprised by how her voice rose then. 'He says that anyone can be happy. You just need to focus on your senses.' She softened her tone. 'And the shape you're referring to is a hexagon and it's meant to represent our senses.'

'What?'

'The hexagon,' she repeated. 'For the six senses. Movement is the forgotten sixth sense.'

Ava had a strange feeling of satisfaction, like she'd successfully defended her lover against some harsh, unfair judgement.

'I don't buy into that stuff. Pop psychology. Self-help. It's really just a money-making thing.'

'Hm. Not sure that's true.'

Sam shrugged. 'These so-called experts are just preying on vulnerable people. Cashing in.'

Ava felt a hot anger rise to her face, her ears. 'No,' she said. 'What Dr Wandsworth is saying is true. Anyone – if they really try – can overcome their circumstances. If they really, *really* try. They can do it. It's just a matter of putting in the effort.'

Sam didn't say anything after that. In her determination to avoid falling into a dark spiral like her mother, Ava clung on to Dr Wandsworth and his teachings that were now ingrained in her. She reread a section of his book every night before bed, like the Bible, or in the place of the romance novels that brought some women comfort. *The world is here. Will you let it in?* 'Yes,' she whispered to nobody in the darkness of her bedroom, 'yes.'

The long road in front of Ava made her eyes heavy, and her exhausted body finally gave in to sleep.

She woke when they passed a sign for Leicester, her breathing quick and her stomach sore with pain. She thought perhaps it was the tablets causing her discomfort. The coffees maybe. Had she eaten anything? She told Sam to stop at the service station ahead.

'Everything OK?'

Ava couldn't answer. She felt a wave of nausea, her heart pounding like a trapped wing under her ribcage.

At the service station, there was someone in the disabled cubicle and they were taking their time. Sam said he'd get a coffee while she waited.

She repeatedly cleared her throat so that the person inside would know there was someone there, waiting to use the toilet. A bearded man finally emerged without a wheelchair or crutches or an apology and walked right past her.

'Excuse me,' she said.

'Yeah? What is it?' He turned to face her, that dumb look of confusion on a man she'd seen many times before. A sense of entitlement. Ava didn't say anything, and he didn't linger.

The toilet wouldn't flush, and he'd left a mess in there, excrement clogging the bowl. She breathed through her mouth so this dreadful nausea wouldn't materialise.

Sam was waiting for her by the entrance. 'Everything all right?' he asked.

She nodded, but on the road she couldn't get the smell of human waste out of her nose. She felt like it was chasing after her, and when Sam asked if she smelt something, she panicked.

They stopped again, this time at a larger service station. Outside the car, Sam examined the back of her dress as she leant onto the hood for support, shifting the weight of her body on her good leg. Sam said some of the shit from the toilet had smeared onto it. Her skin felt clammy and she heaved a couple of times until she felt bile in the back of her throat, then she emptied the contents of her stomach there by the tyre. Her knee buckled and she lost her balance, falling into the mess.

'Oh, God,' Sam said. 'Oh, God!'

'I'm sorry,' was all Ava could think to say when her stomach calmed. 'Sorry,' she repeated, vaguely mindful of the absurdity of apologising for the body's sudden colourful burst of excitement. The colour here was orange, likely from that packet of carrot batons she'd had for dinner.

Sam helped move her away from the mess, sat her on a

patch of grass. He rushed into the service station to see if they sold clothes, since her dress was ruined.

It felt in that moment as though this whole thing was too big – seeing her father again, returning to London. She brought her wrist up to her nose but couldn't smell the roses from her perfume. She imagined her mother frowning with that crease high on her forehead. She would have said, 'You're not going,' if Ava had shown her the letter, and that would have been the end of it. But she wasn't here, gone without warning.

Sam returned with a white plastic bag and a bottle of water tucked under his arm. He crouched down. 'Here,' he said, snapping open the bottle. 'Drink.'

Their eyes met as she drank the cool water. They were beautiful eyes, deep brown, kind and full of anxiety.

He showed Ava what he'd bought – a Manchester United jersey and a pair of plain cotton shorts – and she had to laugh. These were the clothes she would meet her father in after twenty years.

'Thank you,' she said, forcing a smile. 'These will do.'

'I think red suits you. Better than blue.'

'It's teal.' Ava laughed again, though she wanted to cry.

Sam helped her change, both of them sitting on that patch of grass. He apologised as he unzipped the back of her teal dress.

'What for? You're doing me a favour.'

She remembered that her bra had a big hole in the back and over the years the colour had changed from white to a dirty grey. It was her everyday functional bra. She hadn't thought anyone would see.

He looked the other way as he handed her the jersey. She pulled it over head and found it was ridiculously baggy, at least four sizes too big. It could have passed for a short dress.

The lower half of her body was more difficult. Sam said to use her arms to lift her bottom off the ground while he moved the dress down past her knees, past her ankles. His hands brushed up against the fuzz of her exposed leg, the other mostly covered by the cast. At least none of the mess had got onto her cast. The shorts were loose and long. She tied the drawstring into a double knot so they wouldn't fall down.

'Do you want to save this?' Sam said, holding out the white plastic bag with the teal dress inside, all kinds of foul smells rising from it.

Ava had imagined greeting her father in that dress. She had wanted him to think how nicely she'd turned out.

'Get rid of it,' she said. 'It's not worth saving.'

Sam threw the plastic bag into a nearby bin, along with the rest of the rubbish they'd collected in the car. He used antibacterial wipes on the leather seat where Ava had been sitting with someone else's waste pinned on her like a tail.

She wanted to wail and scream and let loose all of that bubbling dread, but some part of her held back, something learnt from childhood.

'Sam,' she said, her throat burning, and she did her best to appear calm and rational, 'you've gone above and beyond to help me, really you have, and I wish you'd stop feeling guilty now about what happened.' He looked down at the steering wheel, refusing to meet her gaze. 'But I'd like to turn back.'

'No,' he said. 'No way.'

They both sat in silence for a minute while cars pulled in and out around them. Someone parked in the spot next to them where Ava had been ill. The driver stepped out and grimaced. 'Disgusting,' he said. 'Charlie, don't step in that!'

Sam turned to her. 'I've been staying out of this whole thing with your dad because it's important that you make this decision on your own. I didn't want to get involved. But you'll regret it if we turn back now.' He ran a hand through his hair, and a few strands pulled loose from the others that were held in place with all that gel. 'Your father is dying,' he said, his voice softening. 'It'll haunt you if you don't go and at least speak to him. If it was me, I'd want to see my dad. Even if it's just to find some answers.'

Ava knew he was right, that in spite of the years between them, he was the one talking sense.

She nodded, and he switched on the ignition. He said he'd bought her a ham sandwich in case she was hungry. She ate every bite of the sandwich, the doughy bread filling a void. She leant her head against the window and fell into a deep sleep.

When Ava opened her eyes, there were trees above her. They were in London. She asked Sam how long until they were there.

'Not long.'

Ava felt a panic. She was really going to see her father. Her heart was beating too fast and she took one of her painkillers, felt it stick to her throat as she chased it down with what was left in the water bottle.

Sam turned the radio volume down.

'I'm going to help you get into the house,' he said, 'but then I'm going to leave to give you privacy.'

'All right,' Ava said, trying to conceal her disappointment. 'Of course.'

140

She didn't know why she'd assumed that Sam was coming in with her and now that she thought about it, she couldn't see why he ever would. She barely wanted to go in herself.

'I'll be close. In Camden. My dad wants me to meet a potential supplier. It won't take long. I'll come as soon as I'm done. Unless you want me to stay away . . .'

'You don't have to worry about me. Come when you want.'

Before leaving Welton, she'd searched online for her father's house in Hampstead. It wasn't far from her childhood home, just a few streets over. There'd been a boy on a bicycle in front of the house in the street view. It had felt strange, peeking into this tidy-looking street with its residents going about their lives, not knowing she was watching them from her slow computer in Welton. She'd looked for her father, clicked the arrows up and down the street, but there was no point in searching because they'd blurred out all the faces.

They drove through the high street, passing shops and cafés with people sitting outside looking relaxed and happy. Ava felt a strange sense of familiarity. She knew this place, the outline of it, her childhood home, only the details were missing.

Sam turned off into a side street where the houses had a look of privilege about them – soft-coloured, with large circular drives protected by tall hedges or metal gates. There was a general sense of being on guard here, of needing to protect the fort.

Sam pulled into the shingle driveway of a detached red-brick house and parked behind a black Jeep. The house was much bigger than their previous one. It suddenly dawned on Ava that perhaps it wasn't just him in there.

Sam popped open the boot for the wheelchair. He lifted it out and set it on the stones. The street was quiet, a few sparrows looking down from the rooftops like they were on watch. Ava paused for a moment, knowing that she wouldn't be able to wheel her chair along the stones to the front door. It couldn't be more than ten steps, but Ava hadn't practised stairs with Marie. She wasn't supposed to put weight on her leg yet.

Seeing her hesitate, Sam lifted her up, his arms around her waist, and it surprised Ava, the ease of his action, like she was weightless. He asked if it would be OK to set her down on the top step.

'I've laid on worse today,' she said, and he looked at her with a soft smile. Ava wondered if she'd been too mean to him earlier, defending Dr Wandsworth in the car.

Sam dragged the wheelchair over and then touched her shoulder lightly. His hand lingered, and it brought comfort in that moment. She rang the bell, its high-pitched chime echoing through the house. There was movement behind the stained-glass window of the door. Ava recognised the smooth shape of a woman approaching. She felt relief wash through her, the sight of this young woman, a smile on her face, opening the door rather than her father.

'Is this the house of Lee Bridges?' Ava said in a formal voice that didn't sound like her own.

The woman nodded. 'Lee's just in the kitchen. I'm Vivienne.'

Sam crouched over Ava, spoke in a soft whisper. 'Are you OK for me to leave?'

'Yes. Of course.'

Vivienne asked Ava if she wanted to be pushed through, but Ava said she could manage. When she looked behind her, Sam was already in the car.

It was the kind of house they featured in home catalogues, with rugs that were thick and glowing. Every piece of furniture beamed with a sense of purpose. The ceilings were high, stylish copper fixtures hanging from them.

She wondered if he had a wife – if this Vivienne leading her through the house was his partner. She guessed she must be in her early thirties, her own age. Her father had always liked young women – and how else to explain the modern furnishings, the pomp and luxury of this place? Ava had been to her grandparents' house in Kirkby-in-Ashfield, had sat on their tatty sofa. And not even Elena, if she had access to unlimited funds, would furnish a house in this way.

The back of the property was all windows, and the floorboards were splayed with late-afternoon sun as they followed the smell of cooking beef into the kitchen. Here was her father, standing over a hob.

Her throat felt raw when he turned to greet her.

'Hello! Hello!'

His voice was as she'd remembered it. Up, up. It was the voice he used when they had company.

Then his smile flattened. 'What's happened to you?' he said, the excessive cheer gone. He hadn't expected to see her like this.

His face was bearded when he'd always been clean-shaven, and she couldn't help but stare at his pink lips, parted, a question hanging from them. Ava shifted her gaze to the windows behind him, squinted at the light.

'It was just an accident. I'll live.'

She was grateful that he stayed at the hob, didn't try to conjure up some false affection with an intimate gesture like a hug. Perhaps he'd planned to get close but was thrown off by the chair, her strange clothes. She didn't know.

He just stood there, with that surprised look on his creased face. It frightened her, seeing him old.

Vivienne handed her a drink of water with cucumber floating in it. Then she tapped Ava's father gently on the shoulder to say that it was time to add lemongrass.

'What?'

'The lemongrass. It's time.'

'Oh, right. Excuse me,' he said to Ava.

He rushed to the large island at the centre of the kitchen and chopped some long stalks of lemongrass with a sharp-edged knife.

'Did you take the train?' he said, adding lemongrass and coriander to the wok.

'No.' She took a sip of the cucumber water. 'A friend drove me.'

'Does your friend want to join us for dinner?' Lee had his back to Ava, mixing and adding ingredients to the wok, but she didn't mind. It was easier with him looking the other way.

'He's got some things to do.' She thought of Sam nearby in Camden and it made her feel better, knowing he was close.

Vivienne told Lee to lower the heat on the hob. 'It's ready,' she said and gave him another pat on the shoulder – a perfunctory pat, not at all intimate. She took her handbag from the island, before turning to Ava. 'Goodbye,' she said. 'Enjoy your meal,' and like that, she floated out of the kitchen, the sound of the door shutting behind her. *Come back*, Ava wanted to say.

Lee shut off the extractor fan and the room was suddenly too quiet. He scratched his nose, and his wry smile, the one he wore at dinner parties, returned.

'Vivienne owns a Michelin-starred restaurant in Shoreditch. At her age! When you said you were coming to London, I thought, well – of course I've got to get Vivienne over. It's an important occasion. So, I phoned her up and told her my daughter's coming for dinner and she said, "Of course I'll do it. I'll help you cook." So hopefully you enjoy the meal. Do you want more water? Some herbal tea? I've got a lovely rhubarb and ginger blend.'

'I'm fine.'

'Good. Well, it's great that you're here!'

'I don't usually dress like this.' Ava felt it was important to make this clarification.

'OK. Looks fine to me. You *do* look different. Like your mother.'

Ava felt a flutter in her chest.

'I had planned for us to eat outside. I got some new spotlights installed. They've got a nice warm glow to them. And there's the pond,' Lee's eyes widened. 'You have to see the pond. But there are a few steps to get to the patio. Can you manage them? We can eat inside if you prefer. It's up to you. What do you think?'

'We could still eat outside if you want,' she said, taking another long drink of the cucumber water. Her throat felt like it was lined with needles.

'Do you need some help getting down the stairs?'

Reluctantly, she nodded. He offered his arm at first, but when she wobbled and lost her balance, he picked her up as easily as Sam had, her head against his shoulder. He was warm and smelt faintly of cloves.

Ava felt strange. Here was her father, absent these twenty years, carrying her forward like a piece of luggage he'd picked up from a carousel where she'd been spinning, spinning. She leant against the red bricks while he brought the chair.

The back garden smelt of freshly cut grass. The sun was slowly sinking, the bright copper shine of it hitting the eye with sharpness. To the right of the garden was a pond. A big orange fish moved across the water. All this space. She wondered if he still threw his infamous dinner parties. Perhaps it was necessary to keep a place like this so that people would still come.

'There you go,' he said, patting the cushioned seat on the wheelchair.

'Thank you.'

'It's strange seeing you like this. I don't know – I guess I wasn't sure what to expect. It's all so strange, isn't it? When will you be out of the chair?'

'Maybe two weeks.'

'Well, that's not terrible. Did I ever tell you about the time I broke my leg running away from an explosion? It was in the seventies, when the IRA was blowing up everything. Did I tell you this?'

'No.'

'I was on crutches that whole summer.' When she didn't reply, he looked back at the house. 'I'd better bring the food out before it gets cold. It'd be a shame to let Vivienne's cooking go to waste.'

The table was all set up. Napkins neatly folded. Silver cutlery laid out. She wondered if he'd arranged the table himself or if he'd hired someone to put it together.

He walked through the patio doors carrying two plates. The smell of lemongrass and coriander mixed in with the blossom trees.

He sat in the chair opposite, poured white wine, spilling a bit on the table and Ava got a napkin to help, but he told her to leave it.

'Shall we toast to our reunion?' he said.

'OK.'

'Thank you for coming!'

They clinked glasses. A black ladybird landed on the edge of Ava's plate. She batted it away, but it kept returning like a taunt.

With all his energy and talk, Ava had almost forgotten that her father was dying, that his death was what had brought her here. She looked at him and tried to find some weakness in his disposition, but she couldn't see anything. He had aged, yes, and this unsettled her. But he was himself. *Let's go! Let's go!*

'Do you like the food?'

'It's very nice. Is it Thai?'

'Yes. I love Thai food. The street food is best, but it's hard to get anything authentic like that. Even in London. You've got to go to Bangkok for authentic. Have you been?'

'Where?'

'Thailand.'

Ava almost laughed. 'No.'

He poured more wine. 'How's your brother?'

'I'm not sure.'

Lee stopped chewing. 'You're not in touch?'

Ava shook her head. 'He's got his life in New York.' And then, because she couldn't help herself, she asked if Michael had responded to his letter.

'Yes. Well. I'm not exactly shocked by what he said. It's not come out of nowhere, his response. I wasn't exactly good to him. He was . . . a very sensitive boy . . . Anyway, he said he'd rather not.'

Ava was surprised Michael had responded at all. The excitement on her father's face dimmed again, perhaps thinking of Michael. The quiet sound of their chewing unsettled Ava. She preferred her father's erratic hosting to this silence.

She said she had applied to a psychology course. She was thinking of becoming a psychologist.

'Psychology is always useful. As a journalist, you have to understand the human mind. It's how you get the answers you want.' A pause. 'How's your mother?'

Ava put her fork down and it made a loud clanking sound against the plate. Somehow, she'd expected him to know, because he knew everything.

'She was killed in a crash on the M1.'

Lee looked at Ava, his eyes wide. 'No. You're joking.'

'I'm really not.'

'What? I can't believe it. When did this happen?'

'Just last year. In October.'

'No. Your mother . . . when exactly?'

'October fifteenth.'

He stood from his chair suddenly. 'I'm sorry. I just need a minute,' he said and walked over to the pond.

Ava watched him go. He looked shorter than she

remembered, standing over the pond with his hands jammed inside his trouser pockets.

Ava wheeled her way across the lawn. It was difficult on that surface, her arms straining. She joined her father. She looked into the pond and saw life there. The orange fish moved below water hyacinths and a few tiny frogs were visible, swimming along the surface.

'I'm sorry,' Lee said. 'I didn't mean to ruin the meal. I just never thought . . .'

'What happens to the pond in winter?'

'The pond?' he looked at her, his grey eyes flat. 'Well, it can freeze over if it's a particularly cold winter. That can happen. But I keep the temperature stable. The frogs mostly lie at the bottom and hibernate anyway.'

She looked into the pond, imagined those spotted frogs, lying still at the bottom in winter, waiting for their lives to start up again.

'I can't believe your mother's gone.'

Ava nodded, understanding his shock, but also feeling that somehow it had always been in the stars, that her mother would face some untimely end, like she was marked for tragedy.

Lee pushed her back to the table and they resumed their meal. He picked up his fork but didn't eat anything.

Ava asked her father why he'd retired from the paper.

'I was tired of all the bad news,' he said, his voice weary. He took a sip of his wine, as if to signal the end of that line of enquiry.

He cleared his throat, then took another sip of wine. Ava felt that he was building up to something.

'Ava,' her father said, putting his wine glass down. 'I want to make things right with you and Michael.'

Ava stayed silent, her body completely still, as if any movement might set off a torrent of emotion.

'I was never around before. But I'd like to be.' He looked at Ava, so earnest, it made her angry.

'What's killing you?' Her words hung gracelessly in the cool evening air.

'Cancer,' he said. 'The doctor says it's the no-hope kind.' He poured more wine into his glass. 'I won't let it take hold of me. I won't let it get that far.'

Ava thought of an article she'd read years ago about a woman who'd been having a headache for weeks and couldn't sleep at night. She'd heard crackling noises, like the sound of a television when the cable wasn't working. Her GP thought she was overworked and anxious, so he prescribed sleeping tablets, but they didn't make one bit of difference. When she went to see a specialist, they scanned her brain and found three spiders living in her ear canal. The specialist soaked a cotton ball with rubbing alcohol and put it there against her ear until the spiders crawled out, one by one, and she slept soundly after that.

She asked her father if he'd consulted other specialists to be sure of the prognosis, that there was no hope with treatment.

'I have,' he said. 'Let's not talk about that. Let's talk about you. What kind of psychology are you interested in exactly? There are so many areas . . .'

Ava said abnormal psychology. Those stories of people who fell in love with their coat racks. She'd read about a woman who thought she was perpetually falling.

'That, and memory really fascinates me,' she said.

'I'm actually writing my memoirs. I started writing them a year ago.'

'Oh? What are you writing about?'

'The things you would expect. My years as a journalist covering conflict. The celebrities I've met. My childhood. Our family.'

Ava felt cold, as if the temperature had dropped a few degrees.

'I'll get dessert,' he said.

The spotlights were coming on now, a cluster of them by the pond.

Ava wondered what her father had written about their family. Would he describe the arguments? His perpetual absence? Would he write about Sandra Banks? His affair? Would he deny his threats? And suddenly Ava didn't feel much like being there, in her father's garden. She wanted to be back in her mother's bungalow.

The dessert was apple pie and ice cream and her father said he'd made it from scratch, even the ice cream. But Ava had lost her appetite, that unsettled feeling returning to her stomach.

She thought how much this meeting with her father felt like a headline in one of his papers – full of promise and then disappointment. Cancer Cure, Experts Say, and then no cure at all. Maybe in twenty years. The anticlimax of it, a betrayal. An over-promise, the reality thin and dull, like New Year's Eve, surprise parties, the first time you make love. But deep down, at the level of gut and bone, Ava had known she'd be disappointed, coming here.

Ava asked if he'd finished writing his memoirs.

'Almost. The clock is ticking, so I've got to finish.' He held his index finger aloft. 'Do you hear something?'

The faint sound of the ringing doorbell carried into the garden, like a call for intermission.

'That's odd. I'm not expecting—'

'It might be my friend,' Ava said. 'He's got to be up early tomorrow, so we have to get back.'

'But we've barely caught up. Could you stay the night, maybe? I'll drive you back tomorrow myself. I've got three spare rooms—'

'No,' Ava said, firm. 'I'm going back tonight.'

'Oh,' he said. 'Well, of course, if that's what you want to do.'

There was a side door in the garden that led to the driveway. Lee pushed Ava along, neither of them speaking. She just wanted to be home.

In the driveway, Ava made introductions and Sam and Lee shook hands. In that moment, she saw Sam as a man instead of a timid boy of twenty, the way he stood tall, his gaze meeting her father's.

'Do you want something to eat or drink? There's plenty left over.'

'I told you, he's got to be up very early for work, so there's no time,' Ava said, and Sam went along with this lie.

'Very early . . .'

Sam helped her into the car and put the chair in the boot. Her father offered to help, but there was nothing for him to do.

'Just give me a minute,' Lee said. 'If you could just wait one moment, please. Don't go anywhere.' He almost tripped over himself, rushing back into the house.

Sam squeezed her hand. She was grateful he didn't ask questions. She was just so tired.

Her father returned with a Tupperware container in his hands, a slice of apple pie inside it. 'You didn't have your dessert.'

She took the container from him. His thick fingers gripped the window ledge in desperation, his gaze low. 'I'm sorry to hear about your mother. Truly, I am. It means everything to me, that you came.' And then, one last desperate plea. 'I hope I'll see you again. Soon.'

He took a few steps back from the car and stood there with his hands in his pockets again. As they pulled away, his face became blurry, her vision scrambled with tears.

It was just after midnight when they returned to the bungalow and Ava's legs felt stiff and heavy. She'd slept through most of the drive. Sam said there had been an accident outside of Northampton and they'd been stuck in traffic for an hour. Ava asked Sam if he wanted to stay the night at her house, because he looked like he was about to drop.

A strange thought came over her then, picturing the two of them together in bed, his body next to hers. She thought of Dr Wandsworth, writing about the importance of touch, how a simple squeeze could release serotonin into the blood. More than anything, she wanted to feel differently.

'I'll have a quick rest on the couch,' Sam said. And she decided, of course, he didn't think of her that way. To him, she was as an invalid, a burden. He had scooped her out of her own vomit that afternoon.

She thanked him again for driving all that way and said that he was a good friend. He smiled, his eyes barely open. From a hallway cupboard, she brought him sheets and turned off the lights and left him there to sleep.

She took some tablets that made her drowsy. She wanted to sleep and forget.

In the morning, sunlight flickered over her eyes, over the top of that Tupperware container with the apple pie on her bedside table. She thought of her father saying that it was cancer, and then his disappointment when Ava told him she couldn't stay, the Tupperware between his hands.

It was only seven o'clock, and she imagined Sam on the sofa, still sleeping, tired from the drive. She remembered him with the water bottle in his hands, telling her to drink.

In the kitchen, she put the kettle on, and while it boiled, she looked into the sitting room, where the sheets were neatly folded on the sofa. Her eyes settled on those papers from the solicitor, the ones about suing the Ghadimis, there on the coffee table in front of the sofa where he'd slept.

SUMMER

Twelve

Manhattan was hit by a moth infestation in July, holes carving into T-shirts and cardigans and jogging suits. The news that summer was all about the moth invasion, and different theories emerged about where they were coming from. The early spring was to blame. Warmer weather made breeding easy. They were a plague brought down for the nation's sins – *Move your tanks out of the Middle East*, some said, while others shouted, *Ban abortions! Do away with political correctness*. People were having too much sex. The nation was lazy. People needed to roll up their sleeves and get crushing.

A pest-control guy was interviewed on WNBC before they cut to the Gaza Strip, where fresh artillery was being fired. The supermodel Anique Campeau said that her Prada sweaters were completely ruined. 'Holes in all of them.' A camera panned out to all that expensive cashmere lying on the floor like dead corpses.

Michael had been having the same dream of giant Coca-Cola moths all lined up in a neat row, and one by one they flew into a burning house and melted into a big grey sludge, making a stagnant pool in the rubble.

The moths hadn't gotten to Layla and Michael's apartment, but as a precaution Layla washed everything, turned the dryer up to 150 degrees. A lot of their clothes shrank that way and so on a Saturday afternoon they went shopping in the East Village.

Layla tried on different outfits in a small boutique, clothes that showed off her figure, light fabrics in colours and patterns that were bold and vibrant. Jacob was growing impatient.

'Here,' Michael said, handing him a women's fashion magazine. 'Wow, look at this.'

Jacob flipped through the first few pages but quickly bored of it.

'What do you think?' Layla said, emerging from the fitting room in a yellow halter dress.

'Gorgeous.'

'You don't think it's too much skin on show?'

'Not at all.' And then Michael drew Jacob's attention to Layla. 'Doesn't Mommy look nice?' He looked up at her with that same bored expression and nodded obediently.

'Ice cream,' he said.

Layla scrutinised herself from different angles in the mirror, and when she spun around, the skirt flared and twirled with her. She looked like a college girl, stylish and breezy. Michael liked it when she smiled broadly that way, like there was no end to her happiness.

He told her she ought to wear the dress out of the shop. The sales girl cut off the tags.

They got gelato from a vendor outside Tompkins Square Park and sat on the grass there, kicking off their shoes. It reminded Michael of Primrose Hill in London and all those happy people, pale faces craning up to the sun, shoulders bare – celebrating the start of summer after months of wet and cold.

Jacob's face was covered in chocolate ice cream. Michael wiped it clean with a napkin and his son grimaced.

'I've made some changes to my story.' Layla bit into her waffle cone. 'There's a guy now,' she said. 'He wants to settle down, that kind of thing.'

'And Mali doesn't?'

Layla shook her head. 'That's going to be the conflict in the story. Because, right now, my instructor says there's no conflict.'

A little girl kicked a ball and it rolled towards them. Jacob stood up, kicked the ball back to the girl and, for a while, Layla and Michael watched them play together. It was something that intrigued them both, the way their son interacted with people outside the family, a glimpse into the person he would become.

'I'm reading my story in front of the class this week,' Layla said. 'I'm pretty nervous.'

'What have you got to be nervous about?' Michael put his arm around her. 'Just read slowly. No matter how slowly you think you're reading, it won't be slow enough.'

He looked at her with affection. It was difficult to imagine Layla nervous, the big meetings she ran, the presentations and pitches she made to clients.

'Maybe I can practise in front of you tonight?'

'Of course. You can practise as many times as you want.'

She kissed Michael, squeezed his hand. The little girl's mother came over and smiled, and they had the usual conversation.

'How old is he?'

'Just turned two. And your daughter?'

'Same age!'

Michael could read the worry behind Layla's eyes as soon as the woman said that. She would be comparing the girl's size to Jacob's and finding her son lacking.

'Can you believe she was only two?' Layla said a little later, when they were sat outside their favourite Italian place. 'She was twice Jacob's size!'

'She was not twice his size. A little bigger, yes.'

'He's too thin,' she said. 'He needs to eat more.'

'He's in proportion.'

'Have you seen his chicken legs?'

Jacob squinted in the sun, rubbed his eyes.

'I didn't bring his hat,' Layla said, her strained tone, suggesting that she'd failed him in some grievous way.

'Maybe we could move one of those parasols over to our table,' Michael said. But the other diners were using them for shade, so they ate their fettuccini perspiring under the sun. Layla made sure Jacob ate every bite, even when he said he was full.

'No,' he whined.

'Just one more bite . . .'

A block away from the apartment, Jacob complained of a stomach ache. Normally, he would be pleading to be taken to the park where he could see children playing on swings and on those metallic slides, but he groaned and threw up his lunch all over his stroller. He shrieked, tears spilling down his face in shock.

'Oh shit!' Layla said, getting him out of the stroller.

Michael felt the eyes of passers-by on them as he took his now screaming son from Layla and carried him the rest of the way home. 'You're fine,' he said, rubbing Jacob's back.

'Your throat is going to be sore if you keep crying like that,' Layla pleaded with Jacob, but it didn't make one bit of difference. He was inconsolable. It was only when they were back at the apartment and Layla gave him a pacifier that he calmed down.

'I thought we had agreed not to give him that,' Michael said, and Layla turned to him, her eyes like daggers.

'You got any better ideas?'

After they put Jacob to bed, Layla and Michael sat on the sofa together in the stillness of the evening. Layla was still wearing that yellow halter dress, but she was a different woman now from the one in the boutique who had smiled and twirled around. Michael could see evidence of exhaustion across her face, dark circles under her eyes, her skin dull without the sun or the artificial glow of the boutique lights. Her anxiety was hurting her, hurting them.

'He just ate too much,' Michael finally said.

'I forced him.' And then she sat up on the couch. 'It's my fault he got meningitis. I wasn't there.'

Michael sighed. 'It wasn't your fault.'

Layla looked at Michael. A moth flew into their sitting room from the large balcony windows and landed on the wooden floor, almost blending in. She stood up and got a thick thesaurus from a nearby shelf, raised the book high and dropped it onto the moth.

Heat built up in the coming days. The subway was more unpleasant than usual, with the sour smell of people heavy in the busy cars. Michael took the bus into work. He had hoped it would be cooler, less crowded, but he was wrong.

He stood against a rail, people all around him. He thought of another time when he'd been on a packed bus like this. It was in north London. He'd been travelling home from school and a pram had tipped over when the bus jerked to a stop.

A baby, tiny and blind, fell out, wriggling under the feet of commuters, who quietened, dumb with horror. Someone straightened out the buggy. Another scooped up the baby. Everyone's eyes scanned accusingly around the bus in search of the mother who had left her baby like that. A careless woman. Someone who didn't know any better. When a woman stood up from her seat, last to take notice of the commotion, a hush fell over the bus, with only the sound of the rumbling engine in the background as everyone watched her approach.

In her early forties, she wore cream appliqué trousers and a pastel tweed jacket, her hair in a tidy bun with a few dignified strands of grey visible above her ears. No one said a word to the woman. The baby was transferred into her arms, and she rocked it softly on the way back to her seat.

It was then, watching commuters return to their papers, that Michael came to understand something important. The woman on the bus was protected by her privilege.

Michael remembered his father at a parent–teacher meeting. He had been called in because Michael had stuffed a bag of dog shit in the locker of the boy who'd written insults on his arms. His father had tousled Michael's hair affectionately before the meeting. For once, he was proud of his son.

Lee, with his sharp suit, easy smile and casual talk, disarmed Michael's teacher, as if reminding Mr Philips that they were from a good place, a better place than the other 99 per cent. He knew how to defuse a situation like that.

'Boys and their games . . .'

Michael's mother, sitting next to Lee, passed, by association, for someone who belonged to that world. At parent–teacher meetings, she wore silk scarves around her neck, soft and dignified, sitting across from his teachers, and her silence was taken as a marker of quality.

His father used to mock Elena for saying 'cheeses' and 'offen' instead of 'OF-TEN'. He would correct her whenever she got a word wrong.

'Herb. Herb. It's herb with a "h"! I can't stand a person who doesn't know how to say herb!'

Words were important. They were the difference between the truth and a fiction, he used to tell Michael.

Mr Philips and Michael's father moved past discussions on the bag of dog shit and talked about people they both knew. They had gone to the same university. Terrance McLeod, what a dog he was when he knocked back a few pints! Elena laughed along. Mr Philips and Lee discussed the IB curriculum and how the concept-based approach would turn students like Michael into a global thinker. A man of the world. They spoke of the Oxford comma for some reason and his father smiled at Michael dotingly in the chair next to him, though he never looked at him that way at home.

Stifled by the New York heat and his memories, Michael got off a few stops early. He walked the rest of the way to work. The sun sat in the sky like a gold coin, lucky and hot. He found the heat in his office unbearable and was grateful when Dr Susan Barker stopped by in the early afternoon to drop off a spare desk fan. She also had news.

Professor Steven Payne had slept with one of his students. But it wasn't just a sex thing – they were in love apparently, and he was meeting her parents in Connecticut, and they'd bought a Boston terrier together and given it a dog name.

The university had terminated his contract. Dr Larson, the Dean of Humanities, had sat Professor Payne down with biscuits and tea and said that his hands were tied. Of course, he understood all about temptation, and with Professor Payne being young and having that tortured-soul vibe about him, which some students would find attractive, he understood how something like that *could* happen.

And the most astonishing part of all this, Susan said, laughing a little, was that Dr Larson told his own almost-sex-with-a-student story, though nothing had happened, he'd said, not even a dinner. Just thoughts.

Susan reported all of this to Michael, leaning against his office door, clearly amused by the whole situation. And now, she said, eyes twinkling, Professor Payne was training to become a reiki practitioner, and touching was permitted in that line of work, so all was right in the world.

'They're going to pass his Introduction to Public Policy Analysis class to you. Just thought you should know.'

Michael sighed. 'Thanks for the heads-up. And for the fan.' He switched it on, and the air sent all the papers on his desk flying.

An email from Dr Larson confirmed later that morning that Michael would be teaching that extra class in the fall. It meant that he would have to spend a good part of the summer restructuring the course curriculum. He didn't trust Steven Payne, a man who had never kept records and believed in a laissez-faire approach to education, whereas Michael needed things organised.

Sarah Addams sent Michael a message that afternoon saying she had something to give him and would he meet her at a speakeasy in the East Village when he was done with work? He thought of the sketches she'd drawn in the park. He would have them framed and nail them to the wall next to the certificates that told of his qualifications.

Yes, he texted back. *I'd love that.*

The days were getting longer, the light encouraging people to stay out – not that they seemed to need much encouragement in New York. There was something familiar about the side street where Michael was meeting Sarah and it took a few moments for him to remember that Mr Minichelli's pizza place had been here.

As a student, Michael had often stopped there for a quick slice of mushroom and pepperoni. The place itself had been simple, nothing fancy about it, but the pizza had always been hot and full of flavour, and Michael had liked that it was a family-run joint – Mr Minichelli's son would often be doing his homework in one of the red booths and his wife would be sitting across from him, telling the boy to concentrate or there would be no dinner for him. Michael had imagined the Minichelli boy eating three square meals of pizza a day and was vaguely aware now that this thought had been racist.

He walked up and down the street looking for the pizza shop, but it wasn't there, and he saw how its existence wouldn't make sense among the boutiques and shiny cocktail bars – everything served in jam jars here.

The speakeasy where he was meeting Sarah was made to look like a toyshop at street level: teddy bears, jack-in-the-boxes, puppets on strings. On the other side of a distorted mirror inside the deserted shop, a concrete staircase led down to the bar, brimming with people and jazz and liquor.

Sarah was sitting at a table with a peacock feather in her hair, two Martinis in front of her. Michael thought she looked good in her black strapless dress, attractive, like a lounge singer. And then he thought, he shouldn't be there, meeting Sarah Addams. His eagerness to walk over to her was proof of danger. It wasn't until she turned to face Michael that he saw the eyepatch on her right eye, white gauze under it. He told himself that he must investigate this strange thing.

'Don't mind my eye,' she said. 'It's not infectious or anything like that.'

'What happened?'

'It's stupid really,' she said. 'I got into a brawl at a night-club. Someone knocked me out cold.' She laughed. 'I was cutting up a can of Fanta for the sculpture I'm working on and a jagged piece of it flung right into my eye and scratched the cornea.'

'That sounds awful,' Michael said, taking the seat across from her. 'But the pirate look suits you.'

'You think so?'

He nodded, and felt a rush of excitement, sitting across from her. The place was busy with conversation and music and all that noise made the room seem small. In that moment, he felt very old.

'Have you been here before?' Sarah asked.

He shook his head.

'I brought my mother here last week when she was visiting from London. She hated it.' Sarah smiled, touched the blue peacock feather. 'I wanted to repay you with a drink.'

'For what?'

'For modelling.'

Michael laughed, thinking how modelling was the wrong word here – it had to be. He looked at her then, this woman who knew nothing about him. Except, he had told her about his father.

'Have you got moths in your apartment?'

'What? I can't hear you very well,' she said, leaning into him. The music was getting louder.

'Moths. Are they tearing holes through your pyjamas and slippers?'

She laughed. 'No, no moths. I feel bad for them. They're really being demonised by the media.'

Michael shrugged and remembered his dreams, the liquid pool of those Coca-Cola moths lying under all that rubble.

Sarah searched through her large handbag and took out a box of Jaffa Cakes instead of her sketches.

'My mother brought me four boxes. I thought maybe you'd like one.'

'Thank you,' he said, though he'd never particularly liked those biscuits.

'Are you going to meet your father?' she asked.

'No.'

She raised an eyebrow, the one above her good eye, flecks of brown like stars floating in the greenness of her iris. 'I imagine you'll regret it, if you don't see your father before he dies.'

'We were never close.'

People applauded at the end of the song, and the band thanked the room before jumping straight into another one, more upbeat, more saxophone than the last, and

Michael was glad for this interruption. He didn't want to think about London.

'Hey, you never mentioned why you're doing a collection on fathers and sons,' Michael said, leaning over so she could hear him.

She ran her fingers over her glass. The blue polish was chipped on the nail of her index finger. 'I used to have a brother. He died when I was one and my father still hasn't made his peace with it. I wanted to do something for him, so I came up with the idea for the exhibition.'

'I'm sorry. How did he die?'

'He choked on a grape.' Her single eye moved down to the table. 'I don't want to talk about that.'

'Understood.' They both watched the dancing people, and it felt like they were trapped in a strange twilight, there below the cement staircase.

'Will I get to see my "modelling" sketches?' Michael did quotation marks in the air when he said 'modelling', and Sarah nodded her head.

'Soon.'

Then she stood up and pulled him out of his seat and onto the dance floor. Michael hesitated. It had been years since he'd danced in public. He danced in his living room and in the kitchen with Layla and Jacob, to baby songs so that his son would stop crying.

But he danced now, finding his place among the throng of people, their limbs throbbing to the beat of the music. He imagined himself moving smoothly, though he could not be sure. He wanted to look good in front of her. Sarah held herself with confidence, dancing around him, all the time looking at him with that eyepatch.

On the train journey home, she talked about her father.

'He's come out as a homosexual. My mother says they're still planning on staying married, living together as friends.' She shrugged. 'She seems fine with the arrangement. Maybe a part of her has always known. I had my own suspicions. It's my father I pity.' She looked down at her scuffed shoes. 'I think it would be sad, being married to someone you didn't take to bed.'

A man sitting across from them began to sing, his voice loud and operatic. They listened with amazement, shocked that this man, who wore big fleecy socks under his Birkenstocks and had a packet of salami resting on the large swell of his stomach, could produce such a rich baritone. They clapped when he finished.

Outside the station, the air was cooler, but Michael felt himself struggling for breath. The ease and lightness of the evening had disappeared, their existence together more complicated above ground. He worried now, how it might look, the two of them walking back together.

'Shall I walk ahead of you?' Sarah asked, as if she could read his mind. He wondered if this was worse, staging their return like they had something to hide. When he didn't reply, she repeated the idea. 'On the way back to the apartment, I'd like to walk ahead of you.'

'All right.'

Like that, Sarah walked a couple of steps in front of Michael, her stroll casual and relaxed. She whistled a tune from a song the band had played at the bar.

'It's a nice dress you're wearing,' Michael said, and he wondered briefly if her suggestion to walk ahead had been made with this in mind – his vantage point, so that he might admire her.

'Thank you,' she said, and she didn't turn around or change her pace, just kept walking.

It was like a drum, the *thump, thump* of his heart the rest of the way home. When they approached the courtyard between their apartments, Sarah began to whistle a different tune, something delicate and sad to mark their parting.

Michael watched her unlock the door to her building and disappear inside. She didn't look back.

In the stairwell of his block, Michael thought of his father, the way he'd invented excuses and alibis, and had told his mother she was crazy when she accused him of seeing other women. What would he tell Layla if she asked where he had been?

Layla was watching television in the dark sitting room. She had muted the sound, not wanting to wake Jacob, he presumed. She was wearing the yellow halter dress with a navy cardigan over it.

'I'm sorry I didn't call,' Michael said, removing his shoes, the insides of them damp from dancing. She wouldn't take her eyes from the television.

'It's Thursday,' she said.

It took a moment for Michael to realise what he'd done; Layla had her writing class on Thursday evenings, and she hadn't been able to go and read her story in front of the class.

'Oh, God. I'm so sorry,' he said, holding his head in his hands. 'I completely forgot it was Thursday.'

'Where were you?'

'Someone got fired at work. I have to take over his class, so I stayed late to plan.' He noticed then how easy it had been for him to tell this lie, how he had not hesitated.

The blue light of the television screen moved across

Layla's face. 'You know, it's the first time since starting my sabbatical that I've felt like myself again,' she said, her voice low and thin. She shut her eyes and he could tell she was seething with anger. 'That class means something to me.'

Michael sat next to her on the couch, rested his hand on her knee. 'I know. I'm so sorry. It'll never happen again.'

'I miss it all,' she said. 'I miss the meetings, having lunch with people from work. I miss getting praise and doing well. Heck, I even miss the bullshit of the job. All the billing hours and quotas.' She looked at him, tears falling down. 'But what if Jacob gets sick again?'

'I worry about that too. Every day, I worry. But we can't protect him from everything.' He looked at Layla, his heart sinking. 'It's hurting you, trying to protect him. And it's hurting us. I can't even touch a doorknob handle without you chasing after me with anti-bac gel.'

'I want to go back to work.'

'Then go back.'

'But Jacob.'

Michael shook his head. She looked at Michael's hand, a question moving across her face.

'You smell like alcohol.'

'I had a drink after work.'

She stood from the sofa, stood above him. 'You let me down tonight.'

Thirteen

Ava practised the exercises from Dr Wandsworth's book daily. Six exercises, one for each of the senses. When she completed one, she used a pencil to colour in a section of the hexagons on the poster taped to her fridge. The exercises structured her day, and a sense of achievement followed – filling in the hexagon. She didn't know what would happen once they were all coloured in. There were ninety of them – three months' worth. Maybe the exercises would be automatic by then, so she wouldn't need to keep track. She thought Dr Wandsworth would be pleased, like a proud father or husband, seeing the progress she'd made in just twelve days. 'That's how it's done, folks!' He might say something like that, and Ava would smile shyly as the television audience broke into applause.

A great deal of concentration went into a simple task like eating a peanut butter sandwich, when before she'd have wolfed it down. The soft texture of the bread and smooth richness of the spread were details her tongue lingered over. The same level of focus went into smelling a rose from the garden or observing a block of sunlight there on the corner sofa, her eyes catching particles of dust in the air – and there was an awful lot of dust floating in this house. She couldn't say, in truth, that she felt any happier in those times of intense focus, but she did enjoy a kind of temporary forgetting, a pause from thinking about the unpleasantness in her life – the accident, Sam's withdrawal, her father and his slice of apple pie still in its sad Tupperware container in the fridge.

The movement and listening exercises were more dynamic. At first, she'd been sceptical, embarrassed even, playing the book's audio CD with its strange trance music, letting her body do what felt natural, as Dr Wandsworth instructed in his deep, soothing voice. Waving her arms around, rolling her shoulders and head back, she'd felt like a lunatic, but after the first couple of minutes, she began to loosen up and enjoy the sense of freedom that came from moving that way.

Ava's neighbour, Mrs Miller, was watching her through the bay windows during one such session. 'It's great to see you out of that chair,' she said as Ava let her in.

Mrs Miller's large, smiling face looked beyond Ava into the messy corridor. 'Me and the other neighbours are really sympathetic with all that's happened to you – really, we are, darling. It's just – do you think you could hire someone to tidy up the lawn? It's a bit of an eyesore. We don't mind chipping in.'

'Sure,' Ava said. 'I'll arrange for someone to come and cut the grass next week.'

But she had no intention of following through. She'd grown fond of the wild grass and warm blaze of dandelions outside her window, thought it looked romantic and reflected some change in the house, in her. A lightness of spirit.

'Wonderful,' Mrs Miller said. 'I've got to rush off and pick up the boys from football practice. But you look after yourself.'

Ava sat down and rubbed her temples after her nosy neighbour left. She had been suffering from an unrelenting headache for days, and she kept feeling a little giddy, as if her heart might be beating too fast. But when her doctor had asked how she was doing in her last check-up, Ava hadn't mentioned the headache or palpitations, afraid they'd want to keep her in for observation. 'Almost as good as new,' she'd said instead.

The following day, Jane took Ava to a café in Welton, and Ava – without thinking – complained of her headache.

'Which side of your head? What about your jaw, does that hurt too? And the middle of your shoulder blade? Does it feel like you're being repeatedly stabbed with a large butcher's knife?'

'I can't say. I've never been stabbed with a butcher's knife before.'

Jane looked at her gravely.

'Really, I feel fine.'

'It could be a clot. Didn't they say there's a risk of clots after your surgeries and all that time you spent practically bedbound?'

Ava didn't answer, and Jane didn't wait for a response. She took the tea out of Ava's hand and said they were going to the hospital.

A giggle escaped from Ava. 'Jane, you're overreacting. Finish your coffee.'

But when Jane stood up and handed Ava her crutches, she knew it would be pointless to disobey. She took a last sip of chamomile tea, disappointed that her plan to stop in at the bookshop for a light summer read was now spoilt.

In the car, Jane told Ava about her cousin in Cornwall who had suffered from terrible headaches for weeks and was just taking paracetamol to ease the pain and had then had a major stroke, losing all function in her right arm.

'And she was lucky. She could have died,' Jane said, moving into the fast lane without signalling. A driver honked his horn at her and she honked hers back.

'Jane!'

'What?' she said, glancing across at Ava. 'I'm sure you'll be fine. We'll just get you checked out, to be on the safe side.'

Ava looked down at her arm, felt a quick buzz of energy there.

The A&E waiting room was busy for a weekday afternoon. Ava signed in while Jane was parking the car. She didn't want to make someone give up their seat, all these people who were unwell, so she stood by the vending machines and made out that she was interested in the chocolate bars.

A wispy-haired triage nurse took Ava into a narrow curtained area to ask about symptoms and take some bloods.

'Sorry,' she said, stabbing her arm with the needle. 'Your veins keep rolling away. Got plans of their own today!'

It was on her fourth attempt that the dark substance flowed out of Ava, filling those vials that seemed too large, and she changed them, one after the other. It hadn't bothered Ava before, getting blood taken, but everything seemed amplified now, the sensory exercises she'd been practising meant that she could hear the faint rush of blood spilling into those glass vials. She thought how, at any moment, she was going to float up to the ceiling, get stuck in those fluorescent tubes.

'Sorry about all the pokes,' the nurse said, pressing a thick cotton ball into the place where she'd removed the needle.

'It's fine,' Ava said. 'I didn't feel a thing.'

Jane was standing by the reception desk, waiting for her. She took one look at Ava's pale face and bandaged arm and led her to the seating area, flashing sharp looks at a young couple until they gave up their seats.

'How long did they say?'

'I didn't ask.'

Jane tutted. It was hot in the waiting room, and she wiped her face, which was moist and blotched with red. It seemed wrong, being cooped up in this drab building, looking into anxious faces, when it was so bright outside. Ava smiled at Jane, trying to reassure her friend, but Jane thought her face was distorting because of a stroke.

Half an hour in, Jane marched over to the desk, where the receptionists were chatting and laughing – it was just another workday for them.

'Bloody ridiculous,' she said when she returned. 'Two hours at least. I told them you could be having a damn stroke.' She wrapped her arm around Ava. 'Don't worry, you're not.' And then she whispered, 'Forgive me, Jesus, for saying damn.'

Jane had found God last summer, shortly after her husband had left her for a man in Nottingham. She'd come into work one day and told Ava's mother about it, like it was just any old news she was sharing, and then went off to mark down a rack of shirts. She hadn't spoken of her husband since. She joined a born-again church that was above a pool hall, though it was apparently the church getting noise complaints from the pool hall – all that singing and dancing and stomping the devil out.

'God doesn't work quietly,' Jane said.

The pastor was an American from Georgia and people had talked about him for weeks, saying how he was daft, thinking he could convert the English. At first, the neighbours went out of curiosity, and now a good number of them were part of his congregation.

'It makes me feel safe,' Mrs Miller had said, 'being in his presence.'

Ava wasn't sure then if Mrs Miller had been referring to Jesus or the pastor. She didn't like the way the pastor looked at her in the grocery store, like she was next on his list, but there was a pull there, something in his southern drawl, his circuitous way of speech.

When Ava had been in hospital recovering from her injuries, Jane had said that she'd asked the pastor to pray for her. On Friday that week, they were having a prayer service and she was to be included. It was strange, she thought, being part of an event that she wasn't physically attending, especially given that her belief in a soul or spirit was hazy at best. Ironically, or perhaps not ironically, she'd had one of the worst nights on that Friday, the pain so large she'd been vomiting into a bucket for hours.

'That's a kind of healing,' Jane had said, 'getting rid of all the toxins.'

A couple of porters brought out fans, which got the air moving around the waiting room, but Ava found it worse than the stagnant heat, the way the fans threw around the smell of sick people onto each other. Her heart fluttered.

'You're going to be all right,' Jane said as Ava moved

her fingers to her chest, and she began to really worry then.

She thought of Dr Wandsworth's handsome jawline, imagined him sitting next to her instead of Jane, telling her to focus on her senses. But the fluorescent lights were too bright here, the smell unpleasant. She wanted to shut everything out.

An hour and a half into the wait, Jane brought up the pastor's son while she filed her nails down. 'I think he's just your type. He's clean, works at that garage on Days Road. He did my tyres last year and gave me a special discount.'

'Well, sign me up,' Ava said, and Jane looked pleased and carried on talking about how he had once carried her groceries all the way to her car when she'd had to park a fair distance from the supermarket because it was a Saturday and everyone was out shopping. He'd even put the bags in the boot for her.

Ava knew that Lindsay Scott from the Lancôme counter had given the pastor's son a blowjob in the back of his car, that he had asked her for anal, but she had refused. 'One step too far,' she'd said.

Ava's eyes felt sticky in the heat. Jane had done this before, dropped hints about the eligible men at her born-again church to lure her in. Ava didn't trust her judgement – she thought Kyle was handsome too, a good catch. Clean boys – this was all Ava could hope for at thirty-one.

A nurse finally called Ava's name and took her and Jane through to an area with curtained cubicles.

'Make sure they've checked for clots in those blood tests,' Jane told the nurse as she went to find Ava's results. At work, Jane still gave Ava instructions on putting up sale signs and folding cashmere sweaters. She couldn't help herself.

Perched on the hard hospital bed, Ava thought of her mother, how she'd died without anyone there to hold her hand, crushed in that two-door piece of junk on the M1 outside of Northampton. Where was she going? Not to work or Spinolli's. For months, Ava had tried to work this out. Elena had hated driving on the motorway, found it stressful to make the half-hour trip to Matlock, and here she'd been, on the M1, with all that alcohol in her blood.

'You expect too much from me,' Elena had said, days before she'd been killed in that crash. She had relapsed and made a spectacle of herself in the doctor's surgery. She'd been waiting for the results of a mammogram and in her anxiety had bought a bottle of gin and drank half of it before her appointment.

Ava had had to leave work early to collect her mother. The receptionist said they had a zero-tolerance policy for abuse. Everyone had to wait their turn.

'Of course,' Ava had said. 'I'm so sorry . . .'

And then the receptionist had said the mammogram results were benign so that Elena wouldn't return.

In the car, Elena had said, 'That's a relief.'

'You didn't have to call her that.'

'Well, that woman *is* a cunt.'

Ava had pulled the car over on a residential street. 'Do you hate me?'

Elena had laughed – a light, dismissive laugh – and she'd looked out of the window. Her silk blouse was wrinkled at the waist. 'What's this, Ava? Don't be ridiculous . . .'

'Why did you do it?' Ava shouted.

Elena's smile disappeared in an instant. 'I tried my best. I really did. But today was hard.'

'Not good enough.'

Ava could never understand her mother's relapses. How she could give up on all her progress. She'd been dry for nearly eight months. Ava had told herself that when her mother made it to a year, she would leave. She would live someplace else.

Elena had kicked the dashboard, a flash of pain across her face. 'You think I want to be this way? You think I enjoy *this*? That I like slipping back?'

She had cried for a few minutes, then used the rear-view mirror to apply a fresh coat of lipstick, a light plum colour. She used her pinkie finger to wipe away the excess and then said she'd like to go home.

Jane looked at her watch now, exhaled dramatically. She huffed and sighed to no end about the wait and when she started complaining about the healthcare system, Ava tuned her out and thought of Sam. She wanted to call him.

They'd sent a few texts back and forth after London. Neither of them mentioned those papers from the lawyer. He'd told her about a new drama show she should watch and perhaps he could come over and they could start season one together. Ava had wanted to say yes, and maybe they could touch each other after that. A quiet stroke, a squeeze, an exchange of warmth.

But Ava had told him she needed space. Too much was happening in her life. Sam had said, 'OK. I'll be here when you're ready,' but she had decided not to contact him again.

Because there would always be this struggle in her mind: he had hit her with his car. He felt indebted. She would always second-guess his intentions and it seemed too much to risk, getting close when she could never know for certain if guilt was guiding his hand.

A young doctor pulled the curtain back and introduced herself so quickly that Ava didn't catch her name. A hot flush rolled through her as she anticipated what the doctor might say, how she might want Ava to have more tests, an operation. She couldn't bear the thought of being a patient again.

The doctor's eyes were cracked with red, like she hadn't had a decent night's sleep in weeks.

'No sign of clots,' she said. 'But your BNP is above normal.'

'BNP? What in God's name is a BNP?' Jane asked.

Ava felt dizzy as the doctor explained that a BNP test measured heart function. Her voice seemed distant, an underwater thing.

'How high above normal?' she asked.

The doctor reviewed the chart. 'We expect numbers below a hundred and yours was four-hundred and thirty-two. It could be worse. I've seen numbers over ten thousand.'

'Did her injuries cause this?' Jane asked.

Ava was glad her friend was there because she couldn't think of what to say. Her hands were trembling slightly, so she clasped them in her lap and looked to the doctor to provide some clarity. She didn't understand what she was being told.

'It's possible, but not necessarily.' The young doctor flicked through the papers on her clipboard. 'You might have always had some underlying heart condition – if that's what's going on here. I can't confirm anything with just this test. But certainly it's possible that your injuries have exacerbated things, putting further strain on the heart. We'd need to do a cardiac ultrasound to have a better idea. Find out what the heart is doing.'

The tibia. The pelvis. And now the heart. Ava felt in that moment a deep betrayal – her body conspiring against her when she'd thought it was on her side, all that time she'd dedicated to physio and those exercises from Dr Wandsworth's book.

The young doctor pressed two fingers against Ava's wrist, taking her pulse, and her touch brought calm. Ava was in the right place, at least.

'When can we do the test?' she said. 'The cardiac ultrasound?'

They booked her in for an appointment in two weeks' time.

'It's ridiculous that you haven't got an earlier appointment available,' Jane said with sharpness. 'Is there a more senior doctor we could speak to about this?' And, here, it was obvious by the way the young doctor's eyes shifted that she had lost her patience with Jane.

It was late afternoon when Ava was discharged. They walked back through the waiting room. Here was a pregnant woman, and the man sitting next to her rubbed her back. An elderly man in a wheelchair to the far left of the room stroked the shoulder of a middle aged woman. Ava thought about Dr Wandsworth and his teachings. His exercises on touch. It was not enough to squeeze her own hand. She longed for someone to touch her, admire her body.

Jane dropped her back at the bungalow and said she'd call in the morning from her shift to see how she was doing. 'You'll be all right, you know that, don't you?'

Ava had lost count of the number of times she'd said that. She forced a smile. 'I'm not worried.'

★

Ava phoned Kyle from the shoe department the following evening and asked if he would come by. He said he would make his way as soon as his shift was over.

When he arrived, he apologised for not having anything to offer, like flowers or chocolates.

'There's no need for that,' she said.

She asked if he wanted a drink of water and he said he was well-hydrated. Since there was nothing more to discuss, Ava told him why she'd asked him to come by.

'I wanted to propose something to you,' she said, trying her best to sound natural and breezy.

He leant forward, and Ava thought how his hairline had receded since their date in January.

'I was wondering if you would consider having a physical relationship with me.'

His thin mouth opened as if to speak, but no words came out. Ava thought how it might be necessary now to explain, or else he might get wild ideas of them planning holidays together when she had no intention of making a boyfriend out of him.

'I think it's important to be touched. Wouldn't you agree?'

At first, he looked confused, but then he nodded his head, too many times. 'Well, yes, definitely. I mean, sometimes I touch myself, but it's not really the same.'

'No,' she said, her eyes moving down. 'No, it isn't.' She forced a smile, when her mouth was trying to do something else – that tendency towards a grimace, her nostrils flaring like they needed more air. Kyle's stance didn't change, and it was like they were talking about sales figures over lunch.

'I need someone to do that for me,' Ava said. 'Touch me. Do you think you could manage it?'

Again, he nodded his head like one of those bobble dogs on a car dashboard. 'Of course. I mean, I would love to do that.'

Before he'd arrived, Ava had shut the curtains in every room, made sure there was no light to reveal what she was doing and who she was doing it with. Absolute darkness was necessary. Even the hallway lights were off now, and Kyle said he couldn't see where he was going as he knocked into something.

In the bedroom, he stood awkwardly by the door, waiting for a signal from her

'You're all right to lie on the bed,' Ava said.

He took off his shoes, left them neatly side by side at the foot of her bed. For a while, neither of them moved. It was almost impossible to make out the expression on his face, which was what she had planned. She just wanted someone to touch her, but his breathing was loud and quick, and his breath smelt like he hadn't eaten.

'Are you sure about this?' he said.

'Yes.'

'I don't want to hurt you, with all your injuries.'

It was Ava who moved first, running her hands over his unremarkable chest and he moved his head closer to hers.

'It might not be such a good idea to kiss,' she said. 'It might confuse things.'

'Right,' he said. 'Right.'

She shut her eyes to forget that it was Kyle lying there on her bed and for a few moments it worked, and the warmth of his touch felt like it was mending some deep brokenness. Dr Wandsworth was right – it was possible to acquire happiness through the senses. But the further they went, the more impossible it was to ignore that it was Kyle doing the touching – his fingers slender and trembling, no real force behind his touch.

He apologised for not being a very large man when they both undressed. Ava took the condom she'd left out on the nightstand, gave it to Kyle. Earlier, she'd taken a bus to Boots in town, bought a box of condoms, and it had been thrilling, selecting it from the shelf, queuing up with it at the cash register, refusing the offer of a bag. She'd felt proud, empowered even, buying this box of ribbed condoms. When she'd run into her neighbour Mrs Miller outside the shop and she had asked about the lawn, when it would get mowed, her eyes had moved down to the box and she'd stumbled over her words, and Ava had been pleased. She'd offered Ava a ride back to the bungalow and she'd accepted Mrs Miller's offer, that box of condoms sitting on her lap in the passenger seat.

Awkwardly, Ava and Kyle fumbled into each other in the total darkness of the bedroom and it took a while for Kyle to get the condom on.

Whenever Ava was close to forgetting that it was him lying next to her, and then on top of her, he asked a question about her preferences and his small voice broke any illusions that he could be someone else.

'What about like that?'

'Yes,' Ava said, though his touch was completely off the mark.

She was grateful when he said he was close to climaxing. He made many apologies about how quickly he had reached this stage and promised it would be better once he'd let go of some pent-up frustration.

The sounds he made were truly awful, like a cat shrieking in pain. And then he said, 'Oh, that was great.' And he kissed Ava's nose by accident, thinking it was her cheek, because it was so difficult to see anything.

Almost immediately afterwards, Ava switched on her bedside light and reached for her crutches. Her eyes took a moment to adjust to the light and when things came into focus, it was something she wished she could unsee, the way he lay shrunken and naked, almost quivering, on her bed, the filled condom hanging from him.

She smiled sympathetically. 'That was nice,' she said. 'Maybe we should both get dressed.'

It was difficult to get him out of the house. At first, he asked if she wanted to try again, convinced that he could fully satisfy her now. And when he saw that she had no interest in that, he said how beautiful she was, how he looked forward to seeing her again and perhaps they could have dinner beforehand and catch a show.

When Ava finally had him standing by the door, he leant in to kiss her on the mouth, but she kept her lips pressed together.

'It would be a bad idea to tell anyone from work,' she said.

He nodded and smiled widely. 'Of course.' And then he made a gesture with his hand, like he was zipping his mouth shut and throwing away the key.

In the morning, Ava felt a sinking dread. That sense of a loss. But the loss of what, she wasn't sure. What she knew for certain was that she wanted no memory of the night before. She threw out the box of condoms and piled other things on top of the bin. Half-eaten bags of crisps. Food that was going off. She kept her father's apple pie. There was a little mould there on the crust.

In the bath, she sponged her body around the cast. She decided never to do that again, sleep with Kyle from the shoe department.

She browsed Dr Wandsworth's social media account, as she did most mornings. He looked spotless in those photos – a rare, shiny thing in a world full of Kyles. He was a man of wisdom, enlightened and beautiful. She knew he was holidaying in Matlock Spa, just a half-hour's drive from her house.

When they'd first moved to Welton, Elena had taken Ava and Michael to Matlock Spa at the weekends. They had lunch in nice cafés, went shopping afterwards. Elena browsed the boutiques, tried on things she couldn't really afford.

Ava knew the area well, had recognised an unusual red-roofed house in the background of one of the photos Dr Wandsworth had posted that morning. She could work out where he was staying from there, and she'd narrowed it down to two houses.

Ava would be candid with Dr Wandsworth when he asked what she needed.

'Touch.' She would say something like that, in a matter-of-fact kind of way, and perhaps he would feel obliged to do it, understanding about this need for physical intimacy.

When she wrapped her arms around herself or rubbed her shoulder or held her own hand, as he'd suggested in his book, her loneliness became cold and solid. Ava found those five minutes of practising touch painfully long. It had been worse, fumbling in the dark with Kyle.

But she was convinced that the hexagon of happiness would not carry out its purpose until she could slip into touch, inhabit that sense fully, like she did the others.

In the depths of her underwear drawer, she found a black satin slip. Ava put it on and felt different, more herself somehow. Over the top, she wore one of her mother's summer dresses, because hers were all too large now.

In the taxi, Ava asked the driver for air conditioning. Her hair thrashed around, the open windows messing it up when she'd spent an age smoothing it down.

'Sorry, ma'am, it's broken.'

For the rest of the drive, she smiled with cool determination. There was activity on the river, sailboats, people dipping their rods into the water. The warm summer air encouraged a sense of freedom, and everywhere she looked, children, their parents, cats, dogs – they all seemed to move with lightness; everyone out, having a good time, forgetting that with every passing moment they were approaching their own ends. Hah! She was one of them now, engaged in forgetting, focusing on the moment. She would learn to wield the hexagon of happiness.

'Could you turn the radio on, please?'

The cab driver asked what station and Ava told him anything that played upbeat music.

The two houses that she'd narrowed down as the cottage where Dr Wandsworth was staying were a few miles apart. It would be a challenge to walk between the two on crutches if she got it wrong.

A message appeared on her phone from Kyle, saying how much he had enjoyed last night and how he hoped that they would do it again soon. She immediately shut off her phone.

The taxi slowed on a dirt path, the sound of rocks kicking up underneath the car, trees sheltering overhead.

'Did you say it was this house?' the driver asked, pointing ahead, but there was a family van parked outside.

'No, keep driving.'

It was then, driving ahead in this kind of half-crazed blindness, that Ava began to think how her plan was flawed, deranged even. There were many variables that she had not fully considered, like if Dr Wandsworth was out of the house, or if he took one look at her and shut the door.

'Is it this one here?' the driver asked.

'Maybe,' she said, and then with more conviction, 'Yes, it must be this one.' She had spotted the Union Jack waving proudly at the back of the house, as it had in the video Dr Wandsworth had posted earlier that morning.

'Come back in an hour, please,' Ava told the driver, handing him notes for the fare.

The air was fresh here, away from the road. Her mother had often talked about buying a house in Matlock, but all of that talk was nonsense when they didn't have enough money for simple renovations or furniture to replace the old tired pieces.

The house looked like something from a fairy tale, the weathered wood-panelled exterior blending seamlessly into the surrounding woodland. It conjured up images of woodcutters and pixies. Two grey-tailed squirrels chased after each other along the path as if they were playing a game of tag. Ava rang the doorbell.

When Dr Wandsworth opened the door, she was

amazed that it was him, standing on the other side. And then other things amazed her, like how short he was. She had imagined him as a tall man, large in many ways. But he stood only a few inches above her head and she wasn't wearing heels. And then Ava thought how different he looked without his navy suit, dressed in a T-shirt and shorts.

'Can I help you?' he said, and his voice even sounded wrong, too high-pitched to be his own.

'Yes,' Ava said, 'I think you can help me.' She looked into the hallway, hoping he would take pity on her and invite her inside, the way she was perspiring in the heat.

He rubbed his nose, and Ava thought by the way his eyes were cloudy and red that she had woken him from a nap.

'I'm lost,' she said.

Ava felt foolish, standing in front of him. How had she been so naïve to think that she could just float into his day like dandelion fluff blowing in the sky? He was a celebrity, an expert on a topic. Who was she?

'I'm lost,' she said again, feeling the full weight of her words.

'Well, why don't you come in?' he offered flatly.

The interior of the cabin seemed a complete contradiction to its rugged exterior – everything modern and white. The kitchen appliances shone in the sun-filled space where floor-to-ceiling windows looked out onto the River Derwent.

Dr Wandsworth gestured for Ava to sit on a kitchen stool that was completely transparent, like it was made of glass. There were empty beer bottles left all along the kitchen counters, as if there had been a party.

'I'm sorry to barge in on you like this,' she said. From the angle where she was sitting on the stool, he looked even smaller than before. 'I've read your book.'

He smiled broadly. 'Oh, you have? Can I get you a drink?'

'Water would be great. Thank you.'

While he ran the tap, she noticed a woman outside sunbathing on the decking area, completely naked.

'Thank you,' Ava said, drinking the water quickly, trying to conceal any look of shock that might give away that she'd seen the woman outside.

The fact that Dr Wandsworth was inebriated only became apparent to Ava now, the way he looked off balance, his eyes bloodshot and the smell of alcohol seeping from him. He lit a cigarette and offered one to her.

'No, thank you.'

She spoke quickly, anxiously, about how she'd been reading his book every night and how diligently she'd completed the daily exercises.

'It's been very helpful,' she said.

He lowered his gaze and smiled to himself; a look of humility, practised, she thought. 'I'm glad you think so,' he said, taking a long drink from his bottle of beer. 'It's meeting people like you who make it all worthwhile.'

Taking the cigarette out from the corner of his mouth, he tried unsuccessfully to suppress a belch. 'Excuse me.'

Ava could see a piece of romaine lettuce stuck between two perfectly white teeth, wedged in there. She forced a smile, pretending not to notice how off-kilter he was. 'I hope you don't mind if I ask a question about your work,' she said.

He fixed a studied expression on his face. 'Fire away.'

'It's about touch.'

He leant forward so that he was only inches away from her face. 'Touch?'

'I'm not sure the recommended exercises are working for touch.'

'What do you mean?' He flicked the cigarette ashes into an empty beer can.

'Well, when I rub my own hand or hug myself, I feel worse at the end of the five minutes than I did at the start.'

'The exercises work better for some people than others, I admit that.' He scratched his head. 'And sometimes things get a lot worse before you start feeling better, like a cold. Haven't you ever heard that expression before?' His face darkened.

Ava nodded. 'Yes, I have.'

Even with his aggressive tone, she persisted with her questions, thinking how she might never have another opportunity like this again; even if he was smashed – she would ask her questions. There was one question, in particular, that pressed heavily against her mind and she was afraid to ask but found the courage, thinking of her mother.

'Is it possible, do you think, that some people will never be happy?'

He looked at Ava, perplexed, like he was deeply insult-ed, his jaw hardening against her. 'Not if you try, no. I don't believe it's possible to be unhappy, not if you truly give it your best shot.'

He flicked his nose, his eyes cloudy with some dark emotion as he paced around the kitchen.

'If you want my honest opinion, I'd say that anyone

who's unhappy is that way because they're lazy, because they want to be that way. They don't stick to the programme. They don't *try* to overcome their weakness. Do you know what I mean?'

His brows furrowed in irritation, and it was apparent to Ava that he'd tired of this visit.

'Lazy, lazy, lazy,' he said. And then his eyes suddenly widened. 'I've got something that might help.'

He disappeared into another room. The naked woman on the decking turned onto her stomach, her bottom perfectly smooth and round like a newborn's head. From here, she looked completely spotless, a demigod, glowing.

'You can have a copy of my latest book,' Dr Wandsworth's voice called out from one of the rooms off the corridor, and he returned a moment later with his book, his smiling face there on the front cover of *Happiness Beyond the Hexagon*. 'I'll sign it for you, if you've got a pen.' He touched his chest as if to feel for a pen, but he had a T-shirt on, no breast pockets there.

'I haven't,' Ava said.

'Well, that's too bad.'

'Thank you for the book.'

He turned then without speaking another word and made towards the decking, greeting the naked woman with a kiss.

The taxi wasn't coming for another half-hour, so Ava stood outside Dr Wandsworth's front porch, deeply shaken. More than the disappointment of not having accomplished what she'd set out to, she felt utterly devastated at discovering him that way, the stark, ugly reality of him.

For a while, Ava watched the squirrels dart around, and then she flipped through Dr Wandsworth's new book.

Much of it was recycled material from his previous work, with a few extra notes on problem-solving.

She thought of her mother. How Ava had often told Elena that she must have derived some pleasure from relapsing. She must have found it satisfying, sinking into that vague, mindless territory, closing herself off from the world. She wasn't trying hard enough; that was what Ava had told her mother.

'Everything all right, ma'am?' the taxi driver asked when she got into the back seat.

'Yes,' she said, and tossed Dr Wandsworth's book out of the window. 'Could you do me a favour? Would you mind driving over that book, please?'

Fourteen

Michael stayed in New York to plan the public policy course while Layla and Jacob went to Chicago. There was a community pool in the suburb where the Zaytoons lived in Chicago and Layla took Jacob every day. Michael missed Mr Zaytoon's barbecues, the ease of summer evenings in their backyard, the sound of chirping crickets – suburban noise, comforting in its familiarity, while Mrs Zaytoon told stories about her sisters in Lebanon, the cosmetic surgeries they were having. 'Every year, I am getting older and they are getting younger.'

When Layla put Jacob on the phone, he didn't speak.

'He's been quiet all day. At the park, he kept stepping on ants. He was doing it on purpose. Do you think it means something?'

'I'm sure it doesn't.'

'I've been working on my story,' Layla said, and then she told him about Mali's sister having a child, and her whole family saying that Mali ought to have children too, settle down.

'But she doesn't listen?'

'Exactly.'

The evenings were long without Layla and Jacob. At first, the quiet brought a sense of peace, walking into an empty apartment where he could be in his own thoughts. But after a few nights of eating what he wanted, reading late into the night in bed, Michael tired of being alone and he didn't like where his mind took him. London or Welton, always someplace in the past. This evening it was Welton.

He thought of Ava and his mother, that last visit home at Christmas. He was in his final year of undergrad studies. Michael's mother expected him to return to England indefinitely in the summer.

She cooked a turkey with all the trimmings and used the good china. She wore a red dress, formal and elegant, like she was hosting a party, when it was just Michael and Ava. Throughout the meal, she spoke of Michael returning to Welton, how she could get him a job in the menswear department until he found his feet again.

'I know where they are,' Michael said.

'Where what are?'

'My feet.'

His mother laughed, batted her hand. 'I was thinking of getting your room painted. Freshen it up for you. A mossy green, if that pleases you?'

Michael felt a wave of sickness, chewing the dry meat, trying to find the right way to say he would not return, that his place was in New York and he'd already begun filling out forms for postgraduate studies.

His sister didn't say much at the table. She had grown shy and strange over the last couple of years, resentful maybe. She had been a child when he'd left, and he missed the ease between them, the way he'd been able to tease and goad her, the way they'd kicked a football around in the garden or played Frisbee in the mornings when Elena had been sleeping in.

'Let's go for a walk,' Elena said, after they'd cleared the table and stacked the dishwasher.

They took the car out to a nearby woodland and it reminded Michael of Hampstead Heath, the walks they did together. The sun was already dim, a small dull circle low in the sky, barely lighting the path, the leaves rustling beneath their feet.

Elena walked alongside Michael, Ava further ahead, in a huff about something – Michael had no idea what.

He had hoped to discuss his permanent move to New York, but Elena wouldn't let him get a word in. She talked about other Christmases, the ones she'd spent with her in-laws in the Midlands. Her father-in-law in the supermarket, rushing over with free samples of juice in little cups, beaming as he handed them over. The juice tasted artificial, too much sweetener. But he loved getting things for free, living off the state fo years after the mines had shut. And the loudness of his body – she couldn't get any sleep. He yawned loudly, coughed like a tubercular, sighed and breathed with a mouth that was always gaping, open too wide. And he ate and ate. There was no end to his hunger.

Her mother-in-law was no better. Her clothes – splashy, the colours and fabrics cheap. She always spoke of bargains, came home with thin plastic bags and took out each item one at a time to tell Elena about the deals she'd found. It had frightened her, the sight of those thin plastic bags, but Lee had listened, indulging his mother with his attention when he barely spoke to his own wife anymore.

'Yes, well, Granny's dead now,' Michael said. 'Why do

you still resent them? It's been . . . how many years? I just don't understand.'

'I was only remembering . . .'

'It's bitter. And actually quite ugly.'

Elena stopped and looked at Michael in shock. He had never spoken to her that way. Her brows furrowed, her mouth tightened, then she sped ahead, away from Michael, past Ava.

Ava looked back at her brother with a question across her face.

The next morning, Michael had tea with his mother in the kitchen. She was still quiet after their walk.

'I won't be coming back this summer,' he said. 'I'll be continuing my studies in New York.'

'For how long?'

'Indefinitely.'

Elena looked at him with disgust. 'After all I've done for you . . .'

She said she'd stayed with their father in spite of the affairs because of him and Ava, had kept the family together for their sakes. She had sacrificed her happiness that way, when she could have lived in the South of France, made a life for herself there. *Doing what?* Michael wondered, but he didn't ask.

She moved on to their lives in Welton, all the hours she'd worked in the department store, her calves and knees sore from standing, marking down sales. She had to deal with rude customers. Someone had once told her to leave this country when she'd refused to refund underwear. Another time, she'd seen a customer touching himself behind a rack of pleated trousers. She had suffered through all of this so that she could feed her children.

And when Michael had been in school – the shame of it – how she'd been made to sit on the other side of the headmaster's desk, like a misbehaving student, while he told her about Michael smoking behind the gymnasium.

'You're exactly like your father,' she said. And she looked at Michael here with real hatred. '*Exactly* like him. Selfish. You only think of yourself.'

'OK.'

'*Exactly* like him.'

'I don't think so. But OK.'

'Like father, like son.'

Michael left the table and walked all the way into town. He went to a pub, nursed a pint for a while. He was flying back to New York the following morning. He'd planned to meet up with friends in the afternoon, but he thought he'd cancel. What was the point in keeping ties with this place, these people?

When he returned to the house a few hours later, he went straight to his room to pack.

Elena knocked on his door sometime later and he said to come in. She held a beautiful navy sweater between her hands. It was cashmere, too expensive for her department-store salary.

'I think you'll look handsome in this,' she said, pale and shy. It was something she often did, pretended that nothing had happened after one of her tantrums. She stepped closer, the familiar smell of alcohol rising from her like an antiseptic fog.

He thanked his mother. 'I'll come back to visit.'

She nodded her head.

He forgot to pack that sweater. It was something Michael often thought about, how she must have cleared out the wardrobe years later and found her gift there, and he imagined the hurt across her face, discovering her olive branch discarded that way.

Ava came into his room that last night and asked what was going on between him and their mother.

'Nothing. The usual things.'

She reached around her brother, held on tight with her thin arms, like she was hanging on for dear life. This sudden gesture of affection shocked him. She had been so sullen and removed during his stay.

'I need you here,' she said. 'You need to help with Mum.'

★

Michael's father sent him another email. He said that Ava had been to see him in London. She'd mentioned that she was no longer in touch with Michael. *What a shame*, his father wrote. Michael didn't read the two paragraphs that followed, just deleted the message.

He stood from the sofa and paced around the sitting room, all the time anger growing hotter inside of him. He had no right. His father had no right to write those words when he had left himself, when he was no better.

Michael walked into all the other rooms. The office, the kitchen, their bedroom, Jacob's room, the toilet, and then he left the apartment.

Sarah Addams was smoking in the courtyard. She waved to him.

'We must stop meeting like this,' she said.

He felt deranged. Didn't know what he should say. Something clever, probably, but nothing came to mind. He walked over to her.

'Are you OK?' she asked.

'Yes.'

'You look a bit frazzled.'

'No.'

The gauze on her eye was gone. He could see a red blob in her right cornea.

'How's your eye?'

'It's healing slowly. It was strange at first, seeing out of both eyes again.' She blew a smoke ring at him. 'I've started working on your sculpture. I've done the outline in wire and I'm just weaving the cans through it now.'

'Can I see it?'

She smiled and stubbed out her cigarette. 'Sure.'

They went up in the lift together. Three large plastic bags filled with cans were crowding the entrance. She said she got the empty cans from a bar close by. She knew the owner. They had an arrangement. Next to the table where she did her work was a wire structure, almost five feet tall.

'It's difficult to see the story when it's still in its skeletal form, without the cans giving dimension and texture.'

Michael squinted at the steel wires, then moved around the sculpture to make sense of them. Was it possible that he was staring at the outline of a giant set of breasts? He shook his head, looked again.

'I don't really see—'

'It's your arse,' she said.

He squinted again. 'What?'

She explained how he'd bent down to tie his son's shoe-lace, and she'd had that view from the bench.

'And why exactly—?'

'It shows vulnerability. That you're doing your best.'

'It's my ass.'

'It's honest.'

Michael had imagined something closer to the moths with the clipped wings, and he felt that this interpretation of his relationship with his son confirmed his ineptitude at fatherhood, that he would forever push and blunder.

Sarah moved to the table where her tools were laid out. 'You can help me build it. I have to cut up all these cans to weave into the wire.'

She offered Michael a sharp crafting knife. He hesitated.

'It's a nice arse if that helps.'

'You think so?'

'One of the best I've seen.'

He took the knife, began slicing through the aluminium.

The blinds were drawn in his apartment, and it was strange looking across, knowing that Layla and Jacob weren't there. No one was going to pull the blinds back, wave hello. He was glad to be in Sarah's apartment where there was light and movement and noise, away from his father's email, telling him, *What a shame.*

Sarah played Cole Porter and gave him a can of beer.

'Did you always know that you didn't want to do the whole family thing?' Michael asked.

'No. When I was a girl, I thought I'd be married by the time I turned twenty. It wasn't until my second year of university that I thought differently. I was in a serious relationship and it frightened me. I told my boyfriend at the time that I wanted to travel and focus on art and he just didn't get it. He thought I was playing a game.'

Her pile of flattened cans was twice the size of Michael's and he watched her thin hands, the way they moved effortlessly.

'He proposed, and I had to break his heart. It was awful.

I told myself that I wouldn't do it again. The serious relationship thing.'

'Can't you do both, art and a relationship?'

She shrugged. 'Yes. But it's more fun this way.'

Michael nearly sliced his finger open with the knife. 'I think Layla wishes she had a life like that.'

'A life like what?'

'She started this writing class and wrote a story about a woman in her late thirties who doesn't want to settle down.'

'It could mean nothing.'

'The story is so obviously about her,' he said, reaching for another can of beer. It was terrible stuff, that beer, but the can was a shade of beige, and he guessed she would use it to make a convincing ass – his ass.

'She told me from the start that she didn't want children, but I didn't listen.'

Sarah tutted. 'That's naughty.'

'She loves Jacob, of course. But I don't know. Everything feels wrong.'

For a while, they both worked quietly, the sound of the scissors and knives cutting through all the aluminium.

Around midnight, Michael realised he was a little drunk. He was talking about Jacob's meningitis. 'I *need* to be a good father,' he said, his voice slurred, echoing in the room.

Sarah's eyes widened with alarm. 'You've cut your hand.'

'What?'

'You're bleeding. A lot.'

Michael looked down at his hand, the cut just above his wrist, blood pooling and trickling onto the wooden table.

Sarah rushed over with a tin box and wrapped his hand in gauze. The blood seeped through the first few layers, but she kept wrapping.

Her eyes settled on him and Michael found it difficult not to stare at the big red blob of her cornea. It was not a friendship, this thing with Sarah.

She leant into him and kissed his chin. And then their lips pressed together – slowly at first, before something urgent took hold, the push and pull of desire. They reached an understanding of each other that way and didn't need to speak when Michael left the apartment the next morning, both knowing what they'd done could not be repeated.

Fifteen

The estate agent who came to value the bungalow was Karen Myers. On the phone, she said they'd gone to school together, that she'd graduated in the same year as Michael. She had one of those irritating, squeaky voices, like she was ten years old, not a woman in her late thirties. Karen asked how Michael was doing now. Ava said she didn't have a clue and Karen let it drop, her years in sales probably giving her an intuition about when to leave something.

When she came to the house, the large size of Karen was a complete contrast to her small voice. She asked if she should take her shoes off at the door.

'You can do as you please,' Ava said.

She kept on those shiny tanned heels, and Ava wondered if she thought the house was dirty and that was why she kept them on.

They walked through all the rooms and Karen jotted down notes on her clipboard, quick scribbles that were going to mean something when it came to fixing a price.

She had one of those hairstyles that was trendy among the hairdressers of Welton – sharp-edged and brassy with thick blonde highlights running through like a skunk.

She asked about a damp patch dribbling down from where the ceiling met the floral wallpaper in the sitting room.

Ava said it'd been there a couple of years and it didn't seem to be getting any bigger.

Karen wrote something on her clipboard. Ava leant over to see, but Karen kept the clipboard close to her chest. When she was done looking through all the rooms and cupboards, they sat in the living room and Ava offered Karen a drink, but she made a face, like the start of a grimace.

'No, thanks.' She moved her small glasses low on the bridge of her nose and peered at Ava as if she were a therapist and Ava her patient. 'Why is it that you want to sell *now?*'

Ava didn't think she needed to give her an answer, didn't think she had any business asking. 'It's my mother's house,' she said. 'I want a fresh start.'

Karen nodded. 'It's a shame your bungalow isn't on the other side of the road, facing the river.' She pointed out of the window with her big finger. 'But even if it had the views, it needs a lot of work doing to it. And it's not just cosmetic work, like removing that mirrored wall. The bedrooms aren't exactly huge and the roof needs work.'

Her blue eyes scanned the sitting room and it bothered Ava, the way they moved around behind those small glasses, as if she were judging everything at once.

Her valuation was much lower than expected. Ava thought then of all those headlines in the *Messenger* about London booming, people selling their houses for double the purchase price, when her mother's bungalow had only appreciated a few thousand pounds.

'Even then,' she said, coughing into her hand, 'it might not sell.' She put a painted fingernail to her chin and then her eyes lit up. 'I'll tell you what. There's a young Cornish couple who've just moved back from abroad and they're looking to buy a house that's a project, get their hands dirty. If you want, I could arrange for them to come and have a look.'

'Yes. That would be fine.'

She didn't seem too fussed either way, so it was a surprise to Ava when she rang only two days later to say that the Cornish couple would like to view the property, and would next Wednesday be all right? Ava told her yes, and immediately arranged for a cleaner to come in, since she couldn't manage on her crutches. She pulled down the poster from the fridge with all the hexagons and threw it in the bin. She'd donate Dr Wandsworth's book to the charity shop.

Jane came over on Tuesday evening to give her a hand with the clear-out. She was wearing a bright pink T-shirt from the year the department store had done a run for cancer.

'Kyle's been asking about you,' she said as they put her mother's clothes into large plastic bags, ready for collection.

'Oh?'

Jane's eyes narrowed. 'Any idea why he might be asking?'

'No.'

Jane said Kyle was a sensitive young man, a good man. Clean. Ava knew that even with her scolding, there was heart at the centre of everything with Jane, that she was soft where it mattered.

'I'm not returning to Green's,' Ava admitted.

Jane's hands and eyes were busy sorting through the piles, deciding what to donate, what to throw. 'I thought that would be the case,' she said finally. 'If you need part-time work, there's always a job for you at Green's anyway.'

In Michael's room, they kept nothing. Her brother who couldn't turn up to their mother's funeral. She took a kind of pleasure in throwing him away. His Walkman and cassette tapes, his school things. In the bin they went.

When they had finished, and Jane was ready to leave with all the bags in the boot of her car, Ava threw her arms around her friend. At first, she could feel Jane's whole body tense up from the surprise of this gesture, but then she loosened and squeezed back.

'You've got me, darling,' she said, before gently pulling away and wiping her eyes. 'You've got to know how much your mother loved you.'

Ava searched her mind for evidence of love. She could easily find other things: Elena's dependency on her. Criticisms she made about Ava's appearance in the name of self-improvement. 'It's hard to remember sometimes,' she said.

When the Cornish couple came to view the bungalow, Ava stayed in the kitchen. She could hear the estate agent, her tone different from the other day, describing the *period features* and *potential*. Walls could be knocked down, an extension added at the back. A basement dug out. Imagine, she said: a pool table, a home theatre for entertaining. Such things were possible when you had vision and some pocket change. She was selling them an identity, the story of who they could become. But Ava could never see past her mother here, so it was time for her to go.

Ava lingered in the kitchen and listened nervously. The couple came in and said hello and Ava smiled and left them to explore. From the hall, she could see them looking through kitchen cupboards and they carried on to the back garden, reappearing at the front of the house, where they stood and talked to the estate agent. When they pulled out of the driveway, Karen waved goodbye as if it were her house.

'It's hard to tell what they thought,' she said. 'They were making all the right noises. But you never know.'

Later that afternoon, Ava called Karen to say that she could slash the price down further if the couple were keen. She just wanted to sell and be gone and forget.

★

Sam stopped by late one evening. He was growing a beard and looked much older with it. She hadn't seen him in almost four weeks. Ava wondered if he'd come to confront her about the lawyer's papers. She didn't care; he was at her door.

He said, 'It's *so* good to see you out of that chair!'

She wanted him to say, 'It's so good to see *you*!'

'I saw the for-sale sign in your front lawn. Are you moving?'

'I hope so. If anyone makes an offer.'

He smiled – was she imagining sadness in his smile, the thought of her gone?

'Where are you moving to?'

She shrugged. 'I don't know. Somewhere with a better broadband connection. Maybe Sheffield so I'm closer to campus. I've been accepted on the psychology course.'

'That's great. *So* great!'

He looked into the hall and asked if it was a good time

to talk. She invited him in, offered him a drink, but he said he wouldn't stay long.

He sat on the sofa with his coat still on. Ava thought he was going to bring up the papers from the lawyer. She felt a flutter in her chest, anticipating this confrontation.

But he talked about London.

'The guy who I met in Camden – the supplier – he's offered me a job. We really hit it off. He's got a big shop there. I think I'm going to do it.'

She suddenly felt flushed. 'You're moving to London?'

'Yeah. In a few weeks.'

'What about uni? Haven't you still got a year left?' She felt like a mother saying that.

'I'll look into transferring to a London uni. Or I'll take the year off completely.'

Ava tried to fix a more pleasant expression on her face. 'OK. Yes. I can see how that could work.'

He said he liked Camden, had walked around that day she'd been to see her father. He had a falafel at the food market, walked along the canal. The opportunity was there, and he wanted to do something different. For himself. Away from his parents.

He looked at her then, touched her shoulder, his hand warm and fine.

'You're the first person I've told about London.' His hand moved down her arm, and she welcomed his touch, moving closer to him on the sofa.

He was leaving. There was no danger of attachment. Why should Sam be different from other men she'd found attractive, other men she'd wanted to take to bed? He wasn't different – this was what she told herself as she leant into him and kissed his cheek. His lips were close and she hovered there, lingered for a few seconds. He looked down and then his eyes slowly shut and she felt the pressure of his lips. Ava returned his kiss with force, their mouths opening, curious. Exploring this potential. He moved his hands along her shoulders, her spine. There was strength to his touch, and she wanted him to always touch her.

Her heart was beating into her ears, her wrists, but the cardiac ultrasound seemed distant then, her time as 'patient' far removed when Sam's tongue slid along her collarbone.

His excitement encouraged her. She liked hearing him say that she was a real woman, whatever that meant. She told him to remove her top, her pyjama bottoms.

She also said, 'Fuck me.'

He hesitated. 'I can't stay, though. After. I've got to go unload a shipment at my parents' shop.'

She laughed, tousled his hair. 'You don't have to stay after.'

He kissed her again. She was surprised by his proficiency, the way he used his tongue. And when he moved inside of her, it took everything to delay pleasure, to make it last. They were both desperate for release, and when the moment was close, Ava warned Sam.

'I'm close too,' he said.

It was rare for her to climax with a new man the first time in bed with him. They both lay still on the sofa, her ear against his racing heart.

'I have to leave,' Sam reminded Ava only a short while later. 'Do you need help getting dressed?' he said.

'No. I can do that.'

He gently covered her naked body with a throw and

kissed her forehead like she was a sick child in bed. 'I'll text soon,' he said.

There was an empty feeling in her stomach. After Sam left, Ava looked in her fridge to see what there was to eat. On the middle shelf was the Tupperware container with her father's apple pie. It looked dry and cold. Inedible, the mould spreading. She thought of her father with that container between his hands, the apology written on his face, urging her to take it.

He had sent her an email shortly after she'd been to London: it was good to see her again! Did she like the apple pie? Could he visit soon? He hoped so!

She shut the fridge door, finding nothing there that appealed. She did the crosswords, increasingly agitated. Her mind was on Sam. It made her angry, the longing she felt for him. He had warned her about needing to leave, and yet she had expected him to stay, which was unreasonable, really. She checked her phone, but there were no messages, and so she returned to her crosswords.

A little before midnight, Ava dialled her father's number.

'This is Ava,' she said, her voice pitched high with formality.

The groggy voice on the other end brightened. 'Ava?'

'Yes. Did I wake you?'

'Oh, no,' he said, and he cleared his throat. 'Well, yes, I *was* sleeping. But I'm happy you've called.'

'I was just doing the crosswords.'

'Oh?'

'I was stuck on a four-letter word. The clue is biotech crop.'

'Biotech crop?'

'Yes.'

'Biotech crop. Bio techcrop,' he said, trailing off a little. His breathing crashed into the phone and he went quiet for a while. 'Four-letter word. Bio-crop. I don't know this one.'

He asked what she had been up to and she told him about trying to sell the house.

'Change is good. You know what you should do? Travel. I can make a list of places for you to visit. I know this great spot in Fiji. Maybe we can do a trip together. Italy? Provence? My insurance is terrible, though. This whole terminal illness thing makes it almost impossible to get decent coverage. How's your leg?'

'OK. It still hurts, though.'

'Pain is awful.' He trailed off again. 'But you've got a lot to look forward to, don't you? A potential move and that psychology course?'

'Sure.'

'Why are you really calling?'

She sighed. 'I'm not happy. I'm finding it exhausting to keep pretending.'

He cleared his throat. 'Well, it's natural. Unhappiness is a natural part of being alive.'

In that moment, when he didn't try to talk her out of her unhappiness, it was easy to warm to him, to keep talking.

'There might be trouble with my heart,' Ava said.

'What kind of trouble?'

'I'm not sure. I've got a scan on Tuesday.'

'When?'

'Early Tuesday morning.' Ava went quiet. And then she

said, 'I want to be more of an open person. I keep shutting people out.'

Her father said nothing, and after a while she said, 'Hello? Hello?' and realised that he was snoring, that he'd fallen asleep.

The night before the scan, Ava lay awake for a long time. She kept thinking of Sam. The pressure of his lips. His excitement. He had texted her the following morning and said nothing important. She hadn't responded. Because what would she say? What was the point? He was leaving. Her heart was sprinting through the night. She was convinced the cardiac ultrasound would reveal some terrible defect.

In the morning, she dressed in loose clothes. A blouse she could easily unbutton at the front, a wraparound skirt. It was raining outside, a soft rain, too light for an umbrella. Jane had offered to drive her to the appointment, but it was the same day that they were bringing in the autumn line for Liz Claiborne and she would have to go through it meticulously. It would be a long, tiresome day for Jane, so Ava had made other arrangements, told her she'd already booked a taxi. In truth, she didn't want her there, talking about Jesus, telling her how everything would be all right.

The taxi driver opened the back seat of his musty-smelling Ford Escort and Ava was grateful for his silence during the car journey. It was something she found difficult, people making conversation early in the morning, before she had the chance to understand her own mind.

At this hour, there were only a few other cars on the road. The river was flat and grey, no boats moving across it. It only took twenty minutes to get to the hospital when it usually took forty. Ava followed signs to cardiac investigations and checked in. The secretary, his eyes trained on the computer screen in front of him, told her they would call her in soon. When she turned to find a seat, Ava saw her father.

He looked tired, greyer than when she'd seen him last. But he was dressed in a crisp white shirt and he smiled when he saw her and stood from his seat. Slowly, she walked over to him.

'I hope you don't mind I'm here.'

'I don't mind.'

They sat in the waiting room and looked ahead, neither of them turning to face the other. Ava felt relieved, seeing her father again.

'So you found me.'

'I know how to find people.'

He took her hand, and she was surprised by the ease of their intimacy. For the first time in days, she felt her heartbeat slow a little.

When they called her name to go through, her father squeezed her hand.

'Do you want me to come in with you?'

'I'm OK.'

The warmth of his touch was still there in her palm as she followed the technician into a small room with a bed, a bulky machine next to it.

The technician was a man with a thick, sandy moustache, and when he spoke, he did so quickly and efficiently, his moustache moving and his lips momentarily disappearing beneath it. He explained that she needed to take everything off at the top and put on the gown he gave her.

'The gown needs to be open at the front,' he said,

speaking at her forehead. 'Once you've got it on, you can lie on the bed.' He left the room to give her privacy. She did as he instructed, swimming in that large hospital gown, and it was only a moment before he knocked on the door and Ava told him to come back in.

He turned the lights down like they were going to make love and then settled himself on a squeaky office chair next to her and typed information onto a screen. He asked for her full name and date of birth and then took the ultrasound probe, covered it in a thick jelly and pressed it hard against her chest so that it felt like it was bruising her skin. Intermittently, he clicked buttons on the keyboard to take pictures.

He explained that the gurgling was the sound of her pumping heart, a deep underwater noise that filled the room, her heart an alien thing.

'Take a deep breath,' he said. 'Good, and hold.' He continued clicking buttons, pressing the probe harder into her to capture pictures in black and white, images of her heart beating colourless on the screen.

Ava thought of her father in the waiting room, how he had travelled all this way to see her, and then it didn't hurt so much when the technician pressed down with his probe.

'Another deep breath,' he said, 'and hold. Now look up.' He moved the probe to her throat. She wondered if the technician could capture this feeling of calm in his pictures.

He wiped the probe with a tissue and said the test was over. Ava asked if he'd found anything. The technician said that he couldn't tell her either way, that it was the specialist's job to explain. He tore off tissues from a giant blue roll, told her to wipe her chest with it to get rid of the sticky gel, and it reminded Ava of the time she'd been with Steve Ross shortly after secondary school, when he had released himself onto her chest and then offered her double-ply tissues.

She changed back into her blouse when the technician left, and it took longer than it should because she kept getting the buttons wrong.

In the waiting room, Ava's father had his eyes closed. He looked like a patient, waiting to find out how long he had left.

She touched him gently on the shoulder. His thin paper lids flittered open.

'How did it go?'

'Fine. They won't tell me the results now.'

Lee stood from his seat. 'Let's have breakfast.'

They went to a place that did a full English for a fiver and sat across from each other in a red plastic booth. The large windows looked onto the busy road leading in and out of Welton. The traffic was already building up with people rolling down their car windows in the heat.

Lee leant across the table. 'Do you remember Primrose Hill?'

'Yes.'

'I went for a walk at the weekend and sat at the top of the hill.' He smiled, boyish suddenly. 'It just reminded me of us. When we used to go.' He sat back against the red plastic. 'I was thinking, if I'm feeling OK, breathing and all, and if you're free, maybe we could have a picnic there for my birthday in October.'

Ava heard herself respond automatically. 'Yes.'

She'd liked their picnics there. And sledging when it snowed. And the thought of her father celebrating his last birthday on his own was too depressing. She would go.

'Brilliant,' Lee said. 'Lovely. I'll collect you from Welton.'

'You don't have to drive all this way.'

He shrugged. 'It's only three hours.'

The waitress brought tea and coffee.

'How are your memoirs going?'

'I've nearly finished the first draft. I've just written about the week I spent with Liza Minnelli in Queensland. It's more the personal-life stuff I'm finding difficult.'

'Things about us?'

'Well, yes.'

Ava wondered then if all this recent contact wasn't just research, material he could use for his book. A way to rewrite the past. Would he call this chapter 'The Reconciliation'? A paragraph or two about his birthday on Primrose Hill?

The waitress returned, balancing too many things between her arms. Two big plates piled up with meat, eggs and beans, different bottles of sauce. Ava felt the opposite of hungry.

'I'd like to read your memoirs,' she said.

'Sure. If you're interested. I'll send you what I've got. It's a bit . . . rough in places.'

'What do you mean?'

'Well, the writing. It's an early draft. And it's unflattering.'

'For who?'

His eyes widened. 'Me, who else?'

Lee started eating, cutting up the sausages, coarse-textured food that he put into his small pink mouth.

218

Ava picked at the mushrooms at the edge of her plate. They looked like they'd come from a can.

'I've been thinking. It's a shame you and Michael have lost touch. Maybe I can help in some way.'

'He didn't come to her funeral. But he sent flowers, so.'

Lee stopped chewing, shifted his weight. 'Maybe it was too hard for him—'

'It was hard for *me*.'

Ava swallowed, could feel her heart beating in her throat. She thought of the technician pushing there, taking a picture: here was grief and disappointment.

'I only meant that he's probably still thinking of you and your mother.'

'Is this your attempt at an explanation? Why you left? Why you didn't come back?'

'I thought it would be easier.'

'For yourself.'

'For *everyone*,' he said, low and firm. Ava remembered this tone – he had used it with Elena when they were in a public place. Discreet but cutting.

She felt the air pulling out of her.

The waitress came over and asked if they'd enjoyed their meal and they both nodded. Lee made a sign with his hands for the bill.

'Of course, I was an idiot,' he said. 'Of course. I'm sorry, Ava. What else can I say?'

She looked at a smudge of brown sauce on the table instead of his eyes.

'Send me your memoirs.'

Sixteen

When Layla was seven months pregnant, she'd bought maternity lingerie – a black lace camisole with a matching thong. She'd emerged from the bathroom, a little shy, clambered onto the bed and kissed Michael.

'What's the matter?' she said when he drew back. 'Is it because I'm huge?'

'No, of course not.'

'Then what? Why are you pulling away from me?' Michael's eyes settled on her bump, the big balloon swell of it under all that lace.

'You're worried about hurting the baby.' She sat up, frustration moving across her face. 'I can't believe this. I thought we were going to be different. You told me we weren't going to be like other couples. Sex in different positions. You said that.'

'There's only a little while to go now. Don't you think it's risky?'

'*No*,' she said, drawing out the word. 'Where are you getting your facts from? The seventeenth century?'

She rolled out of bed, put on her robe and left the room.

She pretended to watch television, the way she often did when she was angry.

'I'm sorry. We can try again—'

'Things are already starting to change,' she said, her eyes not moving from the screen. 'You promised they wouldn't change.'

Michael turned off the television, but her gaze was still fixed ahead. 'Some things *will* change. For both of us. I mean, we're having a baby. Of course things won't be exactly the same.'

She shut her eyes, rubbed her temples. 'I know they won't be *exactly* the same.' For a while, neither of them spoke. 'I just don't think I have what it takes to be this person. A mother. I don't have that instinct in me, like Bonnie does.'

'You're the best person I know,' Michael said, and she looked at him with doubt. 'If there's anyone who can succeed at this, it's you.'

She smiled a little then.

'I'm worried too, about being a good parent. I'm lucky I've got your help.'

'I *have* improved you. Remember that terrible sweater you used to wear when we first started dating? And those white leather shoes! What were those?'

They laughed in the dark, and she led him back to the bedroom, showed how his apprehensions about hurting the baby were unfounded. It was Michael who woke up hours later with pain in his stomach, the worst pain he'd ever felt, and Layla led him to the car, held his hand in the hospital bed when they said it was appendicitis.

'It's always about you, isn't it?' she said, sitting in the

chair next to the bed, and Michael laughed, and it hurt even to laugh.

While he recovered from surgery, Layla took a few days off from work and they played Scrabble, invented a theme version of it. Food at a Carnival. Things You Fear. People You Admire. They contested each other's answers. Who fears mayo? Some people do, Layla said, holding on to the scoresheet. They both wrote YOU for people they admired.

★

Standing at the arrivals gate at JFK, waiting for his wife and son, Michael felt a sweeping sadness, thinking about where he had spent the night and how he had changed their story.

He'd come to the airport two hours before their flight was due to land because he couldn't bear to be in the apartment with those large windows looking onto Sarah's building. People came and went through the arrivals gate, some happy to be home, others tired and alone, just wanting to get to their next destination, and Michael was there through it all, waiting.

When Layla and Jacob finally walked through the arrivals gate, an hour after their flight had landed, Michael felt on the verge of collapse. Jacob saw him from the other side of the barrier and pointed, his face lighting up. Layla let go of his hand and he toddled over to Michael, who bent low to receive him. That dark birthmark on his right arm, the way his hair flopped a little at the front when he ran. He was light, too light. Had he always felt so weightless?

'Sorry it took so long,' Layla said. 'Our bag was literally the last one on the belt.'

He took the suitcase from her and she kissed him, and Michael felt knots tightening in his chest when she pulled away.

'I'm so tired,' she said.

'Let's go home.'

While their taxi stood in rush-hour traffic, the driver spoke to them about his dreams of putting on a Broadway musical. 'It's going to be something like *Rent*,' he said, 'but without the AIDS. That part's a real drag.'

'I've been writing myself,' Layla said, slumped in the back seat, stroking a sweaty curl away from Jacob's sleeping head.

'Oh yeah? What are you writing about?'

'A woman in her late thirties who doesn't want a family,' Michael answered for her. It surprised him, the childish spite in his voice, when he was the one who'd wronged her.

Layla looked at him, wounded, then turned her head to the window.

'My girlfriend's all pissy because she thinks she's Scarlet, the main character in my play. I told her, maybe some version of you, but not *you*,' the cab driver said.

At the apartment, Layla went straight to bed, but Jacob was restless after his nap and wanted to play with all the toys he hadn't seen in the last week. He dived into his pirate-ship box and said he was hunting for treasure. Michael played along, invented for himself a mean rival pirate, Toothless Joe, who was looking to get to the treasure first. Jacob laughed, but there was also fear in his eyes, a nervousness to his laughter, confronting Toothless Joe. What struck Michael was the honesty of his fear – and it materialised in the form of tears when Michael spoke in a deep, gravelly voice that reminded him of his own father's. He wondered whether all sons were afraid of their fathers.

'We're just playing. It's a silly game.'

Jacob hesitated when Michael reached out to comfort him, staying in his cardboard box, until his father said he was Toothless Frank, a pirate who was kind and fair.

Michael needed to tell Layla. This lie was too big. He couldn't function. At work, he stared at his computer screen for hours. He couldn't make sense of the words in front of him.

He stopped in to see Dr Susan Barker. She spoke of her latest research and he was glad to just listen.

She'd divided participants into two groups. One group, she explained to Michael, was shown pictures of conventionally attractive people with their straight smiles and strong jaws and perfect Hollywood cheekbones.

'Out-of-my-league-type people,' she said, pulling up some of the pictures on her computer screen.

The other group was given pictures of misfits. Those poor unfortunates with hair growing out from the tips of their noses, black fur on their tongues, big spots and moles and pockmarks ingrained into sallow skin. Features that were jumbled up like a cubist work.

'Third nipples, that sort of thing.'

When she showed Michael those pictures, he winced, and it bothered him, this wincing, because he had thought of himself as a different kind of person.

Dr Barker went on to explain that each group was then made to write a short essay, either on the topic of community or individuality. Consistently, a higher percentage of those who were shown pictures of the attractive people wrote about community, and those who got the full horror show wrote about individuality.

'It's how vulnerability works,' she said, throwing her creased hands. 'We draw a firm line of separation between ourselves and those we perceive as vulnerable and different. We're scared to death of these people because we recognise our own vulnerabilities in them. We are disgusted and terrified of being vulnerable!' She looked at Michael, who must've seemed so lost in his own mind, because she said, 'What's the matter?'

Michael wanted to tell her, 'I've cheated on my wife. I'm a terrible person!' But it mattered to Michael, what she thought of him.

'Nothing. It's just so hot in my office, even with the desk fan. I can't get any work done.'

'You want another fan?' She stood, and from the large metal cabinet behind her desk retrieved another fan. 'Take it,' she said. 'Stay cool.'

At home, Michael found reasons to discredit each opportunity to tell Layla. She was waiting for a phone call from her mother, or Jacob was awake, or she fell asleep just as he was about to tell her. In the cold stillness of the bathroom, Michael shook with fear. She would leave him. She would hate him forever.

Everything else seemed inconsequential, diminished by comparison to the potential of losing his family. He crossed streets without looking both ways.

For the rest of the week, he stayed late at work trying to plan that policy analysis course, went out for runs, avoided the apartment. Once, when he was returning from a run, Sarah Addams gestured for him to meet in the lobby of her building. She'd been smoking in the courtyard.

Michael had not expected to feel relief when he saw Sarah again. But she was the only person who knew.

'It was stupid,' she said, her tone breezy.

'Agreed. *So* stupid.'

'Look, I just wanted to tell you that I'm not going to cause any trouble. I don't have the time or, frankly, the inclination to be trouble. Good as it was, you have a family, and I'd rather not be mixed up in all that.'

Michael nodded again, and felt small, standing next to her. 'I'm sorry. You're really great,' he said.

She smirked, self-satisfied. 'You haven't told her, have you?'

'No. Not yet.'

'Maybe you shouldn't. It was a one-time thing. You don't want to put her through grief for a one-time thing.'

The lift doors opened, and a teenage boy and his yappy dog emerged from it.

'Your installation of the moths – that's me,' Michael said. 'I'm repeating all of my father's mistakes.'

'Perhaps,' she said. 'But I saw something less bleak in the park.'

'You saw an ass.'

'Well, if the shoe fits.'

The lobby door opened, and Michael's heart leapt to his throat, imagining it was Layla, asking what he was doing there. But it was an old man with a walker, and they moved apart so that he could pass between them.

'I've got work to do,' she said, and she crossed her arms and said goodbye before disappearing into the lift with the old man.

'You want me to press six?' the old man said loudly.

When Michael returned to the apartment, it was dark and quiet, but there was a light on in the bathroom. He knocked on the door and Layla said to come in.

She was relaxing in the tub. The bathroom window framed a large, hazy moon. Michael put the toilet seat down, sat there. She had not put any bath foam in so that her breasts were visible, submerged in the water.

'I know you've been avoiding me,' she said. 'It's obvious something's bothering you.'

When he didn't respond, she said, 'The story I wrote – it *is* about a life that I sometimes think about, a life that I wanted for a long time. All of that's true. But I'm happy now and I would never give up this life with you and Jacob. Never. The story is just a story.'

She looked at Michael and smiled and it felt like he was drowning. He noticed the black mould between the tiles on the wall. Beard trimmings scattered on the linoleum floor. Grime and dirt, things growing in damp corners. He wanted to pour bleach over everything.

'If I've been distant lately, it's because of something else,' Michael said, all the moisture gone from his mouth. 'I did something.'

Layla sat up a little in the tub, her eyes wide and unblinking.

'I slept with another woman.'

For a while, the words seemed spoken by someone else, a stranger in the room. The ugliness of them and what they told about him were appalling. But they were true; he had slept with another woman, this was what he'd done.

Layla paused for a moment, stunned, looked down at her naked body, then back to him. She stood quickly and walked away from him, not bothering to reach for a towel.

227

'I'm sorry—'

'Don't,' she said, angry. 'Don't touch me.'

He watched her shut the door to their bedroom and for a while he stood on the other side of it, listening to her sobbing quietly.

Michael thought of his mother, how many times he'd heard her crying behind a shut door, those pained noises filling their London townhouse. The knots in his chest were squeezing tighter now, the pain inside of him large.

Jacob called for his mother. Michael went into his room. 'Go back to sleep,' he said, running his hand over his son's head.

'Story,' Jacob said, but his eyes were already growing heavy, and then they were closed.

The bedroom door was still shut, but he couldn't hear Layla crying. He knocked, then tried the handle, but it was locked. No response.

'It wasn't a love thing,' Michael said.

'What was it then?' her weary voice called out.

Michael leant his back against the door. 'Nothing. It was nothing.'

Seventeen

Ava received two messages: a voicemail from Karen the estate agent and a text from Sam. Karen said that she had big news about the house and would call first thing tomorrow, once she had all the details. Sam said he didn't know why she hadn't responded to his texts. Was she OK? It was his birthday and his friends were throwing him a party that evening, and he would like her to be there, if she could make it. No pressure. He included details of his friend's address.

Ava reread Sam's message several times, in different places – first on the couch, then leaning against the kitchen table, then lying starfish in bed. She held the phone close. When she'd memorised every word of his message, she composed responses. *Happy Birthday! Happy Birthday. Happy Twenty-First Birthday! Happy Twenty-First Birthday.* That was as far as she got. She kept deleting the start of each message, worried she sounded either too flat or too eager, and she hadn't actually decided what her response should be, whether she wanted to go or not. She moved back and forth between saying yes and ignoring the message altogether. It startled her when the doorbell rang. For a moment, she thought it was Sam, that he had come all this way to tell her personally that he needed her at his party tonight. She imagined him standing on the other side of the door. She would take him by the hand, lead him straight into bed.

But it was Marie. Ava had completely forgotten about her physio appointment.

'Your progress is remarkable,' she said, watching Ava stand and sit and move her legs around from side to side. Her lips were bright pink today, her long nails painted blue.

'How does the boot feel?'

'Much better than the cast,' Ava said, remembering the shock of seeing her right leg again when they'd removed the plaster a few days ago and replaced it with the boot. It had looked shrunken and there was a long, thin scar where they'd cut through her flesh to operate. The skin looked dead and there were long stray hairs, some ingrown.

They were nearly finished with the physio session and Ava was desperate to ask Marie for advice.

'Have you ever dated a younger man before?' Ava said.

'How young?'

'Five, ten years younger?'

'Yes,' Marie said. 'I was once seeing a guy who was nine years younger.'

'Did it feel strange?'

'No,' she said with complete confidence. 'It felt good.' She leant forward. 'The young ones are always eager to please.'

Ava knew what she meant. Sam had focused on her the night they'd been together.

When Marie said they were finished for today, Ava

asked if she could drop her off at the shopping centre.

'Sure. I'm already going that way.'

In Clintons, Ava looked through different birthday cards, picked up a few serious ones – candles, balloons, typical birthday things – and then some funny ones, but most of those were to do with age, how old the receiver was, and that was something she was trying not to draw attention to. A thin sales assistant hovered like a nervous shadow. When she asked if she could help, Ava told her no, but she kept looking over from behind the till, so Ava just grabbed the most inoffensive-looking birthday card with a drawing of a cake printed on it.

The card shop was close to the department store. She felt an emptiness in her stomach looking into the entrance of Green's, the place where she had worked for years. She contemplated the yellow signs, the final markdowns, everything from the summer lines now reduced. All those items had started out full of promise and then, as time went on, their values had dropped. Nobody wanted them. It was difficult not to compare herself in that moment to those reduced items. She felt no pull to go inside the store, no desire to say hello to her former colleagues.

At home, Ava found a red dress she'd worn to a school dance when she was sixteen. She knew as soon as she held it up that it would fit exactly as it had done then – she had lost so much weight. She wanted her curves back and considered doubling the padding in her bra. But Sam had already seen and felt her shape. She left the padding in her drawer.

She tried her hair in different styles, and decided it looked best in a plait, tidy and out of the way. In front of the bathroom mirror, which was steamed from her earlier wash, she applied eyeliner, thick and dark against her mother's advice on subtlety, her lipstick bright – a shade Elena would have found offensive in its showiness.

The full-length mirror in her bedroom revealed the reflection of an old person trying to look young, a clown, and Ava decided not to go to the party.

Hours passed. She tried to read a novel, put it aside and picked up another. She couldn't face taking off the dress. All that make-up still on her face. She thought of Sam – his hair, that new beard brushing her cheek.

At ten o'clock, she phoned a taxi. They had nothing available for another hour, so she waited, biting her nails, and went to the toilet several times, added another coat of lipstick, more hairspray, and then the taxi was in the driveway.

The house where the party was taking place was close to Sheffield University. It was a forty-minute journey, but it felt much longer.

'Are you a student at the university?' the taxi driver said.

'I will be. In the autumn.' She felt a rush of excitement, telling him that. 'Do you think you could collect me later on?'

'It's my busiest night. You didn't book a car?'

'No.'

He looked at her in the rear-view mirror, perhaps taking pity because of her boot and crutches. 'I've got a small job close by, around one in the morning. I can pick you up at one-thirty.'

It was better that way; she'd have a quick excuse to get away if things got uncomfortable. She was always looking for an escape route. An hour and a half. Two hours max. She could manage that.

The address led to an old Georgian property, a flat on the ground floor, so at least there was no need to climb up those steep stairs.

Noise travelled through the door. Ava knocked and, of course, nobody answered. They were probably all drunk by now, unable to hear anything over the music. She tried the door and it opened. The sitting room was full of people huddled together in groups. A girl in a thin blue dress was dancing, her feet bare, her smile easy. The room smelt of beer and feet and pot. Ava wondered how many people were living in the house, whether they all got along or fought over bathroom privileges or piles of unwashed dishes in the sink, or too loud sex. Ava had always wanted to experience this type of communal living and had thought she would have been good at it, tidy and quiet. Mostly out of the way, but deeply interested in all that happened between the old, uneven walls.

She looked for Sam but couldn't find him. A boy with a thick beard and his hair in a Mohawk introduced himself as Ahmad. He extended his hand out to her and said this was his place.

'Are you Ava?' he asked, speaking into her ear so that she could hear him. When she nodded, he looked pleased. 'It's great that you made it,' he said, in a way that suggested he knew about her. 'Do you want a drink? A beer?'

'A beer would be great, thank you.'

Ava followed him into the kitchen and there she saw Sam. He had his back to her, but she knew the shape of his head. He was leaning against the kitchen counter, talking to a girl. She was young, blonde, attractive. Ava had tried once to dye her hair that honeyed shade of blonde, her mother's shade, but it had turned out orange, the blackness of her hair not taking to the supermarket dye.

'Here you go,' Ahmad said, handing Ava a cold bottle of beer.

She smiled at him, pretending not to have seen Sam in the kitchen with that girl, who was laughing now, touching his shoulder like he had said something funny. She was going to leave as soon as Ahmad left her side, but he put his arm around her shoulder like they were friends and led her to Sam and the blonde girl.

'You came,' Sam said, his eyes red and hooded, and Ava guessed that he must have been drunk or stoned. He looked down at her leg. 'The cast is off.' He greeted her with a sloppy hug, his whole weight against her.

'Steady,' Ahmad said to Sam, putting his hands on his friend's shoulders and drawing him back.

It was Ahmad who said, 'This is Ava,' to the others standing around. They chatted for a while in the kitchen, although Ava mostly stood around and listened. They were talking about the show *Flight of the Conchords*, which Sam had made Ava watch, and they quoted from the show, sang lyrics and laughed hysterically. Ava smiled with her mouth closed. She must have been the only sober person there. Would her university experience be like this, a repeat of those years she'd spent in a fog, kissing strangers, speaking to people who had nothing to say?

The blonde girl was called Lucie. She leant against Sam's shoulder and it was clear by the way she kept gazing at him and touching his chest that she wanted to be alone with him.

When Ava looked at her watch, she was surprised to see it was already one o'clock. The taxi would be back in a short while.

Ahmad talked about one of his psychology lecturers, how his life would make an amusing offbeat Netflix series, the way he was socially awkward but sweet.

'He reminds me of Tobias from *Arrested Development*,' Sam said.

Lucie laughed and rubbed Sam's arm. Ava felt ill watching the intimacy between them, but she didn't want to appear jealous, so she stood and laughed with the others and even flirted a little with Ahmad.

'Do you want another drink?' Sam said to Ava.

'Yes.'

Sam led her away from the others, through the kitchen and into the back garden, where a few plastic chairs were scattered. He pulled up a chair and told her to sit.

The air was cold, and it smelt faintly of vomit.

'You look fit in that dress,' Sam said, taking something from his pocket. It was a joint. 'Do you mind if I light this?'

'No,' Ava said. 'You don't have to ask.'

He stuck it into his mouth, used a lighter from his pocket and inhaled deeply, then he coughed and laughed, and she laughed too.

'Can I try it?'

He smiled. 'Sure.'

He passed the joint to Ava. She inhaled the rich earthiness of it and coughed, just as he had done, before passing it back, feeling a mild thrill.

'Why have you been ignoring my texts?'

Ava shrugged. 'I've been busy. With house stuff.'

'I thought you were pieing me off.' He pulled his chair closer to hers. 'When did you get the cast removed?'

'A few days ago. It was so weird at first.'

'I would have come with you to the hospital, if you'd told me,' he said, and looked down at the boot. 'Is your leg all weird and shrunken?'

'Pretty much.'

Sam smiled. 'I'm *so* glad you came.'

He smelt of aftershave and beer and dirt. Ava wanted to roll around in him. She remembered the card then, and gave it to him, held the joint in her hand while he read it.

'*Tavalodet Mobarak.*' He looked at her with confusion. 'You want to climb on top – of what exactly?'

She smirked. 'That's *not* what it says.'

He pointed to the card. 'That's what it says in Farsi.'

'I googled it. "Happy Birthday".'

He laughed, and Ava gave him a playful shove. She took another drag, passed the joint back to Sam.

'Thank you. It's a nice touch, the Farsi.'

They kissed. The taste of his mouth was earthy like the joint, which he now held away from her in one hand, while the other rested on her lap.

Ava pulled away, feeling light-headed. 'I need a little air.'

He sat back in his seat, took another drag.

'I think Lucie is into you,' Ava said.

'I'm interested in you.'

'Why?'

He inhaled more smoke, and the joint was much smaller now. 'You know who you are. You're a real woman.'

'Old, you mean.'

'I know what I mean.' He moved the joint to her mouth and she inhaled and said she'd had enough and then he tossed it to the far end of the garden.

'Have you slept with many girls?'

He shrugged. 'Not really. Six. Maybe seven.'

'You're not sure?'

'Eight?' He looked down at the patchy grass. 'What about you? How many girls have you slept with?' He grinned and she rolled her eyes, remembering his age.

'Twenty. Boys.'

He didn't say anything, and Ava wondered if he thought twenty was too many.

'The past is the past,' he said, leaning in to kiss her again, but this time she couldn't relax. She felt panic racing through her. Was it the pot? She thought it was supposed to relax the mind, make you interested in slow-moving clouds and colours on a screensaver. She worried it was her heart.

Ava put both hands on his shoulders, as if she were steadying herself. 'Are you still planning on moving to London?'

'Yeah,' he said. 'I'm going down in a few weeks to look at some flats around Camden.'

Ava looked at her watch – the taxi would be here in less than five minutes. He touched her face, his pupils large, the white shot with red. A sadness fell over her, and then confusion, as she wondered what was the point of this intimacy if he was leaving.

'My taxi's waiting,' she said, and then slowly, using her crutches for support, she stood up from the plastic chair.

'You're joking,' Sam said, still sitting. 'I don't want you to go.'

'I've got a lot going on in my life right now,' Ava said. 'I need to keep things simple.'

He shook his head. 'I don't get you.'

'What is it exactly that you don't *get*?' Her words came

out more sharply than she'd intended.

'You send mixed signals.'

Sam's voice was calm. Ava found it infuriating that he should be so relaxed when it felt like she was slowly drowning.

'You hit me with your car. Things aren't simple.'

'You were going to sue my parents.'

'What?'

'I saw the papers.'

Ava felt a wave of nausea move through her. He knew. 'I was never going to sue your parents. Jane sent a lawyer and he delivered that document.'

'And you kept it because . . .?'

She didn't have an answer. 'I wasn't going to sue your parents.'

'OK.'

'You don't believe me.'

'I do.'

'Right. I've got to go.'

They walked together around the house to the front where the taxi was waiting.

Sam helped her into the car, leant in and kissed the top of her head. 'Thanks for the card,' he said, and then he walked back to the house.

When she got home, it was gone two, but Ava didn't want to sleep. She dialled Michael's number. It would be late in the evening in New York, but it felt important to speak with him, to tell him how he'd ruined her life. All the things she'd given up over the years to look after their mother. A job outside of Welton. A real relationship that might've led to love.

A woman answered, saying hello. Ava hesitated – what

could she say to Michael's wife? They had never met, never spoken.

'Hello?' Her voice came through again, more sharply. 'Look, I know who this is. We have a son. Did he tell you we have a son? Huh? Before he took you to bed?'

Ava hung up the phone and felt sick. She didn't brush her teeth, just fell into bed in her red dress, dipping in and out of hazy sleep.

Karen phoned early the next morning. 'I just couldn't wait to tell you,' she said in her small-girl voice. 'They want to buy your house. The Cornish couple. Cash buyers!' she said. 'But we have to be tactical now.'

Eighteen

The rental car's satnav kept dropping out of signal. Michael got lost a few times driving from Heathrow to Hendon Cemetery, but he was close now. The morning sky lay in front of him in fine sweeping layers of orange and blue, like coloured sand in a jar. Elena had liked making those in summer – telling Michael to add in the green sand, and then she would add yellow, and the next layer was blue. When the jars were filled, she left them in different parts of their Hampstead house, and it felt like they were at the beach. Elena would speak often of Kyrenia in the summer, and the fine sand that slipped through her fingers like silk. She used to bury her father in it when she was little. His legs. His torso.

Michael felt tired. On the flight, he had stayed up and watched a Pixar film that Jacob liked, and it gave him comfort watching those bright characters, sitting in an aisle seat over the Atlantic, thinking of his son. The old woman sitting next to Michael had smiled at him like he was one of those children with a lanyard around his neck, travelling without a family. And she had offered her hand to him later, when there had been turbulence and a cold fear had gripped Michael and his breathing had quickened. He'd taken her hand, embarrassed but grateful. Only when the plane levelled did he let go.

He did not want his life to end. Not the way things had been left at home. The hurt across Layla's face. Her silence as she'd walked around him in the apartment as if he were a ghost, a bad lingering smell. It went on like that for days until she finally said, 'You need to leave.'

Michael approached the cemetery, felt a familiar unease driving through the arched entrance. Elena had taken him a handful of times to visit his grandfather's grave and she had laid down daffodils, held him close. He remembered her tears, her silence.

Michael parked the car and leant against the side of it, smoking a duty-free cigarette. He took his time, listening to the birds. When he had finished with that cigarette, he put another in his mouth, and after his third, he reached for the daffodils on the passenger seat and locked the car doors.

The air was warm, sun falling onto the path ahead. The trees were tall and bright, and it pleased Michael that she was here, in a serene place like this, alongside the father she had loved.

Michael asked a man trimming a hedge about the section dedicated to the Greek Orthodox Church. He said to go right at the end of the path, then left.

A magpie flew past, its long black tail very close to Michael's head. When he reached the Greek Orthodox part of the cemetery, he felt nervous as he glanced at the graves with letters marked on them in a language he'd never learnt to speak or read.

But here was his mother's grave: a slab of grey marble, her name in English and Greek: Elena Agatha Andreadis.

'Mother' and the dates of her birth and death etched there into the stone.

Michael laid down the daffodils.

All the while, he thought of the last night he'd seen his mother. The beautiful navy sweater. Her olive branch.

Michael had smoked half the carton of cigarettes by the time he reached Welton. Driving through the familiar roads, his mind turned to Ava. Would she even let him in? He had sent those flowers but then didn't hear from her. She had every right to hate him, slam the door in his face.

To the left of the road, the river was the colour of the sky, the two indistinguishable so that it looked like the world was dropping off there, and it felt that way, like he was on the very edge of things. And here was the bungalow: the tired bricks, an awful mustard colour, tiles hanging loose in places. He felt a familiar dread, that fear of getting stuck.

A for-sale sign was planted in the front lawn. He thought of his mother, the brightness in her eyes when she'd un-locked the door and said with pride, 'This is home.' The first place she'd bought herself.

The lawn looked like it had not been mowed in weeks and that sense of guilt returned; everywhere in Welton it seemed to follow him, saying, *Coward. Leaving your mother and sister behind.*

Michael parked in the driveway, behind a silver Peugeot. He rang the doorbell and waited. He heard movement on the other side.

The door opened and there was his sister – the darkness of her hair, the downward curve of her mouth. She squint-ed at him in a red dress, eyeliner smeared down the side of her cheek. Michael had not expected to find Ava with a long boot on her leg, leaning into crutches, and somehow, he felt responsible.

'Hello,' he said.

Ava kept squinting as if she did not believe that it was him at the door. Michael leant in, putting his arms around his sister's narrow shoulders, but she stayed exactly as she was, brittle, her whole face one big squint when he pulled away.

'Do you want to come inside?' she said.

In the sitting room, the furniture was the same; the same beige carpets, the same leather sofa, only now it looked like a dead grey heap of leather, no shape to it.

They both stood in the sitting room for a moment, Michael unsure what to do, where to place himself.

'Have a seat,' Ava said. 'Do you want a cup of tea?' Her voice came out foggy, like she'd had a rough night. Michael thought she must've fallen asleep like that, in her red dress.

'I can get the tea,' he offered. 'How do you take it?'

'Black.'

In the kitchen, things had moved around; the fridge was against a different wall, the appliances a pale yellow instead of red. Michael waited for the kettle to boil and keenly felt his mother's absence. It was strange without her in this kitchen, washing plates or discreetly pouring herself a drink.

He returned to the sitting room with the tea. His sister was on the couch by the window where their mother used to sit, her feet up on the coffee table. He placed Ava's tea on a side table where she could easily reach, and he sat at the other end of the sofa.

'What's happened to your leg?'

243

'A man hit me with his car.' A short burst of laughter escaped from her. 'I'm actually in love with him.'

'The man who hit you?'

She nodded.

'Is he abusive?'

'Oh, no. It's not like that. It was an accident. It's how we met.'

'OK.'

Ava pressed down with her index finger in the space between her eyes. 'I can't believe you're here. I would've tidied if I knew you were coming.'

'The house looks tidy. So you're selling it?'

'It's sold, as of this morning,' she said. 'A Cornish couple have offered and I agreed to the sale. They're cash buyers, so it'll move quickly now – at least, that's what the estate agent says. Karen Myers. She says she knows you.'

The name was familiar, but Michael couldn't think who she was. 'It makes sense to sell,' he said, looking around the room, that awful wall mirror showing his tired reflection. 'Where will you go?'

'Maybe Sheffield. I've been accepted to do a psychology course at the uni there.'

'That's amazing!' he said, his voice too loud.

'You're so American now.'

'In what way?'

'Your accent,' she said. 'Your enthusiasm.' She coughed into her hand. 'How's Jacob?'

'He's great. I've got videos if you want to watch.' Michael handed his mobile to Ava and she watched her nephew on the screen, counting to fifteen on his fingers.

'He's big now,' she said, the words catching in her throat. Michael had only ever sent a few pictures of Jacob when he was a baby. But now his son had recognisable features, Ava's own mouth there on his face. She returned the phone to him, looking disoriented.

'I went to Hendon Cemetery,' Michael said. 'It's a beautiful spot.'

'Yes, well. It's what I thought she'd have wanted.' Ava stood from the sofa. 'I'm actually hungover,' she said flatly. 'I need a Panadol and a wash.'

'OK. Fine. Is there anything to eat in the house?'

'No. Not unless you want to be poisoned. We'll have to go out.'

★

Outside, the sky had cleared a little. They went to a café on the boardwalk and sat along the river. The sun, when it wasn't obscured by clouds, brought the river to life, shining down on all that blue.

'How long are you staying?' Ava said, looking slightly brighter after changing out of her dress and washing the make-up from her face.

'Just the weekend.'

'It's a long way to come for just a weekend.'

'I have to get back to Jacob.' He put out the cigarette, replaced it with another. 'How was it? Meeting Dad.'

'Awkward at first.'

'What's he like?'

Ava shrugged. 'Softer, I suppose. He's writing his memoirs. They're being published and everything. Well, if he finishes them in time.'

Michael thought of the speakers at Bar Five and somehow he could not picture his father telling his story, at least not the truth. He would embellish, work towards a punchline.

'Is he really sick?'

'He's got cancer.'

'What type?'

'He won't say.'

Michael sighed. A waiter came to clear their plates.

'Will you see him before you go?'

Michael shook his head. 'I've booked to fly out of Doncaster so that I don't have to drive all the way back to London. And . . . we were never close. We really weren't. He was actually pretty awful to me.'

'I don't remember much.'

'Well, he doted on you. He called me an embarrassment.'

'That was a long time ago.'

'It's all I know of him. It was different with *you*.'

At the bungalow, Ava said she was tired and asked whether he'd mind if she turned on the TV. Michael shook his head. He was tired himself from all the travel and the effort of talking about the past. Ava found an old episode of *Friends*, stretched out on the sofa and quickly fell asleep. But, tired as he was, Michael couldn't relax. He drifted around the house, looked through his old wardrobe hoping to find the navy sweater from his mother, but everything had been cleared out.

He hesitated before going into his mother's bedroom. He switched on the light and it hummed, dim at first, like it was slowly waking from a long rest. Her absence between the mahogany bedposts seemed to confirm to him that, yes, she was really gone from this world.

He had relied too much on the permanence of Welton, the unchanging nature of his mother and sister's existence here. He hadn't factored in death when he'd left, so desperate to get away and make something of himself. He hadn't realised his mother would not live forever. But, more than that, he felt he was to blame. She had been ill, had suffered with alcohol for such a long time, and he had not stayed to help.

The room was mostly cleared of her things, the big wardrobe now empty. But on her dressing table was a box where she had kept trinkets: a black-and-white picture of a man with a tidy moustache. It was Michael's grandfather. Her cross and rosary, a few dried-up rose petals and a school picture of Michael with his hair parted down the middle. Seeing himself among the other items, Michael felt as if he had died like his grandfather. And he supposed that in a way he must've been dead to his mother, the way he'd kept her out of his life in New York.

Michael only had to open the top drawer of his mother's dresser to find the navy sweater. It was folded neatly, the price tag still on it.

He cut the tag off and wore it over the top of his T-shirt, then went to bed, waking up in the early hours in a terrible sweat.

★

When Ava awoke the following morning, the sun was blazing, a big, red circle sitting low in the sky like it might drop back down. Had she imagined Michael in the bungalow? Perhaps the whole day had been a dream, or else she was living in the semi-permanent fog of that joint she'd shared with Sam. Her brother at home after all these years, blowing into her day. It was astonishing. He looked older. Handsome like their father. She had assumed they'd meet again. But she hadn't pictured it like this – her still in that red dress, terribly hungover.

The sound of a lawnmower filled the space between the grey folds of her brain. Looking out of her bedroom window, she saw her brother tidying and trimming, sweating in the heat, and she could not bear it, the sight of him working on the lawn. All the anger that had been missing when Michael had shown up to the bungalow resurfaced now.

She charged out into the garden, still in her pyjamas. 'Hey.' And then louder. 'Hey!'

He turned to see her and switched off the motor.

'Why are you doing that?'

'The lawn's out of control.'

'So?'

'I thought I'd help.'

'No. You don't do *that* –' she felt a searing anger '– *help*.' She imitated his American accent.

'I thought this kind of work would be difficult for you, if not impossible . . .'

'What about other things that have been *difficult* for me? Like staying with Mum while you fucked off to America.'

He wiped the sweat from his forehead and looked up at the sky, searching for what to say. 'I know,' he said, finally. 'I can understand your frustration. But at the time it was too hard to keep coming back.'

'Too hard?' She spat the words at him, unsure whether to laugh or cry. 'I hate that excuse. What about what I wanted? I couldn't just leave her like you did. She needed *us*.'

'I know.'

'Do you? Do you really know? I don't think you do.' Ava's head was spinning, but she pressed on. 'You sent our wedding invitation *three weeks* before the date. Hah!

No offer to come out to New York and meet my own nephew. And the flowers!' She was shaking, her whole body shaking with anger. 'Those fucking flowers with that pathetic note.'

Michael approached his sister slowly. Her posture was deflating, like she was being held up by her crutches.

'Those flowers were awful. I realise that now.'

She began to cry but stepped back towards the house when Michael moved closer. She stumbled slightly.

'I should have come back for the funeral,' he said, and he reached then to touch her arm.

'Go back to your family,' she said, shaking his hand away, and then she walked back inside the house.

Nineteen

It was early evening when Michael's plane landed in New York. Again, he couldn't sleep on the flight, his mind a mess of guilt and shame.

He thought of a speaker at Bar Five, the story she'd told of her burns. She wore a dress with thin spaghetti straps, and all along her neck and the right side of her face and chest, her skin was blistered and raw. The pain kept her awake at night, that or thinking about her ex-husband. She was so afraid it would happen again, even though he had been convicted and was serving his sentence. For a long time, she hated the look of her body. She did not recognise herself in it. She had become someone to look away from, not to stare at. She could feel how hard people were concentrating, trying not to notice her skin. And she'd said she realised then how much people avoided the look of pain, how they were afraid of it, tried to cover it up with light conversation about weather. Very few people asked about the abuse she had suffered. It was a problem, she said, the way people built boundaries between themselves and those who suffered, boundaries to keep the pain at bay, to deny what had happened, to keep themselves safe from guilt.

Michael had thought she'd explained his life in a way that he never could. That it felt that way every time he'd gone back home to see his mother and sister, like staring into a raw blister.

He thought of Ava and how she'd told him not to return. And really, what could he do except leave? Too much damage had been done.

It wasn't a long wait in the customs queue, and he didn't have luggage to collect at the carousel. His carry-on bag was light. The only extra item he'd brought back was the navy sweater.

In the taxi queue, he smoked the last of his duty-free cigarettes. He sent Layla a text to give her warning that he was on his way back to the apartment. She knew he'd gone to England to see his family.

It was August now, and the air in New York was humid and sticky. It felt like he had been away for much longer than a weekend, Welton so far removed from his existence here. And yet, he felt the marks of his visit deeply ingrained in him.

In the taxi, time moved slowly, when all he wanted was to be with Layla and Jacob. Would they be at home waiting for him or would he return to an empty apartment?

It was 7 p.m. when Michael got in. He fumbled through his bag in the hallway, looking for his keys, and then his hands shook as he tried to turn the key in the lock. It wouldn't open. He wondered for a moment if Layla had changed the locks, and his stomach turned, imagining her and Jacob on the other side, just out of reach.

Michael knocked on the door, and there were footsteps on the other side. It was the graphic designer who had moved into their old apartment. Michael apologised for his mistake: this was not where he lived. And he longed for those days before they'd moved up to the new apartment, before life had become complicated with his father's letters, with what he'd done to his marriage.

The graphic designer told him, 'No problem. Come by sometime for lemonade.'

Michael took the hot staircase, walked up two flights, and his keys worked there. The apartment was quiet, but then Layla appeared, looking beautiful in a loose T-shirt and shorts. Michael felt shy, like he was meeting her for the first time.

Her eyes were clear when she spoke. 'It's good to see you.'

She told Michael that Jacob was sleeping, that now would be a good time to talk. They sat on the sofa and Layla moved over to the far corner so that there was a noticeable distance between them, when Michael wanted nothing more than to be close, glued through flesh.

'How was your family?'

'Fine,' he said.

'Good. It's good that you went to see them.' She paused, shifted her weight to the front of the sofa. 'I want to know some things. About the woman.'

'OK.'

'Is she white?'

'Yes, but I don't see how . . .'

'Is she thin?'

'Why are you asking these questions –?'

'Just answer.'

'Yes. She's thin.'

'Younger?'

'It had nothing to do with her looks . . .'

'Answer.'

'Older. She's in her forties. I think.'

Layla's face looked as if it had cracked in half. She nodded, swallowed and clasped her hands in her lap.

'I've been thinking about the future,' she said. 'I want to go back to work. Cut my sabbatical short.'

Michael felt relieved that she hadn't said, 'I want to leave you.'

'Of course. If that's what you want to do.' He edged a little closer to Layla, but she stayed where she was on her corner of the sofa. 'I missed you so much,' he said, his voice full of thick feeling.

Layla looked at him, her eyes wide and sharp. 'It'll take time.'

AUTUMN

Twenty

The bungalow looked strange without furniture. The bareness of it revealed flaws long hidden – cracks behind the sofa, moisture gathering behind cabinets and so many spiders with their webs strewn around like they owned the place. Jane had said that you could slow spiders down by blasting them with hairspray, temporarily immobilising them, and that was when to get your shoe.

The beige carpet was marked with deep lines where the sofa had been and where the imposing mahogany display cabinet had stood for nearly two decades. Elena had hired some young students from the university to move all their furniture into this bungalow. It had been a warm spring day, and they'd had their sweaters tied around their waists, their frames straining under the weight of the old couch. Elena had given them five pounds each and a tall glass of iced tea afterwards.

All those indentations on the carpet and scuffs on the walls seemed now to shout, 'There was a life here! There are ghosts in this house!' The Cornish couple had said that they planned to rip up all the carpets, replaster the walls, put in a new bathroom, instal a peppermint splashback in the kitchen. Ava could understand this need to reduce a place to its bare bones, erase any mark of a previous life. She wished she could return in a year's time to see what they had done.

There were no students in the driveway, no van hired to move her things. Ava had organised a garage sale once her brother had left and it had surprised her, how many people had turned up – some neighbours, like Mrs Miller, just interested in poking their noses in, as if the house were a museum or a peep show; others eager to take the couch, that big cabinet. She needed to get rid of her mother's things. Ava couldn't understand it – who would want their worn-out furniture? But almost everything had sold, and the few items that had been left – a set of coffee tables and two bowing bookshelves – Jane had helped Ava take to the university campus, where students had fought over them.

'All we have to do is leave them on the kerb,' Jane had said, and sure enough, people came and carried them away.

Before she left, Ava walked into each room of the house, her crutches replaced by a walking stick. A sadness washed over her as she thought about her mother, whose presence filled every square inch of this bungalow. She ran her hand along the wallpaper of her mother's bedroom, remembering how she had been brave, that Ava hadn't given her enough credit. She had left London, started a new life for them here. She'd worked long hours to support her and Michael. And there were good memories: their trips to the café on Days Road, sipping hot chocolate after visiting the river in the autumn months, hurling stones and their miseries into it. Ava wished she had trusted her mother's love. It had been there, muffled by the drink perhaps, and by how much they both longed for Michael, but she could see now – it had been there.

Her mobile rang and it was Jane, asking if she needed a hand.

'I've only got three boxes of stuff.'

Jane sighed. 'But you've sold your car. Who doesn't have a car? It's like you're a Londoner. Let me drive you to your new flat at least.'

'I don't need a car in Sheffield. I can walk to all the shops from my flat. I've already arranged for a taxi to collect me.'

'And how exactly are you going to move the boxes with that cane?'

'I've explained to the driver. He knows me. I've used him before.'

'Well, all right,' she said, her tone sharp. 'Seems like you've got everything figured out. When do you think you'll be set up?'

'All the furniture should arrive in a week.'

Here, Jane softened. 'Tell me as soon as you're ready for visitors.'

The driver arrived and greeted Ava with a smile. He remembered driving over Dr Wandsworth's face there on the cover of his new book in Matlock. Ava was glad to see him now.

When he'd put everything in the boot, Ava locked the door and left the keys in the mailbox as Karen Myers had instructed.

In the car, she rolled down the windows. They pulled out of the driveway and she told herself, *This is a house, it's just a house.* But there was her mother, sitting on the wicker chair on the front porch, her gaze across the road on the grey-bricked houses, between which she could catch a glimpse of the blue river – just where she couldn't reach.

★

A few weeks before the move, Ava had been to see the cardiologist, Dr Elisa Marez. Dr Marez had explained that the ultrasound revealed a weakness in her heart function.

'It's likely that your injuries have put further strain on your heart,' she'd said. Ava had tried fixing a calm, reasonable look on her face, though she'd felt like she was falling down an endless staircase. And then Dr Marez had started drawing a diagram, asking when everyone in Ava's family had died.

Ava said her grandfather from Cyprus had died suddenly of a stroke when he was still in his forties. He'd collapsed at the clothing factory where he'd worked in Camden. And it was then, trying to piece together the deaths of the Greek side of the family, that Ava thought how little she knew about them and, by extension, herself. They shared the same blood and tissue, perhaps the same defect. Were her cousins struggling, too, dying young? It was something she thought to do in the New Year, make contact with her family in Cyprus and Greece.

The cardiologist had listened to her heart with a stethoscope, the cold metal permeating through her chest, so that all day she'd felt a chill and worn a thick wool sweater in the dead heat of summer.

'Rest,' Dr Marez said. 'You need to give your heart a rest. The medication could improve things. Some people recover almost completely while taking them.'

Ava's father phoned after the appointment. 'What did they say?'

'The ultrasound was normal. No problems there.'

'That's *great* news . . .'

And hearing her father's relief, Ava knew she'd done the right thing, telling that lie. She saw no point in worrying her dying father.

Ava suffered with a dry cough at night. She was told that this was a side effect of the medication and would wear off with time. She didn't like being awake in the early hours – it was so quiet, she could hear her heart beating, under the covers, under skin and muscle and bone, and a panic would settle over her. She realised she was at the mercy of it, this organ she couldn't control, and she would disappear if it decided to stop.

One night, she had struggled to catch her breath and had called an ambulance, certain this was the end.

'Panic attack,' the doctor had said in A&E, his face expressionless against the bright light of the hospital room. 'It's difficult to tell the difference when there's a heart problem.'

Ava had laughed. Hah! What else could she do? Her body – already failing her – was now playing mean tricks too.

Karen had phoned as Ava was being discharged from the hospital in the early afternoon.

'Ava? Hello? You there? The reception is fuzzy. Listen, I've got a place you might like. Right on the river in Sheffield and it's sitting empty.'

One look was enough, but it was more a feeling than a look. Ava was gripped by a sense of freedom, as if the fear and worry of the last few months, the last few years, was draining away.

Standing in the sun–filled room of the one-bed flat,

a breeze cooling the space, a feeling of lightness moved through her, bringing a calm that hadn't seemed possible in her mother's cluttered bungalow.

'Yes,' Ava had said to Karen. 'I like this place a lot.'

★

It was completely by accident when walking along Orchard Lane in Sheffield that Ava came upon the Ghadimi curtain shop.

She thought of going in to see if Sam was there or if he'd already moved to London. Ava had run into his mother at the supermarket a few days before, had seen her inspecting a turnip in the vegetable aisle. For a while, they'd pretended not to see each other, wandering around with their baskets, eyes low. It was only when they were standing side by side in the checkout queue that it had become necessary for them to acknowledge each other.

Mrs Ghadimi had spoken first, in a quick, agitated way. 'You look well,' she had said, her eyes so like Sam's. But then Mrs Ghadimi's eyes had moved to the cane Ava was leaning on and shame had flashed across her face.

Ava hadn't asked about Sam. She didn't want to hear Mrs Ghadimi say, 'He's gone.' So she had talked about the weather and the new bakery section in the supermarket and when her shopping had been rung through by the cashier, she'd said, 'Tell Sam I said hello,' and left without waiting for a response.

Even if he was there, alone in the shop now, what would she say to him? He had probably moved on to that girl at the party, the way Ava had done when she was younger, moving on, kissing someone who wasn't important. But Sam was important to her. Did he think she was important too?

A box was sitting in front of her flat. She set the groceries on the kitchen counter and returned for the box. Every step took longer, but she managed well enough with the boot and cane.

She opened the box in her sitting room. Packed tightly between blocks of Styrofoam was a delicate vase, almost perfectly matched to the blue of the patterned rug she'd ordered online. A note at the bottom of the box read: *Congratulations on the new flat! Send more pictures! – Dad.*

She had no flowers to put in the vase and decided to go out in the morning to buy a few stems of white roses. She placed the vase on a floating bookshelf above the television where she could easily see it.

There was still some unpacking left to do, and Ava spent the rest of the evening looking through a photo album she'd found in her mother's bedroom when she'd been sorting out what to bring, what to throw. Ava was too young in the photographs to have any real memories of when they were taken. Memories of that time were like a bright, fast-moving light, coming into focus only for a brief moment to reveal a smile or a frown, a soundbite of laughter or a wail of pain and then, blankness. It was then that she discovered a letter behind her parents' wedding photograph. She recognised her father's assured handwriting. He had written to Elena last September, just before she'd died on the motorway.

Twenty-One

They slept in the same bed again, though there was an invisible barrier between his side and Layla's side, and Michael had found out quickly that crossing that barrier had consequences, like sleeping on the couch and more tears. For now, he had to accept that it was enough to be in the same apartment as his wife, the same room and bed, when he could so easily have been living out of a suitcase in a cheap hotel, away from the ones he loved.

He had been leaving work on time, so he could spend as much of the evening as possible with Layla and Jacob. He didn't want Layla to think about what had happened, to wonder where he was or who he was with. But Bar Five was hosting a story evening, and more than ever he felt that he needed to go and listen to other people's stories. He was tired of the ones playing out in his head, the same things being repeated.

He had told Layla that morning that he was going to be home late, hoping that the advance warning would mean she wouldn't worry. She had simply nodded, her face betraying no emotion. He left work early, knowing the bar would be lively, and even at six, he found most of the seats at the front were gone. He placed his jacket on a chair just to the right of the stage and went to the bar, where he ordered a whisky. There, he recognised the woman who had spoken about her daughter Clara. She was drinking a glass of white wine. He approached her, introducing himself by saying he'd heard her story months ago and it had touched him. He asked how the celebration went for Clara's first birthday.

She smiled, a heartfelt smile. 'It was beautiful. She felt so close.'

The bar was already getting full, so Michael returned to his seat.

The first speaker was a middle-aged woman and she talked about her health anxieties. She said she used to avoid leaving her house and would hold her breath when she walked past people on the street. And if someone coughed next to her, she would spiral into panic. She talked about the work she did on herself, catching those anxious thoughts and testing them. Were her fears hypothetical? What action could she take, if any? She had to ban herself from googling symptoms because the diagnosis was always death. A few people in the audience laughed and when she spoke of overcoming her anxiety, they clapped for her.

A middle-aged man spoke next about his sex addiction, and how he was dating someone new but they hadn't had sex yet, even though it had almost been a few months. He talked about all the porn he used to watch and the escorts he had hired. But he had joined a support group and found Pete – a mentor, his new best friend. He felt that he'd overcome his addiction, and at the end of his talk, the room cheered for him too.

Michael thought: what about stories of failure? Those

who had not overcome their demons? Those without a clear resolution, those who were still finding their way? Would people applaud those stories with as much enthusiasm?

He was on his third glass of whisky when the MC opened the floor to the audience, as was the practice towards the end of every event. Did anyone want to share their story?

A hush fell over the bar as everyone looked around to see who would be brave enough to take to the stage. Michael rested his empty glass on the table and made his way to the stage.

'What's your name?' the MC asked.

'Michael Bridges.'

The audience encouraged him with gentle clapping. Then he was alone up there, blinking under the hot spotlight. He flushed, his heart beating fast.

Someone coughed. A woman in a grey suit near the front smiled at him. He swallowed, edged towards the microphone. He could feel everyone's gaze on him, all at once. After years of lecturing, he knew he was a proficient public speaker. But it was easier in the classroom, when the topic wasn't his own life, his guilt.

'I . . .' he began. Then what? What did he want to say? He felt stupid for demanding everyone's attention. Why should anyone listen to him?

He took a step back from the microphone, hesitated for a moment before turning and leaving the stage. He rushed past the people at the bar who watched him go. Outside, every part of him felt flushed and the rain did nothing to cool the heat surging through him from the humiliation.

'Michael,' Layla's voice called out to him.

Michael turned and saw his wife, in a raincoat, her hair pulled back from her face. She was standing in the doorway of the bar.

He thought he was imagining this scene. How else to explain her there?

'I don't understand,' she said, still standing in the doorway.

'I come here sometimes.'

She pulled her hood up, slowly approaching, and when she was close, her sharp eyes met his. 'Why? Why do you come here?'

He wiped the rain or sweat from his forehead – he wasn't sure what was what, still catching his breath from the humiliation. 'I feel like people understand me here. I don't feel like such an asshole. It's hard to explain.'

'Explain it to me,' she said, her tone softer.

They walked home and he told her about his mother being killed in a crash almost a year ago now. The alcohol in her blood. How he had done *nothing* to help. All those years, he could've tried to help. And Ava. He'd left her to deal with it all. He didn't even go to the funeral.

'And, well, my father's dying.' He laughed. It sounded absurd to him, telling Layla about his father. 'Cancer. He's been sending all these letters and emails, and I've just been ignoring them.' He was shaking, his whole body trembling from the shock of speaking the truth.

Layla stopped walking and Michael faced her. She steadied his hands, interlacing his fingers with hers. 'Why didn't you tell me?'

'I'm ashamed.'

'You should have been open with *me*. I thought you were meeting a woman tonight.'

Michael shook his head. 'No. That won't happen again.'

At the apartment, Layla paid the sitter, who counted her money and, when she was satisfied, went home. Layla admitted that she had seen in Michael's emails the ticket he'd purchased to Bar Five and had hired the girl to look after their son so she could find out what he was up to. He thought to say something, to tell her there was no need to investigate him in this way, but he was tired and didn't want an argument.

In bed, Layla said, 'What happened to your mother isn't your fault.'

Michael moved his feet between the cold sheets. He wanted desperately to believe her.

'You need to see your father,' she said, reaching her hand across the invisible barrier, resting it there on his chest. 'If you're serious about making things work with us.'

Layla had taken to going for a walk after dinner while Michael was putting Jacob to bed. She said the walks helped clear her mind. The next evening, she returned a little later than usual. Her hair was wet and she shook raindrops from her coat before hanging it above the radiator to dry. She said she'd been walking five blocks in the rain when a blister on the back of her heel had started to bother her, so she'd stopped in a coffee shop and wrote out a list. She showed Michael her list, written on a napkin.

Ways you could have dealt with your family issues: cooking class, pottery, TELLING ME, yoga, counselling, boxing, seeing them again, NOT FUCKING OTHER

WOMEN, candle-making, writing to your sister and father, writing a story about a guy with family issues.

Michael opened his mouth to speak, to offer his apology, his regrets. To say how he suffered with guilt. But Layla raised her hand and said, 'I'm not looking for a response,' and then, 'I'm going to bed.'

Early the next morning, they took Jacob to nursery. They hadn't taken him back since that dreadful day when he'd fallen ill.

Layla cried a little but said, 'He'll be OK.'

They watched him being led away by one of the teachers, then, when he started playing cars with a girl, Layla squeezed Michael's hand.

Slowly, they walked out of the play area. They stopped in front of the subway, stepping to the side as people rushed past them to get down the steps.

'Good luck today.'

Layla smiled, apprehensive. 'It feels like my first day at school.'

She was returning to work, her first day back in nearly a year. Michael wrapped his arms around her and was so pleased when she rested her head in the crook of his neck. But then too quickly the moment passed, and she pulled away, and they went their separate ways into work.

Twenty-Two

The other people taking the psychology conversion course were all looking to change career paths. Except for one student who was a recent graduate, most were in their thirties, if not older. Ava had feared being surrounded by bright-eyed eighteen-year-olds who didn't know about a world outside of school. But she was sitting next to a woman who'd trained and worked as a teacher for eleven years. And she'd made friends with another woman, Soraya, who was still working in a HR role on a part-time basis. Mature students, the uni liked to call them, though they got up to some immature things, like sweeping all the free condoms at the student union into their hand-bags and leaving them on park benches as they walked home.

Soraya had been to Ava's flat a few times and they'd had drinks in the bar across the way. Once, when a handsome undergrad tried to chat her up, Ava had whispered that her flat was close. He didn't understand that she was teasing him, his small teeth chattering nervously while he talked about needing to get up early for a rugby match the next day. She left her walking stick back at her flat on those nights out and moved a little more slowly.

Ava liked studying on her balcony. The weather had cooled, but she liked watching the river change colour as the sun shifted and dimmed. She was working on an assignment about the ethical considerations of placebo when her father sent his memoirs, a large untitled document attached to a one-line email.

Here they are, he wrote. *See you in a few days!*

Ava tried to return to her assignment but found it impossible to focus. She could think only of the memoirs and what they might reveal about her father, about herself.

She put on a thick woollen jumper and poured a glass of white wine. She began to read. Quickly, she skimmed through sections about his career, his time as a journalist and editor, covering stories of conflict. That was nearly two-thirds of the book.

She wanted to read about a different kind of conflict, so she searched for 'Elena' and the document took her to page 126. Ava had hoped to find love, some intimacy in the story of her parents' first meeting, but her father's focus fell on the IRA bombings. Elena was even introduced in terms of her Greek-Cypriot heritage and the conflict she'd experienced abroad. There was no real indication of who they were together and the life they had shared.

Ava skimmed through the rest of the manuscript, feeling increasingly agitated. She poured more wine, though alcohol interacted with her medication, and she needed to be careful about her blood pressure dropping too low.

He explained the divorce in only a few lines. He said they had argued a lot towards the end, that they had grown apart and become different people. Ava and Michael were mentioned a handful of times, mostly in relation to the difficulties of balancing parenthood and his career in journalism.

Ava wanted to yell at her laptop. His whole account lacked specificity . . . what was he reaching for? She couldn't tell. She had hoped for texture, to understand her father's mind, his motivations, who he was before he had children, who he was becoming now. More than that, she had hoped for an apology – that this memoir was one big apology for the ways he'd hurt his family. But there was almost no regret here, their time together covered in such vague terms. Did she mean so little to him? Were they – she and Michael and their mother – merely shadows, dark and empty, coming between him and his work? She felt more disconnected from him than ever.

She typed 'Sandra Banks' and there were no matches in the document.

The only section that moved Ava was what he'd written about his childhood, specifically about his mother. He wrote about the abuse he'd suffered at the hands of his father. His mother had stepped in when she could to protect him. His mother, who had been the victim of hate crimes in the seventies in the Midlands, when the IRA were terrorising. She'd had a beer bottle thrown at her head in a local pub, had been called 'dirty Irish slag'. She'd felt the need to disguise her accent or else make clear her politics when she stepped into a room full of strangers. Years later, he'd travelled on an overnight flight from Sydney to see his ill mother, but she had died before he could reach her. 'Devastated' – he'd written that emotion well.

Lee phoned later that week to say that he didn't think he could safely make the journey to pick her up from Sheffield and then take her back; his health was deteriorating more quickly than he'd anticipated.

For days, Ava had been thinking about whether to go. He wanted to have that picnic on Primrose Hill. His last birthday. She'd made up her mind finally during the call: she would go. She would ask him about the letter he'd sent Elena. She would watch his face to understand why, after all these years, he'd pushed himself back into her life when she occupied practically no space in his memoirs. Why this recent contact? And why was he asking for forgiveness, asking if she would see him again? Ava would find out the story there, give him a chance to explain, and then she would say goodbye. That was her plan.

Ava told her father she would take the train to London, and then he coughed into the phone for a while, and she felt helpless on the other end.

The train journey to London seemed endless. Ava had a window seat, so she could watch the rolling Derbyshire landscape play out in front of her, blurring when it started to rain and then coming back into focus when the sun found its way through, before disappearing altogether.

At Doncaster station, a middle-aged woman in a big red coat got on the train and sat in the seat facing Ava. It was clear that she wanted to talk, the way she kept looking over. She complimented Ava on her hair, how thick it was, how strong and dark.

Ava smiled politely and stared out of the window, but the woman kept talking at her. 'Why are you going to London?' she asked.

'I'm visiting someone,' Ava said, reluctant to offer any further details.

'Me too.' The woman pulled her thin lips into her

mouth like she might explode. 'I'm seeing a man. We met on the internet.'

She took off her red coat and put it up in the overhead shelf, the sleeve dangling like a corpse. When she sat back in her seat, she asked Ava if she had enough room for her legs. Ava said she was fine. Her walking stick was leaning against the window.

'My mother thinks I'm going to be returned to her in a suitcase, chopped up into tiny pieces.' She smiled. 'But we've been talking online for months now, myself and Ife. It's like he knows me better than anyone. Better than my mother.'

Ava nodded.

'I've booked a hotel, even though he's got a spare room,' she said, like she was trying to assuage her own guilt. 'It's right in the middle of Piccadilly. I've always wanted to go to Fortnum & Mason and buy myself a basket of jams.'

The train conductor came around to check tickets for people who had got on at Doncaster and the woman said the ticket was in her red coat, so she had to stand up and get it from the shelf, but when she checked both pockets, it wasn't there. She remembered the ticket was in her handbag, and the conductor looked bored.

She showed the conductor her ticket and turned to Ava. 'Have you got a boyfriend?'

'I do. His name is Sam.'

'Is he in London?'

'Yes.'

'Oh, how lovely.'

Ava knew that she'd never see this woman again, that there was no harm in indulging her little fantasy, imagining that Sam was her boyfriend and she was travelling to see him in Camden. He would be waiting for her at the station and they would look at each other with happiness from across the barriers. Then they would go straight to his flat, where they would make love intermittently throughout the afternoon while his flatmates were out doing whatever it was that they did in the daytime, and once they'd had enough of that, they'd walk through the city, point to old buildings, kiss under shaded trees and bending lamp posts.

When the train guard announced that they would be pulling into London, the middle-aged woman put on her red coat. She couldn't wait to get there, couldn't wait to see her online boyfriend in the flesh. She wished Ava luck, and Ava did the same.

She waited for the last people in her carriage to disembark before she got her rucksack from the overhead shelf. She leant into the walking stick for support and slowly made her way onto the platform. Her leg was stiff from the journey.

King's Cross was full of movement. People rushing to catch their trains, others just walking at a fast pace with their eyes on their phones.

Lee was waiting for her on the other side of the barriers, his face eager and searching. He looked thinner than he had in August, no colour to his complexion. This was the look of an invalid. She felt happy as he spotted her and waved, but also afraid, seeing him so frail.

'Let me take your bag,' he said.

'I can manage.' She tried to conceal her concern at the flash of his thin wrist slipping out of his sleeve as he reached for her bag.

He nodded, his eyes darting to the exit. 'I'm parked

kind of illegally. If you don't mind, I'll go on ahead and bring the car around.'

After he dashed off, Ava made her way slowly to the taxi stand. She stood waiting next to an old lady gripping her walker. The woman looked over to Ava, her eyes hooded with age. She reminded Ava of her grandmother Katerina, that sense of knowing.

'It's supposed to be awfully cool this afternoon,' she said. And then, 'Don't ever go to Paris in the summer. It smells of piss.'

Ava nodded and was glad to see her father's Jeep. He popped open the passenger door from the inside and she put her walking stick in first before climbing into the seat.

'I'm not a fan of driving into this busy station,' he said, his fingers white against the steering wheel. 'But we haven't got far to go at least.'

Ava felt a dryness in her mouth, having avoided water and tea for fear of having to use the train toilet. 'How have you been?'

'Not great.' As if to prove his point, he coughed – a deep cough that seemed to emanate from the very core of him. He relaxed a little as they left the station and turned onto the main road, but when they hit an area of roadworks with orange pylons, he started coughing again, hacking into his hand.

Ava searched in her bag for a bottle of water. 'We should pull over.'

'It's all right,' he strained between coughs. 'Just hand me a tissue from that box there.'

Ava did so hurriedly. Bright spots of blood appeared on the tissue. He folded it up with his free hand, put the tissue away into his pocket. Ava felt a faint flutter in her chest.

'Should we go to the hospital?'

'No,' he said flatly, his eyes on the road ahead. 'We're going to have a nice day.'

The roadworks cleared, and the streets started to look familiar to Ava. Victorian houses. Tidy lawns. Big trees above them and rust-coloured leaves falling onto the bonnet.

Ava wanted to take him to the hospital. But he seemed so determined to get to Primrose Hill, to celebrate his last birthday. What could she say?

He parked the car on a side street and came around and opened the passenger seat. At once, Ava felt cold, as if the gust of wind had turned her bones into metal. She remembered then the plates and nails drilled into her pelvis, keeping her together.

From the boot, her father removed two large bags filled with food and blankets to lay down on the grass.

'I was going to bring the ball for us to kick around, but . . .' He smiled at her. 'We've both been in better shape.'

She laughed, remembering how she used to play with her father, kicking the ball to him. She'd clung to his encouraging words, those times they'd been out together, away from her critical mother.

Slowly, they began to climb up the hill to get the view of the city.

'I always loved it when we came here,' Lee said.

Ava wanted to take his hand or pat his shoulder, realising how much the trip meant to him. But she resisted, not knowing how to reconcile her father's sentimental mood with his complete disregard for her in his memoirs, and that letter he'd written her mother.

'Michael might be coming. He asked about my birthday. I assumed you told him?'

'Yes . . . he came to see me.'

Ava remembered her brother's face, the pain there, when she'd told him to leave the bungalow. It had surprised her that she'd been capable of hurting him at all. She'd felt satisfied, watching his face crumble.

Ava sensed her breath quicken now as her feet moved a little faster, climbing up that steep hill.

Twenty-Three

Michael thought of the last time he had been to Primrose Hill. His father had returned from his office Christmas party early in the morning. He was drunk. Elena's voice travelled through the walls, insisting that there was the smell of another woman on him. 'It's there on your neck,' she'd said, 'on your balls.'

An hour later, Michael's father came into his bedroom, rocked Michael's shoulder and said, 'Get your coat. It's snowing.' He woke up Ava in the same way.

Their mother appeared at the top of the staircase while they were putting their shoes and coats on by the front door. She was still in her nightdress. 'Where are you going?'

'Sledging. Down Primrose Hill,' Lee said excitedly. 'You want to come too?'

A moment of hesitation. Elena liked getting out of the house after an argument. A family truce held when they were outside of their home.

But her face darkened, the argument not over yet. 'It's seven in the morning,' she said, turning back into her bedroom and slamming the door.

Michael and Ava waited outside for their father while he got the sledges from the shed in the back garden. A light cotton snow fell on their noses and chins. Ava stuck out her tongue and Michael told her she was ingesting pollutants and people's shit.

'I don't care,' she said, taunting her brother by catching snowflakes with her small pink tongue.

Their father appeared in the driveway. 'Let's go! Let's go!' He dragged the sledges behind him as they walked through the blanketed streets, leaving lines in the snow, lines that weren't straight because he was still drunk.

When they got to the top of the hill, the view was immaculate, so peaceful and still, with layers of white settling into Regent's Park, a distant mist rising into a faint sherbet sky. The city in metal stood behind all that winter. For a while, they admired the scene, then Ava said she wanted to sledge down. She did so at great speed, and Michael was relieved when she reached the bottom of the hill, stood up and gave a thumbs-up before starting to make her way back up.

Their father cheered her on. 'Woo-hoo!'

He swayed a little and Michael was sure that if he nudged him he would fall flat on his back, a dead snow angel. They watched Ava slowly climb back up the hill, working her way through the thick snow, burdened by the weight of the sledge.

'I think you should leave,' Michael said to his father. His feet were wet in his shoes. 'It would be best for everyone if you were gone.' He had never spoken to his father like that, but it seemed possible to speak his mind up there with the cold morning unfolding, the white landscape before them. Michael thought of the beautiful girl, Sandra Banks, how she'd returned to the house a second time, asking for Lee with tears in her eyes, a look of desperation across her face. But mostly he thought of his mother, who'd smashed a glass of red wine against the kitchen wall a few days ago, after another argument, and then taken a shard from the floor and cut herself with it. The blood pooling on her forearm – Michael could not forget that.

Lee didn't say anything now, perhaps knowing himself that things could not carry on this way. He kept his eyes on Ava, his favourite thing. When she reached the top, he gave her a high-five. 'Let's build a snowman.'

It was a big snowman, too wide at the base and leaning to one side, but still recognisable as a snowman. There was nothing to accessorise it with, no scarf or coal to offer for eyes, so the snowman remained senseless.

When they returned to the house, Lee and Elena spent all day in the bedroom. At first, Michael thought his father might be sleeping, but then the shouting began. He made ham sandwiches for himself and Ava and turned up the television. It all came to a head in the afternoon. He heard Elena yell, then a crash – something hurled against the wall.

Their father rushed down the stairs with a suitcase. He said he would be staying at a hotel for a few days. He kissed Ava's cheek, squeezed her between his arms, and patted Michael on the head.

Elena came down to the sitting room a few hours later, disoriented, still in her nightdress.

'What the hell happened on that hill?'

★

Michael imagined how it might be, seeing his father again, returning to this place. All the movies he'd watched about

281

family reunions came to mind, the comedy of them. Everyone smiling at each other, embarrassed, not really wanting to be there. There was always a big explosion where dark truths were shared, long-standing grievances aired, but all ended well enough, with hugs and promises to keep in touch. He could not see his own reunion ending that way. He wondered if his sister would leave once she saw him there. He could only hope that she would stay a while so that he might tell her that he needed her in his life, that she was important to him.

At the top of the hill, he sat on the pale grass with his knees close to his chest. The trees below were brushstrokes of autumn and, further still, the city jutted into the grey sky.

It wasn't busy for a Saturday. Just a few families scattered at the top of the hill, with more people dotted through Regent's Park. Occasionally, a dog ran to fetch a ball. And a few runners in their serious running gear were sprinting uphill, calves straining. Michael put a cigarette into his mouth.

He remembered then to text Layla to say he'd arrived safely. He tried to work out the time difference, counting backwards on his fingers. It was early morning in New York. Layla had an important client meeting. Jacob would be in nursery. He took a picture of the view: *Primrose Hill. Missing you both*, he wrote below the photo and sent it to Layla.

He felt a hand on his shoulder. Michael turned back and there was his father, crouching behind him.

Michael was unsure how to greet him after so many years. He thought how his father looked like a dehydrated version of himself. Here was the man he had been so afraid of, old and deteriorating, fragile. He would rather not have seen his father this way. If he squinted, it would have been like standing in front of their grandfather, and he wondered if all men ended up looking like their fathers.

'I can't believe it's you,' Lee said.

'It's me.'

They shook hands.

Ava stayed back, leaning on a cane, unsmiling.

'This is a perfect spot,' Lee said, and he pulled a large checked blanket from one of the bags he'd brought. Michael helped him lay it down, putting a stone on the corner as the wind was blowing it around.

Ava sat on the edge, away from Michael.

'We need to celebrate. This is a moment to celebrate,' Lee said hurriedly, searching through the other bag. He pulled out a bottle of champagne. He had always loved to pop open a champagne bottle in a room full of people.

He coughed, an aggressive cough that made him double up, the bottle dangling from his grip.

'Are you sure you're all right?' Ava asked.

'I'm fine.'

Lee passed around plastic flute glasses. He struggled to open the bottle, but there was the pop, and a little fizz spurted out before he filled each of their glasses.

His hands looked large against the bottle, the hands of an old man, spotted and worn. He raised his plastic cup and said, 'To us.'

Ava said, 'Happy birthday.'

'Thank you. Well. It *is* a happy birthday this year.'

They drank. A chocolate Labrador ran past at speed, retrieving a ball that had landed nearby. Lee unpacked the food – store-bought things: coleslaw, hummus and vegetables, cheese wrapped in prosciutto. He laid out spoons and paper plates and said to start eating.

He turned to Michael. 'How was your flight?'

'OK. Smooth.'

'Good.'

'Ava says I'm a grandfather.'

'Yes.' Michael did the usual thing when people asked about Jacob because it was easier that way, pulling out his phone, showing the latest photos and videos.

Lee set down his plate of food. He reached into his breast pocket for his glasses before scrolling through the pictures slowly.

'Lovely,' he said, smiling at the screen. 'Lovely boy. He looks a bit like Ava, doesn't he? The mouth.' And he drew the shape of a sad mouth into the air. His hands started shaking, holding the mobile. He returned it to Michael.

Grief seemed to spread over Lee's face then, perhaps the realisation of what he'd missed, what he'd given up, and Michael felt a deep satisfaction that his father should regret his life. For years he had wanted to see his father like this, his head bowed, full of misery.

'I know this is awkward,' Lee said. 'I wish it wasn't.' He shrugged. 'But this is how things have turned out. I was not the best father. I know. But anyway, thank you for coming. I'm touched that you're here.'

Ava raised her glass and drank. Their father poured more champagne and when they had finished that bottle, he opened another. Michael began to feel warm from the alcohol, his head a bit lighter, and he leant back a little. He loved this picture of London, the sense of freedom up there on the hill, being able to see so far.

Ava pulled out a wrapped gift from her backpack.

'Oh, what's this? No need, no need.' But Lee tore through the paper like a greedy child. She'd gotten him a knitted scarf.

'Lovely. This is really lovely. Thank you,' he said, wrapping the brown scarf around his neck. It looked like he was drowning in mud. 'I've actually got gifts for you both. I guess you could call them gifts. I wanted to go over some details with the two of you, if you don't mind.' He put a prawn into his mouth, chewed and swallowed. 'You're going to hear from Neil Kirkpatrick soon. He's my solicitor. He'll be in touch in a few days to discuss your inheritance. Everything is left to you two. The house, all my savings. Insurance. Neil will give you all the details.'

'You don't have to worry about me,' Michael said. 'You could give everything to Ava.'

'Don't go speaking on my behalf,' Ava said with sudden sharpness.

Lee looked surprised that his parting gifts were being refused. 'Well . . . you'll both have time to think about what you want to do about the money, whether to keep it or give it away. But it would mean a lot if you used it on yourselves.' Lee turned to Ava. 'On your education,' and then to Michael, 'on your little boy.'

The wind picked up, lifting a paper plate and empty glass into the air. They landed a few feet away. Michael chased after them, and when he returned, Lee was telling Ava a story about their mother. They'd come to Primrose Hill to watch the fireworks one bonfire night – bright bursts of colour lightening up the night sky in different parts of the city. Their mother had loved watching the spectacle. But she was heavily pregnant with Michael and when someone set off a firework close by, she had taken fright and gone into labour.

They all knew the story. But they listened while Lee told it again.

He looked ahead, to the horizon. 'Your mother loved coming here.'

'Why didn't you tell me that you wrote to Mum last year?' Ava said.

Lee looked surprised. 'Oh, well, I'm not sure why I'd need to mention it . . .'

'You had no right,' Ava continued. 'No right to ask for her forgiveness.'

Michael watched this exchange, confused at first. But he thought it made sense, that Lee would've written to Elena, if he'd reached out to them too.

Their father sighed. 'I didn't like the way things were left between us. Your mother was important to me. We shared a *life* together.'

'It doesn't seem that way. Especially not in your memoirs. She's barely a footnote.'

'It was hard for me to write about us.'

Ava sat up a little. 'You paid more attention to strangers than you did to her. To any of us.' Ava took her cane and stood now, towering above their father. 'Did she ever write back?'

Lee ran his hand over his face. 'Well, yes. She did.' He looked up at Ava, his head craning up. 'She wanted to meet.'

'And was it arranged? A meeting?'

Lee looked into his empty lap. 'It was, yes. October fifteenth. But she never turned up.'

'Hah!' But then Ava's face darkened, her mood sharp

like weather. 'Un-fucking-believable. So she was travelling to see you when she was killed on the M1.'

Michael looked at his father, the way he had retreated into himself, sinking behind that brown scarf.

'I wanted to tell you when you mentioned the day of her accident.'

'But you didn't.'

'I worried that I'd never see you again. That you'd cut me out.'

'You were right to worry.' Ava turned and started to walk down the hill.

Their father stood, intent on following her, but he began to cough, and the force of those coughs, racking his chest, almost folded him in half.

He gestured for Michael to follow Ava and managed to croak out his demand. 'Go after your sister.'

Michael hesitated. His father was still coughing with all of his body, as if he were about to expel his lungs.

Lee pointed again in Ava's direction. 'Please.'

Michael caught up with his sister in Regent's Park. She was looking at the metal structure that was the aviary of London Zoo.

'I never liked going to the zoo,' she said. 'All those animals behind fences. It's just a bit crap, isn't it?' She began to cry, tears sliding silently down her face.

Michael stepped closer. 'Jacob loves the zoo in Central Park. You should come. Meet Jacob and Layla in New York.'

She shook her head, wiped tears with her sleeve.

'I just can't believe Mum was going to see him,' she said. 'After all the things she told me about him. He still had this power over her.'

Michael put his hand on his sister's shoulder, and she leant into him. 'I think we need more alcohol.'

He led her away from the zoo and out of the green, through side streets and brightly painted houses. They walked along the canal and surfaced on Camden High Street. More colour and movement there. They sat outside a bar near the lock where a band was playing.

'The guy who hit me with his car moved here. To Camden.'

'The one you love?'

'Did I say that?' Ava shrugged, nursing her beer. 'It wasn't love. He's too young. He watches all these shows that I don't really get.'

Michael lit a cigarette. 'You want to go see him now?'

'No,' she said, her tone softer. 'I'm leaving it. It would never have worked anyway.'

The music got louder, the lead singer of the band cradling the microphone between his hands.

'What's Layla like?'

Michael watched a young couple cross the street, laughing. 'Beautiful. Creative. She's writing a lot.'

'What, like fiction?'

'Yes. One of her talents. She's a lawyer.'

'She sounds too good for you.'

'She is.' Michael put out his cigarette, thinking of his wife. 'You'd like her.'

They stayed for another beer, and watched the light slowly fade, and Michael became aware of more people sitting around them, dressed in denim and leather. The air was much cooler, but at least the wind had died down. He looked at his watch.

'I think we should go see Dad,' he said. 'He looked like

288

he was in rough shape. The way he was coughing.'

Ava kept her eyes on the band.

'I'm sure he never thought she would end up in that accident.'

'That's the thing,' Ava said, laying her palm on her forehead. 'He never *thinks* about anybody but himself. It's always about what he wants. He wanted to go to Sydney. So he went. He wants to see us now. So here we are.'

'If you can honestly say that you're ready to walk away from him, then we'll leave it,' Michael said.

Ava tapped her fingers against the table. 'I can't forgive him.'

'You don't have to.'

'I don't forgive *you*.'

It was dark when they took the Tube back from Camden. The streets were much quieter in Hampstead, the shops already closed. A few lights glowed from restaurant windows and in the distance the shape of people moved between shadows and lamp posts.

'It's weird being back,' Michael said. 'I was expecting to hate it, but I feel a bit nostalgic.'

Ava smirked. 'Remember that snowman we made when Dad dragged us out of bed?'

'It was a pathetic snowman.'

'Fitting,' Ava said.

They walked to their father's house. His Jeep was not in the driveway, but a light was on. They rang the doorbell. No answer. Michael tried the door and found it unlocked.

In the hall, they called out to their father. 'Hello? Hello?'

'I'm just in here.'

They followed his strained voice. He said he was in the downstairs toilet.

'Is everything OK?' Ava said.

'I'm not sure.'

Ava and Michael waited on the other side of the door.

'I took a pill,' their father said. 'It was supposed to send me off. Gently.'

'Send you off where exactly?' Ava said, panic rising.

'Well, into a peaceful death.'

'Jesus.'

Ava looked at her brother, blood draining from her face. 'What the hell?'

'Are you OK?' Michael asked.

'I'm still alive,' he said. 'So it hasn't worked. But I've got some digestive issues . . . Basically, it's hard for me to get off the toilet. And I'm feeling quite faint.'

'Christ!' Ava said, reaching for her phone and dialling for an ambulance.

'Don't worry,' Michael said. 'It's going to be all right.'

The ambulance took their father to A&E at the Royal Free Hospital. They followed behind in a taxi.

When the doctor pulled back the curtain a few hours later, he looked down at his clipboard and said the pill had just been a powerful laxative.

'It explains the loose stools,' the doctor said. 'The dizziness was most likely brought on by dehydration.'

They waited for a nurse to remove the IV line from his arm. Their father, his face drained of colour, apologised.

'I'm sorry for giving you a scare.'

'A scare?' Ava said. 'You were going to kill yourself! The first time we've all been together in years. Did you ever think how traumatised we'd be, discovering your body?'

'I'm sorry. I didn't think—' He stopped himself. 'It's just that I don't *feel* like myself anymore. These coughing fits. And my energy is just gone. I get so tired now.'

There were tears in his eyes. They had never seen their father deflated like that, weary of life, and Michael felt a deep pity for him then. Their father, who had always been up, brimming with energy.

The nurse came in with her practised smile and practised hands, and in a swift motion removed the needle, stemming the trickle of blood with a cotton-wool pad before taping it to their father's arm. They were free to go.

In the taxi, Michael asked his father where he'd gotten that pill.

'Online. I'll be giving it a bad review, anyway.'

'I don't think we can joke about this quite yet,' Ava said.

The house was cold. Michael lit the log burner and Lee ordered pizzas. They sat down in the sitting room, drained, not knowing what to say to each other now.

'We ought to do something to lighten the mood,' Lee said. 'What do good families do?'

Ava rubbed her eyes. 'They play games. Like Monopoly or charades.'

They didn't play Monopoly or charades. The pizza arrived and they ate, weary and silent in front of the television. Ava drifted into sleep in the armchair by the fire Michael had lit. They'd needed the warmth, something to take the chill away.

Michael was sitting next to his father on the brown leather sofa. They were watching a comedian who wasn't funny talk about his receding hairline and erectile problems.

'In your letters and emails, you never apologised,' Michael said, finding the courage to confront his father. 'You called me pathetic. You said I would never be a man.'

'Did I say those things?' Lee laughed. 'It's strange what sticks. I remember, years ago, confronting my own father about something he'd said. "Lee, you're no better than us." I hated him for saying that, because deep down I knew it, of course, but I wanted to be. Better, I mean. And what does that say about me?'

The fire crackled. Michael noticed a large shadow of Lee cast against the wall. He saw how it was pointless to look for an apology from his father, and he turned back to the comedy show.

A new comedian took to the stage who was even less funny. He said to the audience, 'You're killing me!'

Michael laughed, remembering his parents' friend. 'Are you still in touch with Robert Embringham?'

'God, no,' Lee said. 'He used to say that, didn't he? You're killing me! I heard he's gotten himself into trouble. An actress he used to work with has accused him of something.'

'I never liked him,' Michael said.

Lee nodded. 'No. But, you know, he was always a riot.' Lee looked into the fire. 'I miss the dinner parties. They were such fun! I hosted a gala in November and it just wasn't the same. People have changed.'

'How so?'

Lee shrugged. 'I don't know. Everyone's just so serious now. Especially young people.' He leant closer to Michael. His whole face seemed then to animate with life. 'Did I ever tell you about the time I interviewed Keith Summers from Sugarhead?'

'No.'

He sat up a little, energised. 'We got on so well. For the whole week he was touring the UK, I was there on his bus. We stopped off at every McDonald's to get Big Macs.' Lee laughed. 'All that wealth and he just wanted to eat Big Macs. And the screaming people when we'd turn up at a service station to get McDonald's – it was mayhem!'

'I can imagine.'

Lee nodded. 'It really was something.'

WINTER

Twenty-Four

Ava saw Sam at the campus library when she was working on a Saturday afternoon. He was sitting in one of those carrel desks, books piled up next to his laptop, and he looked like he didn't have plans to move for the day. Ava felt such a flutter, watching him from behind a bookshelf. He was typing away on his computer, flipping through his pages of notes.

He looked different, stubble on his face, his hair worn shorter. She preferred him this way. He looked like a scholar, a tasteful shabbiness to his clothes, with patches on the elbows of his jumper. It had crossed her mind to approach him and ask what had happened to Camden. What had kept him back?

She wanted to tell him about all the changes she'd made since they'd seen each other last – the move, her course, everything that had happened with her father and Michael. She wanted Sam to see her without crutches, without a walking stick, her own legs propelling her forward, and perhaps then his guilt would be appeased, if he thought of her at all now. She still thought of him, thought about that night they'd spent together.

But Ava kept her distance. She continued to stack the shelves with books from her metal trolley. It was work that she enjoyed doing, because it meant that she came across unusual titles, subjects far removed from her life – from the Inquisition to seventeenth-century European law and Greek philosophy. Occasionally, when it wasn't busy, she would take a book up to the fifth floor where there was an old, worn chair in a corner by the window and read for half an hour or so, before she thought the head librarian might wonder what she was doing.

Closer to exams, the library was brimming with people revising and researching so that they could write their essays. Soraya had told Ava that some students came to the library when an essay topic was announced and checked out all the books so that others didn't stand a chance with their own papers. She didn't know if this was true, and suspected Soraya was being a little dramatic, but Ava made sure to set aside the books she needed for her own work well in advance. It was one of the perks of working at the library.

She did most of her studying off campus, at cafés where the natural light and gentle hum of people talking seemed to lighten denser topics. There was something about being in a room full of strangers that Ava found deeply appealing. She liked to imagine their lives, what they hoped for and dreaded.

She was enjoying her course and had become especially interested in memory. It had fascinated her to learn about the anatomy of the brain, how everything was filed and compartmentalised like the books in this library – only the books could be altered, new words added to them, others taken away. They'd done experiments to show the power of suggestion, how long-term and short-term memories could be manipulated, and it made her wonder how many of her own memories were true.

By 5 p.m., the end of her shift, it was already dark outside, the days much shorter now they were entering winter. Ava felt more like herself when the weather was cooler, not as dizzy as she'd been in the summer months. Her cardiologist, Dr Marez, said this was because her medication dropped her blood pressure, but the cold helped to raise it back up. Ava had been to see her a few weeks before. She had been told that her heart function had improved and that her heart was on the borderline of what would be classified as normal, though just a little larger. The left ventricle was still slightly dilated. She'd need to keep taking the medication, but it was good news. The cardiologist had smiled, surprising Ava, who had not believed her capable of a smile. She was pleased with herself, Ava realised. The side effects of the tablets had mostly worn off and it was just one more thing she did in the morning, taking those pills, brushing her teeth, applying eyeliner when she got ready for a day of classes.

As Ava left the library, she thought of Sam, probably still up there on the third floor. She felt agitated, knowing he was close, just within reach. A wind kicked up the dead leaves scattered along the asphalt. It was the season she enjoyed the most, winter. The layering of clothes, lights strung up in darkened streets, snow falling in American films about Christmas. She buttoned her coat – it was cold – and walked to the campus café over in the next building. It was always buzzing there: poetry readings, political-awareness campaigns, discussions, debates.

She managed to secure a table by the window. Soraya

would be joining her soon. A boy with hair in his eyes sang and played the guitar in a corner of the café, his music inoffensive, easy enough to ignore. She opened her textbook. One of the articles assigned for her course had to do with assisted suicide, and she thought then of her father and that dud pill. A month after that, she'd received a call from the hospital to say her father was in a grave condition and that she should come. She'd rushed to see him, all the time remembering the passage she'd read in his memoirs about rushing home to see his dying mother. He hadn't made it. His flight had been too long. But she'd got there in time and held his hand. She thought of her father often, when she caught a glimpse of the blue vase on the floating shelf above her television – the one he'd picked out for her and, always, she kept a white daffodil in that vase.

Michael had returned for the funeral and had leant into his sister for support. When Michael and Ava were alone in a pub, after the wake, both quite drunk, they confessed to each other how they felt relieved that it was over, and their shared sentiment diffused their guilt a little.

Ava looked now at her watch. Soraya was twenty minutes late for their revision session. It wasn't like her not to be on time. Ava checked her phone and saw a handful of messages from her, saying how she'd been sent home from work because she'd been vomiting in the toilets all morning. It was probably that stomach bug going around campus.

Ava was starting to read the first case study when Sam Ghadimi approached the table.

'Hello,' he said, smiling softly. 'Do you mind if I sit?'

Ava flushed, feeling suddenly like she was wearing too many layers.

'Sure,' she said. 'No, I don't mind.'

He unzipped his coat and left it on the back of the chair where he sat. His shoulders were broader, and Ava wondered if he'd been using his membership to the campus gym.

'I've seen you around here,' he said.

'Have you?' Ava wondered why he hadn't said hello. Had he been avoiding her? And why then was he approaching her now? She pushed back the sleeves of her tatty grey jumper and thought how tired she must look after an afternoon of work. She was between eyebrow threading, which was not so great either.

'I didn't want to encroach on your space. Are you studying?'

'Yes,' she said. And to prove that she wasn't just posing as a student, she pointed to her textbook, open on a page with nearly every paragraph highlighted and her notes in the margins. 'I've got exams next week.'

'Me too. Four of them.'

He asked what had happened with her father and she explained about seeing him and Michael and about scattering her father's ashes in a woodland near the house where his mother had been scattered. Sam listened thoughtfully, his whole body leaning forward, absorbing her words, and Ava felt shy and nervous in his presence.

'I'm really sorry,' he said. 'It must have been very difficult.'

'It was, but Michael was there.' She flipped her hair back, and it bothered her that she did that. 'I'm living in a flat nearby. It overlooks the river.'

'Really? That's exciting,' he said, and then he opened his mouth like he was about to speak again, but he stopped, and Ava wondered if he was going to bring up the night of the party and their argument about the solicitor's papers, but he said nothing and Ava was glad.

'I'm living close to the library with friends.'

'What happened to London?'

He scratched his head. 'I thought I'd finish my degree first. I've joined a few committees here and I'm working in student housing. It's kind of nice.' He looked at his watch and she was afraid he was going to say that he had to leave. Instead, he seemed to relax into his seat. 'Have you got any plans for the Christmas holiday?'

'I'm going to New York to see Michael and his family.' She thought of Jacob, the times they'd spoken over video chat. He had been timid at first, running away from the camera, but last week he had shown her all the toys in his room. Her computer was full of pictures of him.

'You look good,' Sam said.

'Well, I feel more like myself anyway.'

Ava wondered if it would ever be possible for them to be friends, to go to cafés and bars together like this without expectations, only to enjoy being in each other's company.

'I don't want to keep you from your work,' Sam said. But he made no attempt to move, his coat still hanging on the back of his seat.

'You're not keeping me. My brain works better in the evenings.'

'Are you still on the same number?' He looked at his phone, scrolled through his contacts.

'Yes,' she said, 'that hasn't changed.'

'What about the old flip phone?' He smiled.

'That's still the same too.'

'I *do* need to head out. I've got an early start to the morning and, unlike you, my brain works best first thing.' He held Ava's gaze for a moment, and she could tell that it meant something to him, seeing her again. What exactly, it was difficult to tell. Maybe just the satisfaction of seeing her well, unbroken.

'It would be great to catch up again.'

'Yes,' Ava said, 'maybe after Christmas when I'm back from New York.'

'We could go to the beach in Brighton. Smoke that joint.'

Ava remembered their kiss at the party, the earthy taste of his mouth.

He bent over, his big arms around her, his warmth and the faint smell of aftershave on his neck familiar to her.

When he left, she couldn't concentrate on her work, couldn't stop thinking of him and how much lighter she felt after seeing him again. It was hard to explain, only that she felt now there wasn't this niggling thing buzzing in the background.

There was no sense in staying where she couldn't concentrate, so she left soon after Sam. She put her earphones in and listened to chapter two of the introduction to Greek she had borrowed from the library – so far she knew how to say hello and ask for the toilet. She had made contact with a cousin in Cyprus through social media a few weeks earlier. Delia was in her late twenties, single, and took a lot of pictures of her dog. She said Ava could stay with her for a long weekend in February, and Ava had accepted her invitation.

On her way home, she stopped off at a supermarket to pick up a few things for dinner and, walking past a bookshop, she saw Dr Wandsworth's book in the window. She had to laugh, remembering the smallness of the man, that piece of romaine lettuce stuck between his flashy white teeth. What Dr Wandsworth had failed to say in his books, she thought, was how it was easy to live through your senses – to look and smell and touch – when the sights and smells and textures were fine. She would pay a lot of money to watch Dr Wandsworth live through his senses in a room full of shit instead of his shiny appliances.

When she got in, the flat felt cold. She turned the heating on and boiled water in a pot for pasta. She listened to Sam Cook in the evenings. It made her feel like she had company, his voice so full of life. She had been eating her dinners overlooking the river with a gentle flickering candle in front of her, but it was too cold to leave the balcony doors open now, as she'd done all the way up to October, and it was all darkness out there, except for the few lamp posts along the boardwalk below.

A message came through on her phone from Sam.

He said how nice it was to see her and how he would like to be friends. It reminded Ava of being in school, getting a message like that. She responded, saying she would like that too.

By the time the water had boiled, she had received several long paragraphs from him. He said that he didn't like how things had ended between them, that he shouldn't have brought up the papers from the lawyer. He'd just been stoned and frustrated. He didn't know what she'd wanted from him.

She wrote back, saying she knew what she wanted now. Would he come to her flat?

She sent that text and waited.

The heat on the hob was too high, steam and water spilling out. The quick buzz of her phone – a message waiting. Ava tried to move the pan but burnt her fingers, the hot water scalding them. She turned down the hob and picked up her phone.

He said he still thought about that night they'd been together. He asked for her address.

Ava clutched the phone to her throat, her chest – the places where the technician had pressed down with his probe, taking those black-and-white pictures of her heart.

She sent her address. Sam was coming to her place.

Waiting for him to arrive, Ava surveyed her flat. Every cushion and candlestick she had chosen. There had been a few hiccups. The toilet overflowing, a big mess spilling out of it, the boiler breaking down and a leak from the flat above, turning her ceiling brown. She had foolishly tried to repaint her ceiling white with a long roller one weekend, her arms and back straining so she could barely move the next day. She had put up a sign at the university and paid a first-year to do the rest of the job for her. She managed.

While the music played – a song about Cupid and his bow – Ava thought of Sam in the cold, making his way over, his new hair, his lovely eyes. She stayed on the sofa, her legs dangling comfortably from the arm, and she listened to the music, watched the warm stillness of the room with all of her attention.

Acknowledgements

I would like to thank a number of people who in one way or another helped bring *Out of Touch* into the world:

My brilliant agent Camilla Bolton and the dedicated team at Darley Anderson for your advocacy, guidance and heart.

My wonderful editors Jennifer Kerslake and Lettice Franklin for their invaluable support and guidance. The amazing team at Weidenfeld & Nicolson for bringing the book together.

Leone Ross for her immense support and thoughtful guidance when the novel was still taking shape.

My friends in London and abroad who were always keen to talk about 'the book', but also there to distract me from it.

Maureen, Sinead and Imelda for your love and encouragement.

My sisters Hengameh and Houri, and my talented grandmother Homa, for their love, belief and guidance.

My parents Hayedeh and Houchang for their unwavering belief in me.

And Simon, for everything.